PRAISE FOR THE
GUARDIANS OF ASCENSION SERIES
BY CARIS ROANE . . .

"Caris Roane powers into the paranormal romance genre with a sexy, cool, edgy, romantic fantasy that gleams like the dark wings and lethal allure of her Guardians of Ascension vampires. Prepare to be enthralled!"
　　—*New York Times* bestselling author Lara Adrian

"Roane's worldbuilding is complex and intriguing, and in addition to her compelling protagonists, she serves up a slew of secondary characters begging to be explored further. The Guardians of Ascension is a series with epic potential!"　　　　　　　—*Romantic Times* (4½ stars)

"A super urban romantic fantasy in which the audience will believe in the vampires and the Ascension . . . fast-paced . . . thrilling."　　　　—Alternative Worlds

"A great story with a really different take on vampires. This is one book that is sure to be a hit with readers who love paranormals. Fans of J.R. Ward's Black Dagger Brotherhood series are sure to love this one too."
　　　　　　　　　—Red Roses for Authors Blog

CHAINS OF DARKNESS

CARIS ROANE

St. Martin's Paperbacks

This is a work of fiction. All of the characters, organizations, and events portrayed in this novel are either products of the author's imagination or are used fictitiously.

CHAINS OF DARKNESS

For information address St. Martin's Press, 175 Fifth Avenue, New York, NY 10010.

ISBN: 978-1-250-03530-1

Printed in the United States of America

St. Martin's Paperbacks edition / July 2014

St. Martin's Paperbacks are published by St. Martin's Press, 175 Fifth Avenue, New York, NY 10010.

10 9 8 7 6 5 4 3 2 1

To the fabulous Felicity Heaton, good friend and fellow author, who has helped me climb this mountain

ACKNOWLEDGMENTS

Many thanks to my editor, Rose Hilliard, for her hard work on the Men in Chains series, and to my agent, Karen Solem. A special thanks to my copy editor, Laura Jorstad and her careful eye. And to Danielle Fiorella, as always the artwork reflects the series beautifully!

CHAPTER 1

Claire Turner hid at the end of a long cavern tunnel, deep in the shadows. Her nerves were like fire on her skin. Guards moved in and out of a nearby prison cell, some with whips and Tasers, others with cleanup gear. The air smelled damp and musty as though death came often to this part of the world.

Her heart slammed against her ribcage. She'd been thrust into a secret cavern-based vampire society with the task of rescuing a prisoner, a famous warrior called Lucian, from his captivity.

She didn't even know where she was exactly. Rumy, the small Italian vampire who had left her here, had said something about Malaysia. He'd dropped her off just minutes ago, told her to trust her instincts, then insisted repeatedly that she'd be fine, just fine. Like hell.

She took deep breaths. She couldn't believe she was doing this, risking her life by agreeing to what now seemed like a ridiculous plan. What did a social worker from New Mexico know about running covert operations?

But Lucian had become the key to finding her best friend, Zoey, who had been abducted two years ago and was now caught in some kind of sex slavery in this part of the world. According to Rumy, Lucian was the only vampire who could help find Zoey.

Lucian. She could feel him now and even sensed his location, and all because of the single strand of small, dark metal links she wore around her neck: blood-chains. She carried a matching chain in her pocket and once Lucian put it on, he'd have enough power to break out of the prison. Or at least, that's what Rumy said he hoped would happen.

Several guards left the adjacent tunnel that led to Lucian's cell, leaving only one behind now, but she wouldn't be able to make her move until Lucian was finally alone.

None of the vampires even glanced in her direction, which meant they couldn't see her, another reality she struggled to comprehend. Despite the fact that she was a mere human, the blood-chains she wore had some-how sparked an innate ability she possessed to create something called a "disguise" and which acted as an invisible shield around her.

So much was at stake in this moment that her heart thumped in her ears. If she failed to rescue Lucian and was caught, she'd probably be sent into sex slavery her-self or even killed outright. Though given a choice, she was pretty sure she'd prefer the latter.

More than once while waiting, she'd thought about going in and wrapping Lucian up with the same disguise that kept the guards from seeing her. However, any guard who happened to enter the prison cell and found Lucian gone would shout an alarm. No, the moment she extended her disguise to include Lucian would have to be the same time she left with him.

She drew a few deep breaths trying to get calm. Then as the last guard left and disappeared down the hall, she moved swiftly through a short adjoining tunnel that led to the large cell lit by torchlight. Moving off to the right, she entered a sloping pit that ended with a smooth wall.

And Lucian.

The sight of him stopped her cold. He sat completely naked on a small patch of cement, chained to the wall. His wrists and ankles were shackled, chains hanging between. Another chain, locked onto the back of his left ankle, secured him to a thick black iron loop bolted into the wall behind him. The arrangement restricted his movements by about ten feet in any direction. If she'd doubted the story Rumy had told her about Lucian and his brothers, and their abusive father, she didn't anymore; only a monster would treat his son like this.

She knew Lucian from the photographs Rumy had shown her as well as by the new vibrations of the chain at her neck. The chain recognized him, allowing her to siphon his power, clear evidence that the chains held a magical quality. Even her vision seemed to have improved in the dim, torch-lit cave.

But hearing about the man and seeing him in person were two very different things. She hadn't understood the size of him before. He was physically imposing and on some level, even beautiful. He had to be at least six-five. He had short dark hair that set off strong cheekbones, giving his face a sculpted appearance. His lips were full and sensual, his jawline angled, and his nose straight but with a slight curve at the bridge. His shoulders were broad and heavy, his arms ripped, his hands large and fleshy.

His thick, straight brows, however, were drawn together in a tight line as he rocked his head slowly back and forth, his lips moving over words she couldn't quite make out.

Rumy had told her Lucian would probably be suffering from a kind of madness that vampires experienced when their blood-needs weren't met on a regular basis. With his eyes closed and muttering unintelligible things, he seemed to be in exactly that state. At Rumy's suggestion, she'd brought a vial of blood with her that would help clear Lucian's head so that he could focus better.

At the same time, Lucian looked like any other male in her world. Her gaze dropped to his muscled thighs and as if on cue, he lowered his knees to stretch out his legs. Very male.

She looked away. It seemed invasive to be staring at him.

She fingered the single blood-chain at her neck, and realized she really could sense what he was feeling, the depths of his despair, his rage, and even his madness.

The same chain would create the powerful bond once Lucian wore the matching set. She still couldn't believe she was about to bind herself to a vampire, but through a process she couldn't begin to understand, the chains would make it possible for her to form a tracking pair with Lucian. If she wanted to find Zoey, this was the only way. And right now, she'd do whatever the hell Lucian wanted her to do, if it meant locating and rescuing her best friend.

She called to him. "Lucian, can you hear me? Rumy sent me. I've come to take you out of here. Lucian?"

Lucian struggled to make sense of what he'd just heard. A woman had called to him, or maybe he'd just imagined it, another illusion. The blood-madness was killing him.

"I'm here to your left. Can you see me? Try to focus if you can."

There it was again, the same voice, a melodious sound, very feminine.

He shifted his head in the direction he thought the words had come from, struggling to see her. His vision came and went because of his debilitated state, but suddenly she was there, near the far wall. A woman, human by his reckoning, standing just beyond the torchlight. He had no idea who she was.

His captor and father, Daniel Briggs, had kept him in a state of intense blood-starvation so that he suffered from recurring episodes of dementia and distorted vision.

He blinked several times, working hard to hold the image. The woman appeared to be cloaked behind an intricate disguise, something only a vampire could create. Yet how had a mere human accomplished a design like that?

But with his next breath the scent of her blood reached him, and the sudden craving he experienced cramped his stomach. He couldn't repress the groan that followed. What he wouldn't give to take from her vein.

A protective instinct rose as well, the warrior part of him that always put the welfare of others above his own. "You need to leave, woman. It's not safe here. Daniel will be back. If he finds you, he'll kill you or put

you to work in one of his sex clubs." He lifted his manacled wrists. "And in case you haven't noticed, I won't
be able to lift a finger to help you."

He needed her to know something else as well: that
he was Daniel's spawn. Within him, he'd always felt
the same nature at work, the one that could easily bru-
talize others. The same instincts had made him a good
fighter, he knew that, so he wasn't completely disgusted by who he was; just grateful that the darkness
he carried around with him had an outlet. Given his
blood-madness, given that he wasn't in control, he could
hurt the woman.

"Lucian, please listen to me. I'm here to get you out
of this prison. Rumy sent me because I have a gift for
making disguises. We're just not sure if it will protect
us from Daniel."

He lifted his head. "I can hear Daniel coming now.
He's not far away. You have to leave."

Footsteps sounded on the stone floor. He looked up,
barely able to make out the faces of the men who entered from the tunnel to his left, not far from the
woman. The guards had been coming in and out, cleaning him up, making him presentable. His vision cleared
once more and he recognized Daniel, who had a couple
of guards and a med tech with him.

"Give him two ounces," Daniel called out. "He's spiraling from blood-madness and I need him coherent."

Daniel's voice always sounded like he could give
seminars on positive thinking. The bastard was charismatic, charming, and filthy rich—in a literal sense, because he'd made his fortune off the backs of anyone
who came near him. He saw nothing wrong with in-
flicting pain to get what he wanted.

The more pain the better.

As the guards advanced, Lucian's mind slipped away.

Ancient memories surfaced, of being bound to Daniel's table, enduring his "corrective punishments," as he liked to call the torture he inflicted on his sons. He wanted Daniel dead. More than anything in life, he wanted the bastard dead.

He struggled in his chains, straining to get at Daniel. But what could he do, bound as he was?

One of the guards got a little too close and four centuries of battle experience took over. Lucian slid onto his side, kicking out with his foot at the same time. He connected with the guard's leg and sent him sprawling. The man shouted in agony, his knee shattered.

The other guard backed off.

Lucian leaped to his feet, once more pulling at the chains, trying to get to his father.

Daniel smiled. "Just Taser him. I haven't got all night."

The uninjured guard drew his weapon and fired.

As a searing pain shot through his chest, Lucian roared. A terrible electrical charge followed that caused his arm and back muscles to seize, then spasm.

The Taser.

Vampires and electricity didn't mix.

He fell to his knees, rolling onto his back. The charge paralyzed him long enough for the tech to come at him with a needle-less syringe and to slowly insert two critical ounces of blood deep into his mouth. He sputtered, struggling to swallow, but the blood tasted so good and at the same time began having a positive effect.

The moment his lucidity improved, he started calming down, though his body still jerked with aftershocks. The paralysis, though beginning to fade, kept him immobile.

He shifted his gaze to the far wall, to the human who

had been talking to him, and there she was. She hadn't been a hallucination after all. Better yet, Daniel couldn't see her. The woman's disguise held, and for the first time in months hope rose that he might just make it out alive.

For a long moment, he stared at her. She was dressed simply in jeans, a light-green T-shirt, jogging shoes. She was beautiful with deep-auburn hair that flowed in waves past her shoulders. Her creamy skin gave her an almost angelic appearance. Her nose was straight, her cheekbones high and strong, yet she watched him with tears in her light-brown eyes. No doubt she wasn't used to Daniel's barbaric ways.

Yet what surprised him was how clearly he could sense her emotions—as though he had some kind of connection to her. She was frightened by where she was, but there was something more, a powerful determination to do what she'd come here to do.

He remembered now. She'd spoken of Rumy; Rumy had sent her here. If all went well, this might just work.

He glanced back at Daniel, who stared at him with arms folded over his chest. Daniel really didn't seem to be aware of the woman, even though he was one of the most powerful vampires in their world. He'd reached the highest form as an Ancestral, those vampires with tremendous power who tended to rise to positions of leadership or, in Daniel's case, autocracy. Daniel all but ruled the vampire world.

And with that much power, he should have seen the woman.

Yet he hadn't.

Was it possible she really could get him out of here?

The dose of blood eased Lucian and helped him to start healing the debilitating effects of the Taser. Even so, his body felt raw, reminding him of the torture he'd endured over the past year in the prison he'd previously inhabited. Daniel had brought him here, along with his brother Marius, but he'd quickly separated them. Lucian had no idea where Marius was.

Daniel called to him. "Is your head clear now?"

Lucian sat up, swiveling to face the man who'd sired him. His father wore an expensive, tailored suit of dark-blue silk, a goatee trimmed close, with his short, dark hair slicked back. His eyes were light blue with a hint of green, not quite teal, but lighter and flecked with gold. He defined all that was evil in their culture.

Lucian despised what his father stood for. "What the fuck do you want anyway?"

"I want you to return to me, Lucian. That's all I've ever wanted from you and your brothers."

"I know you have Marius imprisoned here somewhere, but where's Adrien?" There were three brothers in all. Recently a human female had taken Adrien from their previous, shared prison, but he hadn't seen him since. He didn't even know if Adrien was alive.

"I'm not here to discuss Adrien. I want to talk about you and what I can do to persuade you to join my ranks."

"Not a goddamn thing."

"You're being absurdly stubborn for a prisoner in chains."

Lucian just stared at him, letting him feel his hatred. The man had been his torturer as a child. He would die before he ever joined Daniel's ranks.

Daniel gestured with a sweep of his hand. "Let me be specific. I need help finding the extinction weapon. It seems you and your brothers all have a special kind of tracking ability, and with just a little effort I know you'll be able to find it. Join me, Lucian, help me gain a weapon that will allow me to rule our world for the next millennium, and you can share in that power. Just think what that would mean for you: the position of prominence, the enormous wealth. And together we'd be invincible."

"I'll never return to you. And after four hundred years, I don't understand why the fuck you're still asking. My loyalties lie with those who seek justice and equality in our world, not monsters who enslave and torture the innocent."

Daniel's eyes narrowed to thin, unreadable slits. But Lucian knew that expression well. Nothing good would follow. "I don't think you're getting the picture. You'll do this for me and like it or you'll die, Marius with you. It's that simple."

"Then kill me now, Father, because I'd prefer death to serving you and I'm sure my brother would feel the exact same way."

Daniel pulled his lips back, revealing the sharp points of his fangs. He moved in swiftly, before Lucian could get out of the way, then placed a hand on top of Lucian's head. An excruciating stream of power flowed from Daniel's hand, once more paralyzing Lucian.

"This is just the beginning, my son. I have more in store for you. Trust me, little by little I'll tear you down until you will do anything I want you to do. For now, feel my power."

Pain ripped through Lucian, traveling down his spine and into his legs. He roared once more, then fell back unable to breathe, to think, to move. It took several seconds before he could finally make sense of his surroundings once more.

"Good. You're back. And now I have another piece of persuasion for you." He pivoted slightly and snapped his fingers in the direction of the tunnel entrance.

* * *

Claire felt some kind of vibration in the air shift, some level of Daniel's intention. He turned toward the arched doorway behind him, where two large torches cast a glow at the end of the cave. He waved an arm and once more snapped his fingers.

Guards appeared, one on either side of a man they dragged behind them. He was naked like Lucian but covered in grime. She wasn't sure of the color of his hair because he was filthy, including his face, which was bruised and bloody.

Lucian leaned back like he'd been hit. He rubbed a hand over his face, narrowing his eyes as though he couldn't see well. "Marius, is that you? What have you done to Marius?"

The guards dropped the vampire at Daniel's feet.

"You sure you don't want to join me, Lucian?"

"Never." He leaned forward on his knees, his gaze fixed on Marius. His head wagged back and forth again. Claire had a strong sense that he couldn't see his brother clearly.

"Well, that's too bad, then." Daniel leaned down and, taking a blade from his pocket, sliced open the man's throat. The victim thrashed, his hands to his throat, blood leaking everywhere.

As Marius collapsed, Daniel stepped out of harm's way. Apparently he didn't want blood on his expensive suit.

Shouting sounded through the pit.

On instinct, Claire covered her ears, aware of the reason a few seconds later: Lucian had started bellowing like a wild animal, straining against his chains. "Marius! My brother! Marius!"

Claire felt his pain because the chain shared it with her, letting her experience Lucian's horror. He was losing something infinitely precious.

Her chest started to hurt.

She tried not to look at Marius, who now lay still, but whose blood had created a lake near his head. Instead her gaze drifted to Daniel, who watched Lucian's suffering with a half smile on his lips, his gaze hooded.

So he got off on his son's suffering. Of course that much had already been made evident to Claire in the recent exchange.

"It's just you and me now, Lucian. Marius is gone. Adrien is holed up somewhere with the woman who bound him up and subdued him. Become an Ancestral and rule beside me. You'll forget this pain, and you won't believe the power you'll wield. It's intoxicating."

Claire knew Daniel's words were wasted. She could feel Lucian's venom. He hated his father, wanted him dead.

Daniel skirted Marius's body. "Say you'll join me, Lucian. I have a thousand slaves here and you'll get all the blood you need. I can feel your starvation, and I want to take care of you. That's what you've never understood. I have tremendous compassion for you."

Lucian, still prone, strained once more against his chains trying to reach his father. "I'll see you in hell first, Daniel."

But again Daniel touched the top of his head. The powerful warrior rolled onto his back, his body seizing again.

Through a mist of tears, her hands pressed over her mouth, Claire watched Daniel revel in the pain he caused his son. He stood over him, both arms spread wide, staring down at Lucian's body, a smile on his lips.

At last, Lucian must have passed out, because his eyes closed and his body grew lax. For a moment she thought Daniel might have killed him, but Lucian's chest moved up and down. Only then could Claire finally breathe.

She held her disguising shield tight, fearing that Daniel might suddenly realize she was in the cave. If he ever turned that level of power against her, she wouldn't survive for the time it took to blink.

Fortunately, with a sheen of perspiration on his forehead and a satisfied dip of his chin, Daniel turned and left the space. The guards and med tech followed after him while a cleanup crew hurried in.

She turned away as two of them carted Marius's body out; the rest set to cleaning the floor. Powerful emotions moved through her: the grief that Lucian would now experience, and the horror she felt at watching a man killed in front of her eyes. She knew enough to let the sensations flow, as hard as they were to bear.

She would have a lot of processing to do later, but right now she had to get Lucian out of the cave.

With the last of the blood cleaned up, the crew left. Claire waited until the hall beyond grew quiet. Finally, she hurried toward Lucian, her disguising shield tight around her.

She withdrew the vial of her blood from the pocket of her jeans, then dropped to her knees beside him. Uncorking the small plastic tube, she held it beneath his nose, hoping he'd catch the scent.

At the same time she smoothed her hand over his forehead. "Come back to me, Lucian. Let me take you out of here before Daniel returns. Please wake up."

She thought about what he'd said, that he was loyal to those who sought justice and equality. Here was a man who deserved so much more than what life had dealt him.

His head began to shift, first left then right. A moan left his lips. "Blood," he whispered.

When his lips parted, she began easing the blood into his mouth, then stroking his throat to encourage him to swallow. Little by little the vial grew empty.

"Lucian, can you hear me?"

He finally opened his eyes and stared at her. "You're the human, the one I saw earlier."

"I am."

"My God, your blood tastes the way you smell, like sweet herbs. And there's strength in you. Great strength. But who are you?"

Claire stared into Lucian's smoky-gray eyes and for a moment got completely lost in what he'd just said to her. She'd never heard a more beautiful compliment.

"My name is Claire. Rumy sent me here to help you."

Maybe it was the chain she wore, or that she admired how he'd stood up to his father, or his kind words—but suddenly he became more than merely the vehicle by which she could find her friend. Something inside her began to warm to him, a sensation that brought heat to her cheeks.

He sat up and took several deep breaths. He winced suddenly and shaded his faced with his manacled hand. "Marius." He whispered. "Oh, God, Marius."

As much as she needed to get him out of the cave, the sooner the better, she had to give him just a little space to recover from what for her had been a horrifying spectacle. She swallowed several times, her throat tight.

In addition to the sudden swell of grief, she also sensed that he was working hard to recover from Daniel's most recent assault. He was still in a lot of pain.

After a moment he lifted his face to her, but his gaze dropped to her neck and he frowned. "You're wearing a blood-chain."

She nodded. "*Your* blood-chain, Lucian. Rumy said

that being bound together through the chains would be the only way you could leave this cave, but I don't know exactly what he meant."

He glanced down at his manacles. "Rumy was right, because these shackles are preternaturally enhanced with Daniel's power." He lifted his gaze to hers. "The blood-chain bond will expand my abilities, give me what I need to break free. But tell me what Rumy told you."

"That we'll have a proximity issue, with about a twelve-foot reach, which means we'll have to be close to each other for however long we're bonded in this way."

He lowered his chin. "And? Surely he told you more than that."

"Rumy was very specific that you'll be in a blood-starved state. You'll require a recovery period, and I'll have to donate."

"And you're okay with that? Because the sense I'm getting is that this is all new to you."

"Very."

"Then why did you come here? Why would you put yourself in this kind of danger?"

Claire needed him to understand the whole picture, especially the promises Rumy had made. "Two years ago, my friend Zoey and I were abducted from a club in Santa Fe. I've been held captive all this time in Florida at Daniel's command. But Rumy got wind of it, suspecting that I might have the ability to forge a tracking pair with you. Does this make sense? The 'tracking pair' thing, I mean?"

He nodded. "It does. It's very rare in our world, but I'm starting to get the picture. Rumy helped you escape, didn't he?"

"He did, but he insisted that I search for your blood-chains first. When I actually found them in my captor's office, I finally believed everything he'd been telling me. You have to understand, until three days ago, I didn't even know about your world except for vague rumors some of the staff mentioned now and then. I thought it was all gossip."

Lucian scowled. "So Rumy sent you here wearing the blood-chain intending for you to bond with me."

She swallowed hard. "Yes. He believes that Daniel orchestrated my capture and that he'd fully intended one day to use me for exactly this purpose, to become part of a tracking pair in order to find the weapon he's after."

His frown deepened. "What did Rumy tell you about the blood-chains?"

"That when they were created, they were infused with your blood, which makes them specific to you. He also said that you had tremendous power and that once you put on the blood-chain and we bonded, that you'd be able to break out of these shackles." She glanced down at the horrible, heavy iron bands around his wrists and ankles. Lifting her gaze back to his face, she added, "And I hope more than anything that it's true."

Lucian searched her eyes. "But what's in it for you?"

Claire's throat seized and her eyes filled with tears. "I need help to find my friend, Zoey. She's lost somewhere inside your world." Images of her best friend from childhood suddenly came to mind. Zoey was so different from her in almost every way. She had short, jet-black hair, for one thing, and large blue eyes. They'd lived on the same street and been in and out of each other's houses from the earliest time Claire could remember. The moment Rumy had told Claire that Zoey had probably been trafficked into the vampire slave system, she'd set her course. She had to find her if it was the last thing she did. "Rumy's convinced Zoey was auctioned off as a sex slave. If you and I do form a chain-bond, and it turns out we really can track things, then I'll need your commitment to help me find Zoey. That's what's in it for me and Rumy assured me that you'd be willing to help."

Lucian wrapped his arms around his knees and closed his eyes. "Fuck. This isn't right, not on any level."

She reached out to him, touching his arm. "Lucian, I don't have the luxury of thinking in terms of whether this is right or not. I only want one thing, to find my friend. I have no idea if she's alive, but I can't leave your world without knowing one way or the other, without making an effort. This seems like the only way."

He put a hand to his abdomen.

"Are you still in pain, even though I just gave you some of my blood?"

He nodded, then lifted his gaze to hers once more. "Again, this won't be simple, and you could get hurt in the process. There will be times when I'll be completely out of control, do you understand?"

"You're talking about your recovery process."

"I am."

"I know and I'm still okay with it. I just need your promise that if we do this, you'll help me look for Zoey."

He met and held her gaze for a long moment, as though considering all that she'd said. She sensed not so much his deliberation as a rebuilding of his commitment. "We'll need to find the extinction weapon," he said at last. "That's the commitment I need from you. We'll hunt for both, for Zoey and the weapon, whatever it takes, but I can't let my father get hold of a weapon that has the capacity to destroy every last vampire on the planet. Do you understand? Will you make that commitment to me?"

She didn't hesitate, not for a second. "Absolutely."

He put his hand to his chest. "I can sense that you're speaking the truth." He rose slowly to his feet, this very naked man, this powerful warrior.

He overwhelmed her as much by his sheer size as by the strength of his commitment to end Daniel's reign of terror.

He held her gaze. "Then I'll bind myself to you."

She dipped into the pocket of her jeans and pulled out the matching blood-chain. "Let's do it."

Lucian struggled to remain focused on the human and on her intentions. His thoughts wanted to fix themselves exclusively on Marius's death and his burning desire to hunt Daniel down and destroy him. But he couldn't do anything until he got out of this prison, which meant he had to turn his attention to more immediate issues, like the weapon and to helping Claire find her friend.

He met her light-brown eyes again, caught by their unusual shade, and dipped his chin once. She extended her hands, and as he lowered his head to give her a better angle he felt the vibration of power that both sets of chains held.

She quickly slid the second chain over his head, lowering it onto his neck. Her gentle touch reminded him that for over a year he'd known only brutality and isolation.

He met and held Claire's gaze once more, but this time she came into sharp focus. Her auburn beauty struck him all over again; he had the sudden awareness that if circumstances had been different, she was exactly the kind of woman he would have gone for.

She blinked several times as she searched his eyes.

"Rumy showed me pictures, but you're so tall in real life." He watched a blush suffuse her cheeks and sensed a rippling of interest. She found him attractive.

Her gaze skated over his face, then down his neck. She touched his chain and gasped softly. "The vibrations have really grown stronger."

"They have." He leaned close, sniffing her neck and her cheek. "There it is again. You smell like sweet herbs. Your blood tastes like that as well."

Her hands found his arms and slid over his biceps. "Lucian, this is so strange. I can't believe how much I'm feeling from you right now. It's as though I *know* you."

He nodded. "Same here." The sensation disturbed him deeply. She threatened him in a way he couldn't quite understand.

When she pulled away from him, her lips were parted. "I think I'm in trouble here. I'm feeling things that don't seem appropriate. Is it the chain-bond?"

He shook his head. "I've been told that the bond can only reflect what's already there."

She blushed again. "Oh, I see. I guess that makes sense."

The next moment, a jolt of something powerful passed through him.

Her eyes went wide. "Did you feel that?"

He nodded. "Almost like a steel door slamming shut. It's the bond."

"I feel so strange right now. More than just human."

"That would follow. You were siphoning some of my power before, but now it will become a strong, steady flow. Your vision will improve as well." He glanced down at the powerful chains that held him captive. "And now we'll see if the bond will be enough to take care of this part of the equation."

He focused on his manacles, on the charge Daniel had placed within the chains. If they hadn't been preternaturally enhanced, he could have broken out of them two seconds after they'd locked in place. But Daniel's power had made them impervious to his natural strength.

He let his newly enhanced power flow, and little by little he felt Daniel's locking mechanism give way. He applied the full force of his ability, but the resistance to his effort stunned him.

"I can sense what you're doing. I might be able to help." Claire placed her hands on his arms, and that small touch caused his power to surge. The next moment the charge within the shackles fizzled. A little more pressure and the manacles split apart, falling off his arms.

Claire squealed her excitement. "Yes!"

Adrenaline spiked and his heart rate went through the roof. "Hell, yeah."

He repeated the process for his ankles. Once the shackles fell away, he was free.

He stepped away from Claire and turned in a circle. "I haven't had these off in a year. Now just like that, they're gone. They're fucking gone."

Suddenly he glanced toward the entrance to the cell. "Daniel's coming."

Then without warning, his stomach seized once more. Drawing away from her, he doubled over, the pain like fire through his abdomen.

Claire saw that Lucian's blood-madness issue had just resurfaced. "How do we fix this?"

"It's not going to be simple. I'll need to feed from you again soon. But right now I can't even move."

Suddenly she heard running down the hall, as well as

Daniel shouting. She couldn't mistake his voice. He must have divined that Lucian was close to making an escape.

She embraced Lucian and extended her disguise to envelop him as well. "We have to leave."

"I can't, not yet."

She felt the level of his pain. Once more he was almost paralyzed.

"I have you hidden behind my disguise, but can you at least move with me, away from the shackles on the floor?"

He nodded. "I'll try. Just pull me, if you can. I'll see what I can manage."

She took his arm, tugging at him. He started shuffling so that she was finally able to get him back near the wall where she'd originally been standing.

Daniel appeared in the short tunnel entrance and immediately strode to the chains lying on the stone pavers near the smooth wall. "Where the hell is Lucian?"

At least ten guards had followed him inside. The one in charge stepped forward. "He was in here just a few minutes ago. No one went in. No one out except the cleaning crew. I swear it."

Daniel, his flecked blue eyes glowing, turned in a slow circle as he checked out the entire space. He ended up facing the exact spot where Claire stood with Lucian. It was clear that he didn't actually see them, yet he must have sensed their presence, or maybe Lucian's.

"I know you're still in here, my son. I can feel you but I can't see you. Show yourself. I take it you've had help. It will go easier with you if you don't defy me right now."

He started moving slowly in their direction.

Claire rubbed Lucian's shoulders. "You've got to fly

us out of here. Now. Daniel can't see us, but he's coming straight for us."

Lucian groaned loudly as he forced himself to stand
upright. His eyes were narrowed as if in great pain, but
he put his arm around Claire's waist. "Okay."

Having flown with Rumy, she knew the drill and
threw her arms around his neck. She held on tight.

Daniel was only fifteen feet away and moving faster
now.

She shouted, "Lucian, get us out of here." The vibration of flight began.

Daniel lunged the remaining the distance, just grazing her back as Lucian shifted to altered flight.

His words trailed after them. "I'll come after you,
Lucian. You'll never be able to hide from me, and when
I find you, I'll destroy you."

But Lucian had them in the phenomenon called altered flight, allowing them to pass easily through any
kind of solid matter. Faster and faster he flew, away
from the horror of his prison cell, away from Daniel.

Pressed against him the way she was, she could feel
the solid weight of him, not just his physical body, but
what he carried in his soul. Rumy had said that he bore
the sins of his father. Maybe that was what she felt from
Lucian: the weight of all that sin.

In that moment, she knew she really was in trouble.
She hadn't expected to be able to feel so much of what
Lucian felt, to divine his soul. Her quest, which had begun with a need to find Zoey, had just become layered
with elements that disturbed her deeply, that threatened
how she viewed who she was, even what her life should
be. She was a simple New Mexico girl with a degree in
social work and a job rehabilitating prostitutes. She
wanted a husband and a home of her own one day. But

sensing Lucian in this way made her long for things she couldn't put a name to.

As he sped back to Italy, however, the effects of the flight hit her like a brick. Her head once more felt split wide and her stomach boiled.

Can you hear me, Claire?

She frowned. Even though she'd known that telepathy came with the connection they now shared, it was still strange to have another person's voice in her head. *I'm here. Is this real? Are we talking mind-to-mind?* She winced again. Damn, altered flight hurt.

Yes. Mind-to-mind. Sorry about the pain. I can feel that you're hurting. Can't be helped.

I know. But just to warn you, I'll probably pass out when we arrive back in Italy.

Is Rumy expecting us?

At the secret entrance. He said you'd know where that was. Do you?

I do.

She felt him shaking suddenly. *Hey, you all right?*

This fucking blood-madness.

I'll feed you when we get there.

I'm counting on it.

She felt his flight begin to slow. Glancing down, she recognized the familiar Italian landscape below, and despite the pain she realized exactly how much the completion of the chain-bond had improved her vision. The night was dark, but she saw everything as though warmed by the sun in late afternoon, even though it was the middle of the night.

She breathed a sigh of relief as Lake Como came into view. Rumy's extensive sex-club complex ranged well into the surrounding hills, through miles of caverns and caves, invisible to human eyes. She could even see through the heavy disguise that covered the secret entrance to the club.

A tall vampire, in black leather, with an automatic weapon slung over his shoulder, stepped aside as Lucian descended onto the small landing platform.

The moment she let go of Lucian, however, the pain and nausea caught up with her. She fell to the pavers of the landing area, her head spinning.

Her last thought before she passed out was that she really hoped she wouldn't throw up.

CHAPTER 2

Lucian gathered Claire up in his arms, working hard to ignore the scent of her blood. The flight, however, had helped relieve the bulk of his symptoms, and he felt more like himself. Still, he knew the relief he experienced would be short-lived.

For now he'd get Claire and himself to a private room.

He crossed the threshold and addressed the guard closest to the door. "Where's Rumy?"

"In his office. He's expecting you." The guard didn't flinch at Lucian's naked state.

Lucian nodded. He knew the way well. All the brothers had spent time at The Erotic Passage, both for pleasure and at other times to recover from battle wounds. Each had served for decades as a policing force in their world with an eye to bringing Daniel down for good.

Moving into the hall, he veered right, headed up another hall, then made another right. The arched wood door was wide open.

Rumy leaned against his desk, arms over his chest, his gaze falling to Claire. He frowned. "Is she hurt?"

"Just flight sickness, she'll be okay. Looks like we have a couple of issues to deal with. Daniel is after the extinction weapon and Claire wants to find her friend, someone called Zoey. But you know all about that."

"You've summed it up exactly." Rumy held his gaze and smiled. His fangs were permanently on display and he even had calluses on his lips. "So how the hell are you, boss?" Rumy always called him that, though it was in no way a formal designation. He wasn't the boss of much these days. Before he could respond, however, Rumy's gaze once more dropped to Claire. He smiled. "So how do you like Claire? She's got some crazy-ass courage, this one."

Lucian scowled as he looked down at her. "I guess she does. But these blood-chains chafe like hell."

"You mean you don't like being bound, not even to a beautiful woman?"

"Hell, no, and this one's human."

"But strong."

Lucian nodded. "Yes, I'll give her that."

Rumy looked the same, his black curls cut close and oiled. His snug black T-shirt showed off his muscled lean body. The man was short, but he'd forged a powerful place in their society as a linchpin for the underworld. No one touched Rumy.

Even Daniel generally left The Erotic Passage alone.

When a tremor ran through Lucian and he grimaced, Rumy left his place by the desk, passed by Lucian, then held his hand gesturing into the hallway beyond. "I've got a room set up for you both. You can be private, talk a little, get to know each other. I already had your clothes brought in from Uruguay." Lucian had a home there, one Rumy had access to for exactly this reason. Rumy was one of the few vampires on the planet he trusted with his life.

"Much appreciated."

Lucian had been through blood-madness recovery more than once, so he knew what to expect. But it always surprised him how long it took to get rid of the initial debilitating and dangerous symptoms—which could hit at all the wrong moments.

As Rumy headed down one of the restricted hallways in his club complex, Lucian followed him. "So how did Claire come to be here?"

"Daniel held her prisoner in Florida, using her to watch after a boy he'd been holding captive there. That's what she's been doing for the past two years, taking care of him."

"He wanted her as a nanny?" This didn't make sense.

"Daniel never does anything for just one reason. You know about Adrien, right?"

"Not exactly. I saw him a couple of times with the woman who took him out of the Himalayan prison."

"That's Lily. They're together now. She bound him, the way Claire bound you. Josh was her son, the boy Claire took care of. You starting see how this wheel turns?"

"Not yet."

"Daniel chose Lily—plucked her from the human world, just as he did Claire. Both women have strong vampire markers, real potential in our world. Wouldn't you say that's true about Claire? I mean, think about the disguise she made."

"You're right. Even Daniel couldn't see through it."

"Lily had other abilities, but mostly she could track things."

It all began making sense. "So Daniel's original intention had been to use these women to bind us and create tracking pairs."

"Yes. But he's lost control of the process, thanks to Lily and now Claire."

"And he's after the weapon."

"More than the sharp points of his fangs, Daniel wants that extinction weapon. He knows that if he can get hold of it, he can rule forever."

"Over my dead body."

"I've sent out rumors that Claire escaped from her captors by herself but the truth is I helped get her out along with the chains you're now wearing."

"Then Daniel had the chains ready to go, which means he had this planned all along."

"He's a patient bastard. But now you and Claire are here. I'm sure he didn't count on Claire having the ability to create that kind of disguise—and he sure as hell didn't plan on me rescuing her."

Rumy kept them both moving, making turns left and right in what was a real maze of a cavern system. "You've been a good friend, Rumy. I didn't expect to make it out alive."

Rumy inclined his head to the woman in his arms. "You owe your life to her. I only helped get her to Daniel's Dark Cave system, but she did the heavy lifting."

Lucian nodded. "So what do we know about this extinction weapon?"

"Apparently there's more than one. Adrien destroyed the first one, and it looks like Daniel's hot after whatever he can find that remains."

"Is there a finite number? Two? Ten?"

"We're not sure."

Rumy led him through several winding back tunnels near his office, a section of the club complex that only a select few on his security staff had access to. Finally he stopped before a door, then pushed it open. "Here you are."

The room had a basic setup, nothing special, in part because of its medical use. There were even wrist and ankle restraints on one half of the queen-sized bed. The bathroom was close, as was a nearby dresser.

A table and chairs completed the spare decor.

He moved inside and carefully settled Claire on the bed, on the side without the restraints, then removed her shoes. She was still out cold, which was for the best. She'd be hurting when she woke up.

His clothes, as well as Claire's, hung on a nearby rack.

Rumy gestured to the dresser. "You'll find the usual inside. Socks, underwear. The bathroom is fitted up with toiletries. You should be all set."

Rumy took care of the details, but then as the owner of the huge sex-club complex, he had to. "I thought you could use some time alone with Claire, maybe bring her up to speed about our world. I kept the info to a minimum. She didn't know much when I brought her here, and I didn't want to overwhelm her. I guess Daniel had his Florida house staffed with humans, though Claire said there were vampire rumors anyway." He glanced around. "So, can I bring you anything?"

"Claire will need food. So will I, for that matter."

Rumy nodded. "You got it. Anything special?"

Lucian chuckled softly. "A burger would be great. Maybe some fries."

"I'll be back in half an hour."

Rumy took off, closing the door behind him.

Claire stirred on the bed, moaning softly. Lucian reached for his clothes. He didn't want her to wake up and have to face the full expanse of his naked male body again.

He dressed quickly in a pair of jeans and a long-sleeved T-shirt. He didn't bother with shoes, but it felt good to have clothes on after such a long time. For the past year, though at different locations, he and his brothers had been kept in a filthy cave in the Himalayas, naked the entire time.

Tremors ran through him now as he drew a chair close to Claire's side of the bed. He needed blood desperately, but he didn't want to scare her.

Taking her hand in his, he rubbed the backs of her fingers gently. "Claire, I need you to wake up."

Maybe he should have asked Rumy to send another woman to him to get this initial feeding out of the way, but he couldn't. The blood-chains already worked on him, forcing his attention toward Claire. Besides, he'd tasted her blood; selfish bastard that he was, he wanted more of what he'd sampled.

As Claire opened her eyes, she blinked several times. Her head felt like it was trying hard to split wide open.

"Good, you're waking up. How are you feeling?"

She turned and saw Lucian sitting beside her. She lay on a bed of some kind in a small room with very bland beige furniture and white walls.

He held her hand, a comforting gesture given the situation. "I'm okay except for the hammers pounding on the inside of my skull."

At that, Lucian's lips curved. "That's funny. And unexpected."

"I'm not much of a weeper, just thought you should know." She closed her eyes again. "I believe I hate altered flight."

"It can be a real bitch for humans."

The chain at her neck vibrated softly. As she opened her eyes and once more turned to look at him, the depth of his physical need struck her. According to Rumy, he'd been deprived for a long time, at least a year. "Oh, God, Lucian, I'm sorry. Let's get you taken care of. So how do we do this?"

She tried to sit up, but he shook his head. "Just lie still. I thought, if it's all right with you, I'd take from your wrist. It's much less invasive, and you can keep resting."

"Okay. Do whatever it is you need to do. Yes, lying prone for a little while longer will be better."

Rumy had made it clear what being chain-bound to Lucian would mean, so Claire had known this moment would come. But as he angled his shoulders, then leaned over her arm, her heart started pounding. She couldn't believe this was happening. A vampire would soon bite her and take her blood.

She watched his fangs descend as he hovered above the collection of veins at her wrist.

He glanced up at her, his gray eyes darkening with need. "I'll do this as gently and as quickly as I can."

"That sounds good." What else could she say?

She turned her head, wincing in anticipation, but she felt only the slightest prick, then his lips surrounded the wound.

Claire looked back as Lucian began to suck.

The sensual, steady draw on her wrist made her lips part. She'd dreaded donating to Lucian, but now that he took from her, nursing at her wrist, the room started warming up. The soft suckling sound began to remind her of other things.

The first wave of desire flowed over her like the rush of a wave on the seashore. She drew a long breath, as her gaze became focused on the muscled slope of Lucian's shoulders and back. She felt an impulse to cover his neck with her hand and caress him as he took from her.

She gave herself a shake, trying to repress the sudden desire that had taken hold of her, when suddenly, while still drawing her blood, he looked up and met her gaze. *You taste of the sweetest herbs, Claire, though I think I said that before.*

His voice in her head didn't help, either, but sparked her sudden need. *You did.*

His gray eyes were dark with what she knew was a desire that matched her own. She found it hard to breathe and put a hand to her chest.

Thank you for this, Claire. I'm feeling much better. Stronger. And thank you for bringing me out of captivity. I owe you.

"You're welcome." She spoke the words aloud, but her voice sounded hoarse.

Worse, because of the blood-chains, she could feel how aroused he was. The vampire hadn't had sex in a long time. He was very male and would have needs. Even Rumy had told her that much, trying to prepare her.

But her own case wasn't much different. She hadn't been with a man in over two years because of her imprisonment in Florida.

Yet what troubled her wasn't so much that she might end up having sex with the vampire she'd just rescued, but how much she suspected she was going to like it.

A shiver ran through her.

Claire? As he continued to draw her blood into his mouth, he stroked the length of her forearm. His touch was so warm, even gentle against her skin. She didn't mistake the invitation for what it was.

She felt tempted as she never had before and nearly offered up what right now had become an almost painful longing the entire length of her body. But it was way too soon. She looked away from him. "I'm trying to gain my bearings."

Just as you should.

She didn't look at him again while he fed. Instead, she looked anywhere else, trying to ignore what she really wanted to be doing.

The first thing she noticed was that someone had taken her shoes off. Then her eye was drawn to the ceiling, which she realized was quite beautiful despite the bland surroundings. A wave of what looked like light blue granite ran the entire length, but carved and polished to resemble a flow of water.

Good. She had something to focus on besides the fact that she was feeding a vampire and really liking it.

When he finished at last, he released her wrist, licking the small apertures at the same time.

She drew her arm close, looking down at the skin, expecting to see a wound. Instead the puncture marks were gone, and only a slight redness to the skin told her what he'd been doing. "This is amazing."

"We've had thousands of years to evolve. And I've released a serum into your bloodstream that will replace the supply quickly. You shouldn't feel faint or anything."

She shifted to look at him, startled all over again by the fact that she was here in such a strange new environment, sharing a room with a vampire, and that she was bound to him.

He sat back in his chair, definitely more relaxed. His color looked better, and his gray eyes had a brightness they'd lacked before. He was incredibly handsome, which wasn't going to help her desire for him at all.

"I can see that you're feeling better."

He nodded. "Much better. The flight here seemed to help as well. Maybe just being away from that cell."

She glanced down her arm once more, then back to him. "So what's it like? Feeding, I mean."

His brows rose. "I don't know. Like breathing, I suppose. It's just part of my life."

"Of course it would be." She stared at him for a long moment, wondering so many things. She took in his new wardrobe. "You found some clothes, I see."

He gestured with a toss of his hand toward the wall at the foot of the bed, where a tall rack sat. "Rumy had clothes for both of us brought in."

When she'd initially arrived two days earlier, Rumy had given her a few basic garments in addition to the clothes she'd had on. It looked as though he'd since added to her wardrobe. "I can see that."

She glanced around and for the first time noticed the bed was a little different: The far side had what looked like a low steel bar running its length with some kind of cloth attached to it.

She pushed herself to a sitting position. "What is that?"

"Restraints. Though I'll be stable for a while, maybe even a few hours, the recovery from blood-madness takes time, and I'll probably spiral out of control at some point. The bindings will be necessary at least once during the process. But Rumy told you this, right, or some version of it?"

"Sort of. I think he didn't want to weigh me down with too many details."

He glanced at her. "So your name is Claire. What did you do before you were abducted? I mean, who are you? Where did you come from?"

"Santa Fe in New Mexico. Do you know it?"

"Sure. What was your life like there?"

"Well, my family has lived in the area for three generations. I had my own place, of course, but my mom and dad were only a couple of miles from my apartment. My brothers are eighteen and twenty-one now. When Rumy brought me here I went on the Internet and found that they're all doing well. Both the boys are in college." She repressed a sigh. She didn't mind sharing the details, but the conversation was reminding her way too much of her family and how much she missed them. She couldn't imagine how hard her sudden disappearance had been on everyone.

Lucian watched her closely. "And what about your friend, Zoey, were you always close?"

She chuckled, though her throat had started to ache. "More like sisters. We grew up together. Lived on the same street. We even roomed in college. But we're so different, I mean even physically, she's shorter and has black hair, blue eyes. And she has a totally wicked sense of humor. She had really long fingernails though, with jewels on them." When tears touched her eyes, she cleared her throat and changed the subject. "She majored in economics and worked for an investment firm."

"And you?"

"I have a master's in social work. Before being taken out of that club in Santa Fe, I worked with ex-prostitutes, not an easy job."

He frowned. "I'm sure it wouldn't be."

She found it a lot easier to talk about her work rather than either her family or Zoey.

She added, "Prostitution is rarely a first choice for these women. Most of them suffered horrendous childhoods before they entered the profession, so trying to extract them from that kind of work involved treating two layers of dysfunction at the same time."

"We have a similar problem in our world, especially working with the sex slaves we recover. There's always a lot of damage."

She watched his gaze slide to the floor and his jaw flex a couple of times. "What are you thinking about?— because the chains tell me you're really upset. Of course, I can see it as well. What's wrong?"

He met her gaze. "I'm thinking about your friend Zoey and my brothers, what we've all been through, including you. Daniel is the author of all this suffering, and I want him dead. You wouldn't even be here if it weren't for Daniel—and then there's Marius." He shaded his face for a moment as grief swelled over him. She felt ill as she recalled the event. She closed her eyes and let the moment roll through them both, knowing this wouldn't be the last time.

When he drew a deep breath and seemed more himself, she asked, "So what exactly is Daniel's role in your society? I mean, I know that he's in charge right now, but what does that entail?"

"Daniel set himself up as head of the Ancestral Council and now rules our five governing courts. He has tremendous power as an Ancestral. But he also has great wealth because of the sex-slave operation he's built. That wealth has bought him many allies, which is part of the reason he succeeded in taking over the Council. Right now he's damn near invincible."

"And what's an Ancestral?"

"It's the name given to any vampire who achieves a certain level of preternatural power. Only a small portion of our population become Ancestrals, and Daniel's at the top of that food chain."

A knock on the door made her jump.

"Are you okay with someone else coming in here?"

Claire glanced at Lucian, almost startled by the question. For some reason, maybe because of the brutality of the situation she'd found him in, she hadn't expected him to be concerned about her comfort level.

"And now you look surprised. You don't think me capable of kindness or consideration?"

She met his gaze. "I just thought, given what you've been through . . . I don't know, you just surprised me."

He looked away from her, his jaw hardening. She hadn't meant to offend him, but she could see that she'd touched a nerve. She just wasn't sure exactly what it was.

Rumy's voice sounded through the door. "Okay to come in? I brought food."

"Well?" Lucian asked, but this time his voice had an edge.

"Of course. It's Rumy. And I'm sorry if I offended you."

His jaw worked. "You didn't."

Right.

"Come," he called out.

His voice had an authoritative ring. Rumy had told her that Lucian ran a small policing force in their world, protecting as many innocent people as he could from the depredations of Daniel and those aligned with him. Clearly, he was used to command.

Rumy came in, along with wait-staff and a trolley bearing two covered dishes. Her stomach rumbled, partly no doubt because she'd just fed a vampire, but she also hadn't eaten for several hours.

Rumy glanced at Lucian. "You're looking better."

"I feel much better, thanks to Claire."

Later, after he and Claire had consumed a simple but savory meal of burgers and fries, Lucian knew the time had come to get down to business.

Rumy had left so that they could eat in peace, especially since the subjects that would soon be under discussion weren't going to be pleasant. But Lucian now got Rumy on the room's landline and asked him to rejoin them, to discuss how to proceed with finding out what had happened to Zoey and with locating the weapon.

When Rumy came in, however, he wore a serious scowl.

"What's wrong?" Lucian offered Rumy his chair, but the short vampire paced instead.

"We've just had word that Daniel is offering a big reward to anyone who can give him solid information about the whereabouts of the remaining extinction weapons."

Lucian's nostrils flared. "How much is the bastard offering?"

Rumy turned toward him. "Millions, in increments, depending on the value of the information given. That asshole has set up a goddamn tip line."

"Oh, that's bad," Claire murmured.

Lucian glanced at her, then back to Rumy. "Well, the good news is that it won't be an easy process—he'll have thousands of crackpots leaving false information. That alone will slow him down."

"But his organization is big enough to handle it. I think we're in serious trouble. All he needs is the right bead on the weapon, and he'll gain control of everything."

Claire tilted her head. "Do you think he did this because he no longer has you under his thumb?"

"Maybe. This move smacks of desperation."

Rumy rubbed his thumb against the side of one of his always present fangs. He finally sat down on the edge of the bed, facing the table. Lucian's gaze fell to the low steel bar that could be raised to hold one of the restraints. He didn't want the reminder that at some point he'd once more spiral with blood-madness.

"Rumy, is something else on your mind?" Claire asked. "Please, don't hold anything back on my account."

Finally Rumy met her gaze. "Here's the thing, Claire. I have a connection who found out who Zoey went to after she was abducted, because the truth is she never went to auction. Daniel kept her for himself."

Claire put a hand to her mouth. "Oh, God."

"I'm sorry."

Lucian watched tears rush to her eyes—this woman who wasn't a weeper. But he couldn't fault her, not when she'd just heard that her good friend had been at Daniel's mercy for the past two years, if she'd even survived that long. He couldn't imagine a worse fate for a young human female than to be taken into Daniel's Dark Cave system.

Claire, to her credit, straightened her shoulders. "Is there even the smallest hope she's still alive?"

"We have no way of knowing."

At that, Lucian shifted his gaze back to Rumy, and a certain suspicion entered his head. "You haven't told her everything, have you?"

Rumy met Lucian's gaze. He didn't blink, but his tongue flicked out and licked both of his fangs. "I didn't think it was wise."

Lucian's temper shot through his skull and he was on his feet. "What the fuck? Rumy, are you telling me you sent Claire into that pit of hell to rescue me without letting her know the score first? Dammit, she should have had the facts laid out for her before she made a decision to do something that dangerous. You used her."

Rumy spread his hands wide. "I was thinking about you, boss, and about our world."

Lucian didn't care. "The day we set the worth of our society above the value of the individual is the day we've lost the right to survive as a species."

"Lucian, as much as I want to believe that, we needed you here, doing what you're doing now. I didn't know what else to do. Adrien had to go underground to protect Lily and Josh. And you needed out of that hell-hole. Daniel would have found a way to force you to do his bidding."

"You had no right to do this."

Claire felt so sick to her stomach that she struggled to hold down the meal she'd just eaten. Daniel had bought Zoey, and Rumy hadn't told her something so critical that Lucian was actually yelling at him.

And though she'd asked if Zoey was still alive, something about Lucian's outrage indicated that her friend was probably long dead.

She stared at the beige carpeting beneath her bare feet, working at taking in long deep breaths and trying to ease the constriction of her throat.

Lucian paced now, while Rumy sat like a schoolboy in trouble staring up at his teacher.

Claire spoke up. "I want to know everything."

Lucian turned to her and nodded. He stopped next to his chair and crossed his arms over his chest, then turned to glare at Rumy. "Give her the statistics. All of them."

"Fine." Rumy met her gaze, but he'd never looked sadder. "The sex trafficking of humans in our world is brutal beyond description. I don't allow anything like that in the clubs in my complex. There are organizations, like Starlin, that have built empires around trafficking, but everyone knows I disapprove of slavers of any kind. Everyone who works for me earns a decent wage."

"I believe you, but I think you're tiptoeing around the subject. What stats was Lucian talking about?"

Rumy drew a deep breath, his shoulders rising and falling. "In the initial stage of captivity, a small per-centage of humans, about fifteen percent, will not live beyond the two-week mark even if they're treated well."

Claire's throat hurt. "And after two weeks?"

"A second transition occurs at six months, but the survival rate at that point drops to fifty percent."

Claire tried to process what he was saying, but she kept stumbling over the 50 percent figure.

Half.

Half died at six months.

Had Zoey even made it to the six-month mark?

She stared at Rumy, her eyes narrowing all on their own; maybe if she squinted it would help her brain figure this out. "We're talking about a diminishing chance of survival. So what happens after six months?"

Rumy grew very still. His tongue once more made a nervous appearance between the fang-tips then disappeared.

She looked at Lucian. He stared at her from beneath his heavy scowl and thick straight brows.

She felt it again, that weight in him, the heaviness he carried around in his soul that had more to do with the responsibility he felt toward his world than anything else.

He didn't take his eyes off her as he said. "Tell her the rest, Rumy."

She shifted to stare at Rumy once more.

He continued, "By the two-year mark, there's only an eight percent chance she's still alive."

"Eight percent?"

"In a decent situation, eight."

"And Daniel bought her."

"Yes."

Eight.

And Daniel was the one who'd killed his own son, Marius, in front of Lucian.

Once more, her stomach seized. She wasn't even sure her heart beat any longer. It was one thing to not know; another to suspect the worst. But hearing a figure like "eight percent" shifted Claire's perceptions of the situation. These were the hard facts, and given the solemnity that vibrated against her neck, the reflection of Lucian's emotions in this moment, she knew Rumy was telling her the truth.

Lucian drew close to her and took her hand. "He should have told you, Claire."

She stared up at Lucian, her heart heavy. He'd lost Marius today and maybe she'd lost Zoey, though she couldn't be sure. Maybe she should be angry that Rumy hadn't told her everything, but she wasn't. She'd done a good thing, perhaps even a critical one in bringing Lucian safely to The Erotic Passage. If anyone had a chance of ending Daniel's reign, Lucian did.

Rumy's phone rang, and he stepped into the hall to answer it.

"I'm so sorry, Claire. This isn't good news, and again I wish like hell that Rumy hadn't used you the way he did."

When Lucian let her hand go, she rose to her feet. "You know what? I'm fine with it. Because you're safe and after what I saw Daniel do, Rumy's right, your world needs you here right now."

"I think that's really generous of you."

Rumy reentered the room, a slight frown on his brow.

Lucian glanced at him. "Anything we should know?"

Rumy still held his phone in hand. "I've got several calls to return, which is a good thing—one of them might actually be a lead that will pan out. As soon as I heard that Daniel was offering a reward, I alerted my network, asking for any information that might surface about the extinction weapon. Let me see what's going on."

He seemed to consider the situation, then addressed Claire. "I'm sorry for what I did."

"It's okay. I understand your reasoning, and I actually agree with you. Lucian is needed here. You did the right thing."

Rumy held her gaze for a long moment, finally nodding several times in a row. "All right then." He shifted to Lucian. "Listen, let me follow up on the leads. In the meantime, why don't you show Claire the main part of the club." He thcn slapped his pant pocket, dipping inside. He drew out two crimson tickets. "And Eve sent these along."

Lucian glanced at them, scowling. "I'm not taking Claire to a sex show."

Rumy shrugged. "You know Eve. She thinks everyone will love her stuff. But it might be a good thing to expose Claire to other parts of the Erotic Passage because who knows what will happen down the line. At least take her to see the band. Well, keep your phone handy."

With that, he took off.

Claire stared at the tickets, then picked them up. They shimmered. "The Ruby Cave." She glanced at Lucian. "Am I to understand that Rumy just suggested we go clubbing, then hit a sex show?" She didn't know whether she was more appalled or amused. She decided it was the latter and laughed.

"You know, Rumy might be right, maybe not about Eve's show, but let me ask you something. What's it been like since Rumy brought you here?"

"Like being thrown into a giant washing machine during the agitation cycle."

"That's what I thought. So why don't we do exactly what he said? Or at least the first part. The club does have a great band."

"You're serious. But what about the extinction weapon? We should be looking for Zoey." She felt panicky, afraid that if she changed her focus for even a second, she'd miss a critical opportunity.

Lucian put his hand on her shoulder and gave a squeeze. "There's nothing either of us can do right now. Rumy's put out his feelers and he'll get a hit back— you'll see. Then we'll move forward. In the meantime, he is right. We'll both function better if we pace ourselves. This is going to be a tough process that will not resolve itself overnight."

Claire allowed herself to relax into the moment. Her experience as a social worker, which involved managing frequent crises among her clients, kicked in. "You're right. I need to let events unfold and I would like to see more of Rumy's club." She glanced down, looking at her pants. "Are jeans acceptable?"

Lucian smiled. "No. This isn't exactly a casual atmosphere, but no worries." He gestured to the rack near the dresser. "Rumy provided a wide array of attire."

Claire moved to the rack and flipped through several of the dresses, her brows lifting. "Some of these are not fit to be worn anywhere, except maybe The Ruby Cave." She drew out a short black dress with simple lines. "But here's one that might do." She held it to her chest. "Though I have to ask one more time: Are you sure we should be doing this?"

He nodded, and the soft vibration at her neck confirmed what she saw in his face. "This is a good thing. Did you and Zoey go clubbing often?"

"We did. We'd meet up with a lot of our friends, dance, occasionally drink just a little too much." For just a moment she got lost in the memories, but she gave herself a shake. "All right, then, I guess we're heading to Rumy's club."

She gathered up all that she would need and headed into the bathroom. When the chain at her neck gave a tug, Lucian moved closer to the dresser as well, helping with their ongoing proximity issue. "Take your time."

Those words, spoken in just that way, gave her pause as she glanced back at him over her shoulder. He had a wonderful voice, deep and resonant. But he was also very considerate, something she hadn't expected from his kind. "Thanks." She moved into the bathroom, closing the door. This almost felt like a date.

Lucian stared at the back of the door, not quite certain what to think. Was he really taking Claire to the club? It would have felt like a date if their situation weren't so dire.

When Rumy had made the suggestion, his first reaction had been just like Claire's: They had more important things to do than to dress up and listen to a band. But the part of him that had served as a warrior for centuries also knew the need for downtime so he'd put himself in her place.

Claire, though barely knowing anything about his world, had already been abducted when she was thrust into the Dark Cave system to rescue a blood-maddened vampire. And he'd spoken the truth when he said that they'd be wise to pace themselves. The shared chains added a difficult layer to an impossible situation, so yes, he thought this a smart move.

He changed into some clubbing clothes, brushed his short hair, and put on his handcrafted Italian shoes. He then sat on the bed and waited.

But after another ten minutes passed, he felt antsy with a need to be going, to be doing, to be out there battling and taking care of business.

"You okay?" Claire sounded worried.

"Yes, why?"

"It's the chains. You feel, I don't know, distressed."

He sighed. "Pay no attention. I'm trying to take my own advice. It's not easy to let go, not with the extinction weapon hanging over our heads like an ax ready to fall."

The door opened. "I feel exactly the same way."

He shifted in her direction, then stood up.

This wasn't the same woman.

She was Claire but more.

He'd forgotten how beautiful she was, her skin like cream, her lips full. And she was smiling. Despite her situation, Claire smiled, and he really liked this quality in her. She not only made the best of things, she tended to brighten the space around her as well.

She'd added a little makeup that seemed to enhance her unusual light-brown eyes. The dress fit her like a glove, revealing a beautiful line of cleavage, a narrow waist, and a soft curve of hips. She'd chosen a pair of four-inch stilettos so that if he took her in his arms, she'd hit him just right. He was a big man and by human standards, Claire was tall for her species—somewhere near five-eleven.

He opened his mouth thinking words would follow, but nothing came out.

Claire left the bathroom but didn't get very far. Lucian looked at her with his mouth slightly agape, but that wasn't what stopped her. He wore a blue silk, long-sleeved shirt, tailored slacks, and looked like a million bucks. She blinked a few times, trying to gain her bearings. It was one thing to have brought a wounded vampire out of the Dark Cave system, and quite another to be staring into the smoky-gray eyes of one of the handsomest men she'd ever known.

Her heart raced. Maybe this wasn't such a good idea

after all. When Lucian had said that they should pace themselves, he'd made a lot of sense. But she hadn't counted on this sudden, overwhelming attraction she experienced.

Essentially, she now saw him in an entirely new light, as a potential boyfriend, which of course was ridiculous. The man wasn't just a man, he was a vampire, living in a different culture, one that could never mesh with her deep need and desire to return to her life in Santa Fe.

Regardless, she'd agreed to go with him to see Rumy's band.

Reorienting herself yet again, she held her hands wide. "So, how do we do this? Would it be possible to walk to the club from here?"

Lucian shook his head. "Not exactly." He glanced down at her feet. "And definitely not in those shoes. Our room is at least a mile from the club. We'll have to fly."

She put a hand to her stomach. "Oh, no."

But he smiled. "It won't be bad at all. I'll take it really slow for you. I promise, you'll be fine. You won't feel a twinge."

"I suppose I'll have to take your word for it." She then glanced across the room at the shimmery red tickets. "Does it make me a bad person to say I'm just a little curious?"

He laughed. "No, not at all, and I don't blame you."

"Have you seen the show before?"

"A couple of times. Not sure if it would be the wisest move, but we could step in at the back for a moment so you can have a look."

She shook her head, heat climbing her cheeks. "I've never done anything like that before, but Rumy has mentioned Eve several times."

"She's a wonderful person, just very different from what you're probably used to."

At that, she sighed. "Like everything else I've experienced over the past three days."

He crossed the room and slipped the tickets into his pant pocket. "We can decide later." Moving back to her, he held his arm wide. "Ready?"

"I am." When she balanced her brand-new shoes on top of his expensive footwear, and he pulled her tight against his side, there was nothing for it but to slide her arm around his neck and hold on.

But for just a moment, as his gaze caught and held, she felt a powerful sensation of really being in trouble with this man. She didn't know what it was, but something about Lucian just got to her, as though on a deep level his soul spoke to hers and she was listening.

He cleared his throat and looked away. "It might be easier if you closed your eyes."

She agreed. "Eyes closed. Fly at will."

She felt the shift to altered flight and what followed, as he began flying them through solid stone, felt like soft hands barely reaching for her and touching her. She made use of telepathy. *Just tell me when we've arrived.*

Will do.

As promised, the flight didn't take long at all.

He landed her in a space that reminded her of a large hotel foyer with a number of people coming and going, all dressed up. The walls were decorated with extraordinary walls of crystals, all in huge swathes of different colors, violet, light blue, sea green. She could hardly take it in, it was so beautiful.

Off to the left a long counter made of exquisite burl wood served as an information center, guiding visitors to the various venues in Rumy's extensive club complex. At least a dozen women and men served behind the counter answering questions.

"This is amazing," she said, stepping off his foot. "I had no idea."

"I thought it might surprise you."

"To say the least." She glanced down and saw that the floor held an opalescent shimmer. She had no idea what kind of stone it was, but again the design stunned her. She had to do a quick mental realignment: This wasn't just a frightening vampire culture, but an entire civilization.

She glanced at Lucian once more, taking him in and feeling vulnerable yet again. In the back of her mind, she wondered if maybe this had been Rumy's plan all along, to get her to see Lucian and his world in a different light. Rumy had made no secret of the fact that he thought her power could benefit their world, and he wanted her to stay and help their cause.

"Everything okay?" he asked, frowning.

She shook her head, blinked some more. "I'm overwhelmed." The next moment the music started up, though at a distance, with a strong bass beat, very bluesy and sexy.

"I think you'll like this." He held out his arm. She slid hers around his elbow, once more having the weird feeling they were on a date, yet not on a date.

She took a deep breath, hoping to stay centered as he led her down a long hall that turned to the left for a couple dozen yards then opened up into an enormous cavern. On the other side of the vast space, the band was on stage, wearing silver-studded black leather outfits, cut to display muscular arms and chests.

The audience sat at small, linen-covered tables; female wait staff in skimpy black-and-white costumes moved quickly, serving drinks and appetizers. Each of the tables had a single candle, giving the club a romantic appearance.

The hostess greeted Lucian with a broad smile. "So glad to have you back, boss." Everyone seemed to call him by that name.

Yet again, she wondered about him.

The hostess was ready to take them to VIP seating, but he quietly asked for one of the more private booths near the back. "My friend here is rather shy and I'm trying to keep a low profile."

She nodded knowingly. "Of course." She led them down a short flight of stairs. Carved out of a shelf of rock was a row of relatively private booths. Scooting to the center, Claire realized that the design created a layer of privacy that she really appreciated.

Once more, she was grateful. And again, the man was considerate.

Lucian ordered Glenlivet neat, while Claire chose a mojito with sage and honey, her favorite drink.

He couldn't remember the last time he'd done something like this—and not just because he'd been in a prison for over a year.

He didn't date. Ever. He hooked up occasionally, but only for sex.

He sipped his drink and let Claire take in the club. More than once her gaze was drawn to couples who were getting affectionate. For himself, he looked away.

From the moment he'd first engaged with Claire at the Dark Cave, he'd been attracted to her, and from beginning to end this idea of Rumy's to take her to see the band wasn't helping.

His stomach cramped slightly, a faint signal that eventually his blood-madness would come roaring back. Because he'd been through it before, however, he knew he had time. He just wasn't sure how much.

Claire shifted toward him slightly. "I have an idea."

She was so close, and the booth afforded a very private environment. Even the immediate acoustics would allow for conversation.

His gaze shifted to her full lips. He had an idea as well, but he was pretty sure hers was different. "And what's that?"

"Well, these chains have thrown us together in an unexpected way. So, how about we tell each other something, and not necessarily of a serious nature, that we've never told anyone else."

His lips curved. "Only if you go first."

She nodded. "I think that would be fair." She glanced around the club, no doubt thinking.

The music from the band shifted to a quicker beat, livelier. He sipped his whiskey, waiting.

Finally she turned back to him and smiled. "I once dreamed of becoming an astronaut."

He sputtered over his drink. "Seriously?"

She set her elbow on the table and settled her cheek in her palm. "Well, not exactly. I was ten, I think, and had gotten a book with all these incredible pictures of our galaxy. But when I learned that all I'd ever do as an astronaut was travel in a circle around the earth, I gave up my quest then and there."

He set his tumbler down. "I think I know exactly what you mean. The reality simply did not live up to the fantasy."

"Very true. One of the hardest lessons about life, I think."

He held her gaze for a long moment. Claire wasn't a simple woman. She had thoughts behind her thoughts. He liked that about her.

Maybe it was the whiskey easing through his veins, or maybe the trusting light in Claire's eye, but he decided to offer his own never-before-mentioned experience, something no one knew about him. "I have a thing for puppies."

"What?"

"No judgment please. I just do. I've never had a pet, but once when I was young and Daniel had left the compound for a few days, one of the servants had brought in a puppy, maybe ten weeks old. I'd never seen one before—Daniel hated everything that resembled normalcy—and I used to sneak away to play with him. I made up a braided cloth toy and I must have thrown that thing a thousand times, all in secret, of course."

"Why in secret?"

He turned his tumbler in his hand. "Because if Daniel knew that I cared about the dog . . ." He didn't finish the sentence.

"That bastard," she muttered, sipping her mojito. But she met his gaze again. "What kind of puppy was it?"

"A golden retriever."

"Does your kind keep pets, generally?"

"Sure, just not in a place like The Erotic Passage."

She laughed. "No, I suppose not. So what happened to the puppy?"

"He lived deep in the cavern system until he died of old age."

"Daniel never found out?"

"It wasn't that. I chose to ignore the dog, to keep him safe. I think it might have been one of the hardest things I'd ever done."

Claire drew close and put her hand on his back. "I'm glad I'm here, Lucian. And I really do hope that I can help in a meaningful way."

"You already have."

She was so close and she smelled so good. Her blood tempted him; her eyes, her lips, the swell of her breasts.

When she didn't pull away, but instead continued to

stare into his eyes, he didn't mistake the invitation, but he debated for a moment what he should do.

Finally he leaned toward her and met her lips with his own, offering a soft kiss that had her moving into him just little, returning the pressure.

When he drew back, she lifted her glass. "Here's to puppies everywhere."

He lifted his tumbler. "And to the universe waiting to be discovered by young girls."

He clinked her glass and they both drank.

Then his phone rang. After he fished it from his pocket, Rumy's voice came on the line. "You need to get back here. I've got news."

"We'll be right there."

After paying the bill, he took Claire back to their room where Rumy waited for them, pacing once more.

Lucian could feel that he was revved up. "What's going on?"

"I've just received top-notch information that there's an extinction weapon hidden somewhere here in the Como system."

Back at the beige room, Claire found it difficult to process what Rumy was saying, in part because only a few moments before she'd been listening to music, enjoying a drink, and kissing a vampire.

But apparently, the agitation cycle had decided to start up again. She worked to refocus her thoughts away from Lucian, puppies, and her almost-date to once more pursuing the extinction weapon. "And you're sure this isn't some kind of prank?"

Rumy shook his head. "No, this is solid information. You have to remember, I have a spy network more powerful than your CIA."

Claire believed him, yet something didn't feel right.

"If you have this information, isn't there a strong possibility that Daniel will as well?"

"If he doesn't have it now, he soon will." Lucian held Claire's gaze. "Would you be willing to see if we can track it together?"

"Of course." Could they truly form a tracking pair? She'd soon find out.

For some reason, her words stopped Lucian. He stared at her unblinking for a long moment.

"What is it?"

Finally he gave himself a shake, but what she felt from the chains was a strong sense of disbelief.

At that, her lips curved. "Should I be offended that you've thought so little of me? I told you I would help you, but it appears you didn't believe me."

"I'll admit I'm surprised. I thought by now, after all that you've been through back at Daniel's cavern system and even here"—he waved toward the bed, referring to the recent feeding—"you might want to take off and frankly, I wouldn't blame you."

"I won't say the thought hasn't crossed my mind, especially given the numbers that Rumy so recently shared with me. But I want to be here, to do what I can. And yes, I realize that the odds are against my friend still being alive. Still, maybe once we've followed this current lead, we can use the same tracking ability to find Zoey."

"Absolutely." He took her hand once more. "Again, I'm so sorry Claire, about all of this."

She looked into his eyes and believed him. The more she knew about Lucian, the more she saw him as someone very heroic in his world. He wasn't anything like she'd expected, on any level, starting with his sheer size. But he was a good man, one she could trust.

Yet he was also a vampire, something she needed to remember. It wouldn't do any good to get attached to the man, not when her heart still lived in Santa Fe, with her mom and dad and her two younger brothers, where she'd been building a life as a social worker and trying to make a difference in her community. For the past two years, she'd envisioned returning home—and that dream, more than anything else, had kept her alive and moving forward despite her captivity.

She nodded several times, drawing her hand out of his clasp. "I think we should get changed, then figure out how to track this weapon."

CHAPTER 3

Lucian watched the auburn-haired human gather up her clothes and disappear into the bathroom. He was stunned at her resolve. She'd already been through so much and had only recently learned that her friend was probably dead, but she still wanted to help. Where had so much essential courage come from?

He liked Claire—that's what he decided in this moment. From the beginning he'd felt her strength, despite the fact that she looked physically fragile with her pale skin, and the tender compassion that she displayed as her most basic quality. This was a woman who could go the distance.

A woman he'd just kissed.

But he couldn't think about that right now, or how

much the experience had warmed his heart. They had a job to do.

He changed into his battle leathers once more, with a long-sleeved T-shirt. He shifted his attention to this thing called a tracking ability, something the blood-chains were supposed to have created between them. He'd never done anything like this before.

But one thing he knew for certain: In the same way that Claire had an innate ability to create disguises—something the siphoning of his power had allowed her to do—she was the one who carried the tracking gene.

When she emerged from the bathroom, back in her casual clothes, she hung up the black dress, her chin firm. She appeared ready to go to work. "So tell me what you know about the tracking power."

Lucian nodded. He approved of her demeanor and of the vibration in his chain that spoke of her resolve. "For the most part, the capacity to track people and things belongs to you."

"You mean, like the disguising power I have."

"Exactly."

"Okay." She spread her hands wide. "So, how do you think I can access it? What do I do?"

He took her hands once more, connecting his power to her more securely. "Just try focusing your thoughts on the weapon."

She closed her eyes, and his chains vibrated with her efforts to concentrate. He remained very still to let her do her thing.

After a moment he sensed a shift and watched her brows rise, then fall. When she opened her eyes, she shook her head. "For a second there, I sensed something, a definite shape. I mean, it was real. But then it just sort of disappeared."

"Good, that's good. Try again."

She repeated the process. As before he felt the change in her. He could sense how hard she was working to find the weapon, as though reaching through time and space.

At last, she opened her eyes but once more shook her head. "I feel close to the object, but I really do lack the power to complete the connection."

"You know what it is?" Rumy drew close and glanced up at Lucian.

"Don't say it," Lucian snapped, but he could see that his abrupt response startled Claire. "Sorry."

He turned back to Rumy. "I'm not going there. I promised myself that I'd never take that step. It'll bring me too close to being what my father is."

"What do you mean, what your father is?" Claire shook her head, frowning.

"An Ancestral."

"Oh, right. We talked about that earlier."

"If Lucian would take the leap and become an Ancestral vampire, he'd have enough power to take your tracking ability the distance. He could also serve as a judge in one of our courts or rule the Ancestral Council himself."

Lucian let go of her hands and scrubbed his fingers through his short hair. "It's one of the things that level of power would achieve."

She glanced from one to the other. "This is an advanced civilization, then."

Lucian glanced at her. Once more, Claire seemed surprised, which of course did nothing for his habitually short temper. "Yes. We even walk around on two feet and don't drag our arms on the ground."

But she laughed, her light-brown eyes sparkling.

"Oh, come on. You must have seen some of our vampire movies, especially the older ones. You have a reputation in the human world. Which means that I just didn't expect, when Rumy brought me here to what is essentially a sex club, that I'd be hearing about judges, leadership, and Ancestrals. Just please give me some time to catch up."

He squeezed his eyes shut for a moment. "Sorry, I have a short fuse."

"You're allowed."

He glanced at her. Once more the woman had surprised him. "I'm allowed?"

"Lucian, you've been in hell for over a year. If the least negative response you exhibit is a certain level of impatience, I'm impressed beyond words."

Rumy punched his arm and smiled. "She sees you like I do. You've never given yourself enough credit."

Lucian thought they'd both lost their minds. He knew what he was. He lived with Daniel's genes always threatening to take him over and to destroy the good he tried to do in his world. In part, he blamed Daniel's Ancestral genetics for making him the man he was. Daniel had taken all that power and turned it into something evil.

If Lucian ever embraced his Ancestral calling—and he knew he had it within him—what would keep him from becoming just like his father? That much power would tempt anyone.

"All right, fine, think of me as you will, but let's get back to figuring out this damn tracking thing."

"Fair enough."

Once more Lucian took her hands as Claire closed her eyes. She relaxed as much as she could, focusing on the extinction weapon. She had no visual representation for the weapon, so she kept her thoughts trained on what it could do, its potential for annihilation.

As before, an image would arrive at the periphery of her consciousness, trying to break through, then fade away. She centered her mind more carefully on that image. She felt Lucian's power flowing through her now, a sensation she was gradually getting used to. She tapped into that power.

Finally, the image began to take shape, in bits and pieces, sitting in a rough-looking cavern, smallish in size. In the center was a large gray metallic box with vents on the side. Without opening her eyes, she relayed what she saw.

She felt Lucian's corresponding excitement through the vibration of her chain. "Hold that location. That's all you need to do."

"Got it." But the edges beyond the weapon were wavy, as though the rest of the space was hidden behind a disguise. "Wait. Something's not right here. I think there's a disguising shield in place." She opened her eyes and met Lucian's gaze. "Is it possible Daniel is behind this?"

Lucian shrugged, frowning. "I don't know." He turned to Rumy. "Daniel could be here, couldn't he, without your security system knowing it?"

"In some of the more remote regions of the Como system, yes, of course. There are a lot of miles that I haven't explored. Don't really need to."

Lucian frowned. "So this could be some kind of trap."

Claire nodded. "It doesn't feel right to me at all."

"We'll go with your instincts, and cruise the area first to get a good look at the object and the cave. I think we'll know more then."

Claire gulped. "You're talking altered flight."

"I know, but I can take it slow. We won't be exposed like we were earlier in the open air. Mostly we'll be traveling through solid rock and not in a location where other vampires in flight could see us."

She supposed his words were reasonable, but her previous headache still lingered, though not nearly as severe as it had been when she'd first arrived. "Okay."

His lips curved. "You sound doubtful."

She rubbed her temple. "What else would you expect?"

"Point taken." He glanced first at his bare feet, then hers.

Claire smiled. "I guess we'd better shoe up."

Lucian laughed. "Shoe up?"

She shrugged. "It made you laugh, didn't it?"

His expression held for a moment. "Yeah, it did. I can't remember doing that in a long time. All right, Claire, let's shoe up."

Once she had her socks and jogging shoes on and he'd donned some serious steel-toed boots, he held his arm wide for her. As his arm tightened around her waist, she stepped onto his right foot. To feel secure, she slid her arm around his neck, but the sudden physical proximity brought another wave of desire flowing through her.

She became aware of just how male he was, and how much his scent appealed to her. She swallowed hard and focused once more on the task at hand. Knowing they'd be in flight, she switched to telepathy. *So how do we do this? I mean, what do I do?*

Just stay centered on the image and I think you'll be able to direct me. His rich voice pierced her mind, adding another layer of sensation, which she worked to suppress. Rumy had warned her that the chain-bond would enhance all her responses to Lucian, but she hadn't thought she'd be so drawn to him.

She closed her eyes. This time the image came to her quickly, a metallic-looking box, sitting on the floor of a rough-looking cavern. *Got it.*

Now concentrate on finding a path from this point to there.

After a long moment, she suddenly knew where to start. *There's a tunnel straight ahead.*

And just like that, he put them in flight. He took it slow, which helped her headache problem. However, when the first solid wall of rock came at her, she screamed.

He slowed to a stop in a cavern tunnel. *Close your eyes. You should be able to direct me without having to look.*

Really?

Yes. Give it a shot.

Happily.

She closed her eyes and much to her relief, the pathway seemed written on her mind. She continued to direct him down one tunnel after another, a trip that took a long time. *We're covering miles, aren't we?*

Yes, we are.

Finally they drew close to the end point. *Claire, I want you to wrap us up in your best disguise. Can you do that?*

Absolutely.

Claire didn't hesitate. She focused on building the preternatural shield that still hardly made sense to her. But she was definitely growing more comfortable with the process.

Well done, he murmured. *I can feel the strength of it. So how much farther?*

Actually, we're here. The machine is just beyond this wall of rock.

Lucian made a slow pass through the small cavern.

There it is, but I don't see anything else. Do you still detect a disguise?

A very powerful one. I feel like I could see through it if we dropped out of altered flight.

I'm not going to take that chance.

The next moment Daniel emerged from behind what was indeed a serious disguise. He wore a black leather jacket and tailored slacks, a silk shirt—more of his casual look, she supposed.

He stroked his goatee. "Show yourselves. Don't worry. I come in peace." He sat down on top of the metal box.

I can't believe he knows we're here.

That's his Ancestral power.

Lucian, what should we do? I don't trust him.

Neither do I, but he's got something important up his sleeve, so here's how I want this to go. We'll touch down, and you have a quick look around—and I mean quick. If you can see through the disguise and he's brought backup, I'll get us both out of there. Just shout into my head.

Sounds like a plan.

He landed them, and Claire searched the area. All she saw, however, were two women, one of them weak and emaciated, huddled by the far wall.

Daniel just smiled, his arms crossed over his chest.

Lucian squeezed her waist. *Claire, are you able to see through the disguise? What can you see?*

Just two women.

What women?

Right. I forgot that this is my skill and not yours. But they're by the back wall of the cave, maybe twenty feet past Daniel. There's no one else here and I'm sure the women can't harm us. One of them is really sick. I think they both might be slaves.

Daniel narrowed his gaze at Claire. "So you can see through the disguise I created. You have some serious power, Claire. Now tell me what you see."

Lucian interjected. "What do you want, Daniel?"

"I want to offer some incentive for your help, but first I had to find out if you had the tracking ability. It appears you do. And yes, I sent the tip through Rumy's spy network."

Lucian gestured to the box. "So this isn't a complete weapon, maybe just part of one?"

"You've guessed accurately. It's of no use to me. I almost had the plans once, but they got turned over to Gabriel, the one you erroneously refer to as your father. He probably destroyed them."

Claire glanced at Lucian. She didn't know who Gabriel was or why Lucian might have thought of him as a parent. More questions to ask.

Daniel turned his flecked, light-teal eyes on Claire. "Don't you recognize at least one of these women?" He swept his hand toward the far wall.

She searched their faces. The gaunt one, who couldn't be far from death, shifted slightly in her direction as though in pain. She had black hair and her large eyes were very blue. Then she saw the faint resemblance. "Zoey. She's alive. You brought her here." Her heart thumped hard in her chest. Her friend was right there.

On impulse she started to move in her direction, but two things happened at once. Lucian held her tight, preventing her from leaving his side, and Daniel snapped his fingers. With that small movement, the other woman gathered Zoey up in her arms and instantly shifted to altered flight. They both disappeared.

Claire felt dizzy. "What have you done with her? Where is that woman taking her?"

But Daniel only smiled. "As for her appearance,

she's been with me for over two years now and is going through the normal debilitation that your kind generally experiences. She doesn't have long now, but she might survive if you help me."

Claire would have launched herself at Daniel, ready to scratch his eyes out, but Lucian held her in a tight grip. *Don't let him get to you like that. He's taunting you. If you want her back, we'll have to play his game.*

She settled down, working to compose herself.

"Claire has spirit, Lucian. You'll enjoy that in the coming days. A real livewire, but then I knew you'd like her the moment I saw her in Santa Fe. Zoey, on the other hand, was just a lovely bonus. Now, as for my terms, it's simple. If you want Zoey back, then bring me the extinction weapon. Seems like a fair trade, doesn't it?" He stood up. "You won't need to contact me because I'll be watching you both."

Then just like that, he was gone.

Her throat grew tight. "I can't believe she was just here. I barely recognized her."

Lucian drew several deep breaths. At first Claire didn't know what was wrong, but then she felt it. "You're starting to spiral again, aren't you?"

He nodded. "We need to get back. Now."

"Let's go then."

To her surprise, he didn't inquire about return directions; he seemed to know the route even though it was miles long and took a number of twists and turns.

Throughout the flight, she remained quiet, hoping that in doing so, she wouldn't aggravate the growing tension in his body and in his mind.

By the time he brought her to their room, he stumbled as he moved in the direction of the bed. "Claire, you've got to call Rumy, now. You're not safe." He was breathing hard, struggling to get sufficient air into his lungs.

Using the landline, Claire did. "Rumy I need you. Lucian's blood-madness has returned. Please hurry."

"I'm on my way with reinforcements."

"Good."

She hung up, but her hand trembled so badly that she had a hard time getting the handset back on the cradle.

Lucian leaned over the bed, his hands planted on the comforter, his eyes squeezed shut.

She felt myriad emotions swirl through the shared blood-chains—rage and fear, deep confusion, even shame.

She just hoped Rumy would get there in time.

But the next moment the door slammed open and Rumy walked in with three powerful vampires, each almost as big as Lucian.

Claire tucked herself into the corner of the room, which was as far as the chain-bond would allow her to go. The tug on her neck made her wince.

She held a hand to her mouth as she watched Rumy's guards grab Lucian, tackle him to the bed, then work on the wrist restraints. The left restraint was attached to the steel bar on the side of the bed, but another steel loop, located between the halves of what proved to be a split mattress on top of the bed, held the other restraint. The ankles were lashed to the bar that ran across the bottom of the bed.

Lucian snarled and sank his fangs into each of the men in turn as they struggled to secure him. Yelps followed and a mountain of curses.

Lucian's twisted, furious expression, as well as the madness that flowed through the chains, beat at Claire, speaking to her in a constant stream that kept her heart thumping loudly in her ears.

Once Lucian was subdued, all three heavily muscled guards stood back, checking their wounds. Blood flowed from a number of bites. To Claire's surprise, however, each of them laughed.

"Damn, he's strong."

"Always was. Jesus, look how much I'm bleeding."

The third guard chuckled. "I know. I'm gonna need a new shirt."

Rumy's voice drew Claire's attention as he addressed his men. "Aw, you three babies need some Band-Aids? Want me to kiss your boo-boos, make them better?" His medical team moved in, as well as several more guards.

One of the initial guards grinned. "Would you, boss? I'd feel so much better." But he had a chunk missing from his forearm, which he held away from him. Blood had formed a pool on the carpet.

Great. Just what she needed to be looking at.

Rumy jerked his thumb in the direction of the hall. "Stay at your posts, assholes. Let the medics take care of Lucian."

Claire stared at Rumy, still shocked by all that had just happened. Between seeing Daniel again so soon and now having Lucian devolving into blood-madness, she wasn't sure how much more she could take.

Meeting her gaze, he smiled and shrugged. "What can I say? We're vampires. But please don't worry. My men will be fine in about half an hour and the doc here will give Lucian something to calm him down, at least a little. And of course we'll get someone in here to clean things up. You okay, though? None of this is very pretty, is it?"

Claire shifted to look at Lucian once more. "I don't know where to begin. He was fine, then the madness returned so fast and he slipped back into this terrible state."

"If it's any consolation, my experience has been that what he's about to go through right now, over the next few hours, will be the worst of it. He'll have minor bouts later, now and then, but usually a major crisis will help put him on the road to full recovery."

Claire didn't know what to think. She was reminded yet again that this was a wildly different world.

Lucian pulled against the restraints, his back arching off the bed. His fangs still protruded as he snarled at the medical staff. His arms were now tightly secured in the restraints. The setup was a far cry from the chains that had held him captive in Daniel's prison, but Claire hated to see him bound like this again.

One of the medics removed Lucian's boots, then went to work cutting off his clothes in order to make him more comfortable. When the doctor gave him the shot, he settled down a little, but to Claire's mind not all that much.

Once a sheet lay over the lower half of his body, Claire moved to stand at the foot of the bed. Rumy joined her, his gaze fixed on Lucian.

She glanced at Rumy, who'd never looked more solemn. "He's the best of us, you know. He saved his brothers when he was only fifteen and helped them escape Daniel's compound where they'd all been tortured since they were little. From that time, despite what happened to him, he's worked for the four centuries of his life trying to make our world a better place, trying to keep the traffickers, of all kinds, from making the serious inroads they have.

"But he gets little enough credit. Of course having Daniel Briggs for a father has always made the average resident suspicious of him, and of his brothers."

"I know that he's an honorable man." She touched her chain. "These don't lie and I feel it with every breath he takes." Another reason her desire for him seemed ever-present. She liked the vampire.

She then told Rumy what had happened, especially about seeing Zoey.

"Jesus," he murmured. "That must have been horrifying for you."

She put a hand over her stomach and pressed her fingers to her lips. Her throat grew tight all over again. "It was, but she's alive. Only how are we supposed to exchange the extinction weapon for her?"

Rumy put his arm around her shoulders and gave a squeeze. "Don't think about that. The important thing is, she's alive. Later, once you've found the weapon, you and Lucian can figure out the next step."

She turned back to Lucian, who had started to thrash once more. Whatever medication had been given to him clearly wasn't a cure. She felt the agony he suffered even though he'd received a strong dose of her blood. "What can I do for him?"

"Not much. It's the recovery process, sort of like withdrawal. He has to get through it, and he will."

"How much longer will it take?"

Rumy shook his head. "I don't know. Another day maybe."

She could live with that.

Taking a deep breath, as deep as she could get, she placed a request. "Would you please have your housekeeping staff bring me a basin of cool water and a stack of fresh washcloths?"

"Of course." He glanced at her with a warm light in his eye. "And what about you? What can I do for you?"

She smiled suddenly. "A mojito, the best one your bar makes, preferably something with sage and honey. I'm partial to sage especially."

"I'll bring you a pitcher."

She sighed. "Sounds like a plan."

He chuckled and drew his phone from his pocket.

He repeated her orders to his staff, then held the phone to his shirt. "How about dinner? I know you're not hungry now, but you have some hours yet to get through."

"That's probably wise."

"Italian, say in four hours?"

"Perfect."

He spoke once more into the phone. When he hung up, he said, "I'll be back with your drinks."

Not long after Rumy left, the doctor repeated essentially what Rumy had told her, especially that she needed to be alert and patient. Beyond that, Lucian would return to normal in a few hours; this would be the worst of it, followed by less significant episodes over the next few nights.

The team left shortly after so that she was once again alone with Lucian. She sat at the table, watching the vampire moaning and at times crying out. She would be in for a long night.

A few minutes later, however, Rumy returned with a suede wingback chair just for her and stationed it near Lucian's side of the bed. Another waiter brought in a side table, covered it with maroon linen, and with a flourish set a silver tray down that bore a pitcher of what smelled like heaven, along with a tall glass of ice.

He poured the first mojito and garnished it with thin cucumber slices. She sipped, leaned back in her chair, and tried to let go of the nightmare that had, in the past few hours, become her life.

When the basin and clean washcloths arrived, she left the comfort of the chair and her drink, and dipped a cloth in the water.

Lucian now rocked his head from side to side, his eyes squeezed shut.

Lucian. She thought maybe speaking to him telepathically might help.

He moaned, but began settling down. She put the now damp, cool cloth on his forehead. He was sweating, but his neck arched just a little at the feel of the cloth. His body relaxed, and his breathing evened out.

Is that better?

Fire. So hot. Where's Claire? Marius? My brother. Oh, God, my brother.

I'm here, Lucian.

The chains told her he was lost in his grief and in the feverish whirlwind of his thoughts. She didn't know what else to do, so she started telling him what Rumy had said about him. "He's proud of you, did you know that? The leader of the underworld thinks you're the best of all the vampires. I don't know you very well, but I'm beginning to think he might be right. He said you've served for four hundred years."

She continued in this vein and he seemed to relax a little bit more, taking deep breaths, a state that continued for some time. She resumed her seat and again sipped her drink, leaning her head into the wing part of the chair. She was more tired than she realized, and the mojito seemed to magnify her fatigue.

But a few minutes later she watched sweat bead on his upper lip and in the hollow of his throat. He started thrashing again.

She changed out the cloth and wiped all the way down his chest as well as his arms. The more she touched him, the more he seemed to calm down.

She continued to talk to him. She told him all about Josh, what it had been like to care for him for two years, how close she'd gotten to him, how often they played video games, and how much she missed him. She added that Rumy had given her an update on the boy once she'd arrived at The Erotic Passage: He was back with his mother and seemed to be thriving. "Adrien's become a father to him, did you know that? At least that's what Rumy said. See what you accomplished, Lucian? You kept Adrien safe, and now he's able to keep Josh safe and Lily. You did good."

He released a deep sigh, his brow still pinched, eyes still closed, but his body no longer spasmed and his breathing had once more settled down.

She returned to her seat and topped off her mojito.

Much later, between ministrations, dinner arrived. When she caught a whiff of the fresh bread, the pasta, and the salad, her stomach growled like she hadn't eaten for a year. Being a blood donor in the vampire world and taking care of a sick warrior was hard work.

As soon as the wait staff left, she gobbled her food. Of course, it looked like she was eating for two now, a thought that made her smile because it seemed so absurd.

She glanced at Lucian, now lying peacefully on his back, his eyes closed, his arms at last slack in the bindings.

She munched on antipasto, swirled a bite of spaghetti Bolognese on her spoon, bit off a chunk of bread, and basically devoured her meal without one thought to manners.

It helped to be working on her third mojito between bites.

Of course, just as she was starting to relax, his legs began to thrash.

Lucian could smell the woman's blood. What was her name? He couldn't remember. He couldn't really focus.

He was unable to reach her, either, which filled him with rage. Something held him back.

More chains. He was covered in chains head-to-foot, bloody chains.

He thrashed, trying to break free of them.

Something cool landed on his face then traveled down his chest, easing him.

He was so hot. He walked through hell, flames licking at him constantly.

He couldn't see much, but images flashed through his mind, of Marius as a little boy. Of Adrien. They were laughing. Sometimes Daniel would be gone for days at a time and they could relax, their wounds healing.

Lucian always structured their play and made his brothers study between times of torture. One day they'd leave, but until then, Papa would return, chaining them to wood tables, teaching them how to be men by slicing them open.

More images flashed of his mother smiling at him when he was very little, holding him close, telling him over and over how much she loved him and always would. She'd been human and died when he was four. Adrien and Marius each had different mothers, who had also died when the boys turned four.

Daniel had killed the women because his boys needed to learn how to be tough, not to whine or cry.

The fever raged once more.

Another cool bathing.

Was this his mother tending him?

No, his mother was gone.

Who, then?

He took in a deep breath, and the woman's blood called to him. Something vibrated at his neck.

More heat.

Another cool wet cloth.

A soothing voice spoke to him, about the wonderful meal she'd just eaten of pasta and salad, then something about sage mojitos.

After what felt like centuries, his mind cleared and

at last he was able to open his eyes. Only a single lamp burned on the nearby nightstand.

He glanced at the chair next to his bed. A woman rested there, her knees curled up, her lips parted as she leaned against the side. She was asleep.

His nostrils flared.

He could smell her blood. His stomach cramped. He moaned and the woman's eyes opened.

She glanced at him, leaning forward. "You're awake. And you're finally present; I can see it in your eyes. How do you feel?"

He couldn't remember her name. "I need to feed. Now." His voice was hoarse, like he'd been screaming. Maybe he had been.

She scooted her legs off the chair and stood up. She drew the chair close to the bed. "Rumy told me only to offer myself to you like this." She extended her wrist to show him.

Claire—yes, her name was Claire—rose from the chair and held the back of his head. She brought her arm close to his face.

His fangs emerged, descending rapid-fire. He struck then sucked hard.

In quick stages this time, as her blood flowed into his mouth, the cramping eased and his hunger abated. After a few minutes he released her wrist.

"Thank you." He closed his eyes and fell asleep.

Claire drank from a second, less potent pitcher of water that Rumy had brought her about an hour earlier. How sweet it tasted, the exact thing she needed to fill up her reserves.

She could see that Lucian had fallen asleep; he was actually resting. He seemed different now, less panicky, more satiated. She sensed he was on his way to recovery, if not completely out of the woods.

And suddenly the need for sleep fell on her like a hammer.

She rounded the bed, her feet dragging. She'd have to sleep next to him because of their constant proximity issue, but Lucian wouldn't be able to reach her because of the restraints, so she felt reasonably safe. She slipped off her shoes then—still wearing her T-shirt and jeans—crawled beneath the covers on the far side.

The world fell away the moment she closed her eyes.

CHAPTER 4

Sometime later Claire awoke to Lucian moaning. She turned toward him and her increasingly improved vision warmed up. He looked better, but he seemed to be in some kind of distress.

The chains suddenly spoke to her. He was no longer suffering from the deprivation of blood, but from something else.

Her body seemed to know and responded accordingly, as warmth climbed her cheeks.

She slipped from under the covers and rounded the bed to the other side. He was wide awake and lucid, but his lips were parted.

Claire. His voice was sensual within her mind. *Be with me. Please. I need you.*

She'd wanted him from the first, but this was new territory.

She felt flushed and hot. They were alone, in a private room, and the door was locked. Only the dim lamplight burned.

She wanted Lucian. She valued and respected him, which caused her own need to soar. And the time with him at the club, especially the kiss they'd shared, had somehow opened the gate for her.

Her gaze slid down to his chest, his pecs heavy with muscles, his nipples in tight beads.

The single sheet that covered him had formed a tent at his groin. And he was still in restraints.

She licked her lips.

Lower the sheet. I want you looking at me. All of me.

She hesitated. It was one thing to feed Lucian, to give up her lifeblood, but another to engage with him physically. Part of her knew she shouldn't—if she had sex with him, she'd become much more attached than she should.

Yet she wanted this with Lucian more than she wanted to be careful and wise. As one enthralled, she picked up the edge of the sheet and slowly peeled it away from his body, taking it all the way to his bound ankles.

Lucian came from her mind unbidden. *You're beautiful.*

I love that you're looking at me. I've wanted this. From almost the first moment I saw you in the cave, I've desired you.

She nodded as her gaze became fixed on his erect cock, then on the line of hair leading toward his navel.

His abs flexed and released.

His hips rolled. He turned toward her slightly and arched his hips so that she watched his cock thrust.

Her body responded in kind, clenching deep.

"I can smell your sex, your desire, Claire." His voice came out in a soft purr. "Please come to me, give me release. Your blood has eased the madness, but now I have a new kind of agony."

Maybe it was because the vampire used his manners; Claire would never be sure. But some kind of meet-your-vampire's-needs insanity took over her mind. She reached down to the hem of her T-shirt and pulled up and up, stripping slowly. His gaze raked her face, the slope of her neck, then drifted down to her breasts.

She leaned over so he could see her cleavage. His lips parted and his gaze fell to half-mast. She moved closer, leaning over him from the side of the bed.

With her bra still on, she eased her chest down to his lips and watched his tongue emerge. She lowered herself until he could lick the swell of her breasts.

He groaned. *Claire. My God. Claire. More.*

She reached back and unhooked her bra, tossing it aside. She fed him a nipple. He latched on and suckled. And it felt so good.

Look at me. His voice in her head commanded her.

His eyes had a wild look, but very different this time from his earlier blood-crazed expression. Each tug on her breast brought an answering pull deep between her legs.

Claire couldn't blame the blood-chain. She needed this, too, and she needed Lucian now.

She slid her hand down to his hip, lower, until she could stroke the crown of his cock. He moaned and suckled her breast harder as she ran her thumb over the wet tip, then slid it lower to caress the ridge, playing with him.

Desire shot through her, demanding more. Claire had never experienced anything so erotic in her life. Not only was her own desire heightened by their chains, but she could also feel what he was feeling. Panting, she pulled back, then slipped out of her jeans, losing her thong at the same time.

He watched her, breathing hard now, deep gulps of air, as his gaze flew over her body.

She leaned over his cock and took him inside her mouth.

His back arched and he groaned so loud that she was sure he would come just like this. She drew back, giving him a moment. When he settled down, she returned, sucking gently, letting him feel the pleasure of what had been denied him during the year of his imprisonment.

Blood and sex.

The touch of a woman.

His most basic needs.

"Enough." His hoarse voice filled the room.

She didn't wait for instructions or permission but climbed up on the bed. She swung a leg over his hips and mounted him. He was a big man with a big cock, but Claire was more than ready for him as she glided down on all that enormous, wonderful girth.

She closed her eyes as she seated herself. She heard his breathing, very light gasps, as if he was afraid if he felt too much, he'd spend himself way too soon.

She eased up and savored the length of him, then slowly lowered herself again. She gave herself to enjoying what felt so completely forbidden.

Sex with a vampire, a man who was essentially a stranger to her.

His hips flexed as he pushed himself inside her.

"Do you want me to release your hands? Can you control yourself right now?"

He nodded.

Maybe she shouldn't have, but she took the risk and

released the restraints, freeing his hands. She needed more of him, his hands touching her, fondling her. She wanted all of him and the moment his hands grasped her hips, she planted her fingers on his abs and slowly glided her hands up.

"Claire," he murmured, his voice hoarse.

She lifted her hips at the same time, feeling the length of his cock once more: pleasure on pleasure.

She moved faster as her fingertips reached his mouth and he groaned, his hips flexing again. His hands dipped low, grabbing her bottom and holding her firmly. He took over, thrusting up into her, increasing the speed.

She leaned down and kissed him, bit him, sucked on his lips until they parted.

She took his tongue in her mouth and suckled him.

He pushed into her harder.

His arms wrapped around her back, pulling her closer. She wanted to be closer. The vein in her neck throbbed and a different kind of need rose. She shifted her face away from him, which put her throat in close proximity to his mouth.

His tongue licked the length of her neck, over the vein.

She groaned as he thrust and as his tongue teased her sensitive skin.

She wanted more of the forbidden. She wanted him to bite her while her hips worked him hard.

Lucian rode the edge of ecstasy as he never had before. The blood-chains and his recent starvation worked together to forge a passion that moved like a roll of thunder through his body.

He drove into Claire, his cock rigid and ready. He could release at any moment, but he needed more from the woman straddling him.

His tongue repeatedly stroked above the vein that carried all that he'd needed desperately for over a year.

His blood-madness was gone, but the cravings he felt were almost as powerful. One thought dominated all others: Even above releasing inside her, he wanted more of what was in her veins.

His fangs descended. *Give it to me, Claire. You know you want to.*

I do. More than anything in the world.

He licked and she arched into his tongue, pushing against the little flicks he gave her throat.

She moaned as she rode him, her hands on his shoulders.

Come closer.

She arched her neck, creating the right angle. He teased her with the sides of his fangs, up high enough that the sharp tips wouldn't cut her.

She groaned. *Do it. Please. I want you to take your fill, take what you need.*

He knew she meant what she said, because the chains vibrated against his neck. He sensed she'd become desperate, just like him, longing for the experience that would bring them even closer together.

Come for me first. Your orgasm will flavor your blood. Come for me.

He sped up his thrusts, anchoring her even harder with his hands, keeping her pinned close to his groin.

She gasped for air now. *So close. Damn, I'm so close.*

I'm fucking you, Claire. And I'm going to drink from you as soon as you let go. Just let go.

The combination of his words and the feel of his cock deep sent Claire over the edge screaming. He drove faster and harder, wringing pleasure from her body.

He strove to hold on, knowing how much better it

would be if he waited. He wanted to come while he drank from her neck. He ran through a couple of algebraic equations in his head just to calm down a little as her satisfied body slowed and she relaxed against his chest. He surrounded her with his arms.

Holding her close, he tried to remember just how long it had been since he'd held a woman like this. Too long—maybe a decade or more prior to his imprisonment. Most of his couplings had been brisk and didn't involve any kind of intimacy. He didn't put much stock in love in any form, but after what he'd been through, her body and the soft mounds of her breasts soothed him.

His starvation pressed him forward and he nuzzled her neck. She shifted but kept her throat close. "Will you let me drink from you, Claire?"

"Yes. God yes. I need more right now."

"More like this?" He stroked her deep with his cock, then withdrew almost all the way out before he plunged back in. He'd been right about her; she was ripe as hell.

"Yes, just like that." She breathed in gasps, ready for him again.

"I'm going to bite you now."

She cried out. "Lucian. Yes."

He cupped the back of her neck, his hips moving in short strokes, the way he would attack her vein. His fangs protruded to their farthest point, his lips easing away from the sharp tips. Saliva pooled in his mouth, ready, so ready.

Do it came as a sharp command from her mind.

At almost the same split second he bit down, and her blood spilled into his mouth.

His rational mind receded to a dark quiet place and what was pure vampire moved to the front. A beast of thousands of years of evolution emerged, groaning as he sucked, driving his cock into her hard as he drank her down.

She groaned heavily in response, her voice hoarse and loose, savoring what was happening to her.

He thrust faster, but just as deep and hard. Each time, her pelvis ground against him. Her blood glided down his throat, powering him, feeding the vampire, the entity that required her blood. She tasted of the moon and water, of the earth and stars, all that was life.

Come for me again, Claire, and I'll come with you.

He moved faster and her breathing grew shallow and quick, brisk pants. He continued to drink from her neck. How much had he taken from her? He didn't care. He just needed to feel her pulling on him as she came again.

He drove faster, sucked harder. The power he felt now spread to each limb so that he became one quick movement, drinking her down, driving his cock.

You're close, aren't you?

Yes, so close.

He pumped faster and a series of sudden cries left her mouth, then her back arched and she screamed. He kept his mouth fixed to her neck, still drinking.

He grunted, pushing harder and faster. His lower back tightened, and suddenly the orgasm rushed through him, a stream of pleasurable fire. But he kept drinking and on the sensation flowed.

Her cries continued to fill the air. *Lucian, my God, Lucian. So much pleasure.*

Ecstasy filled him as he released over and over, pumping into her.

Her blood was doing something to him, something miraculous, and he felt himself winding up again. As he pumped faster still, once more her cries splayed over his shoulder.

Keep sucking on me, Lucian. The sensation is making me come again.

Oh, God, yes. Same here.

He fired into her once more from the depths of his body and groaned in a steady cry against her throat.

Finally she grew quiet in his arms, maybe too quiet, but he still kept drinking from her, unwilling to let her go.

He didn't want to stop.

Lucian, I can't open my eyes.

Her body felt heavy on him now, more than just the lethargy following orgasm.

The blood that now flowed into his mouth had grown thin. Too thin.

His rational mind came powering back and with a jolt of adrenaline, he released the serum that would rebuild her blood supply quickly.

Oh, God, he'd taken so much.

Claire. Claire.

But nothing returned to him.

He drew back. She was limp against him and pale, deathly pale. Suddenly he felt very weak as well, and his blood-chain no longer vibrated. To his horror, he realized Claire was close to death. But if one died, so did the other. Had he just killed them both?

He felt for her neck artery with his fingers and waited to feel the pulse of her beating heart. Nothing. He pressed harder. Fear worked in him now, fear that he'd let the beast he knew himself to be take over and kill the woman who'd brought him out of captivity.

The weakness he felt told him the truth of what he'd done.

Shame crept over him. He'd lost control. He'd been unaware of how much blood he'd taken because no part of him could think.

Claire, come back to me. Please. I'm sorry. So sorry.

He rocked her. He felt weak as well, when her blood should have given him enormous strength. She walked close to death, treading the shores, almost lost.

The only hope he had was that his serum could reach her marrow and produce red blood cells fast enough that her heart wouldn't give out and her brain would get enough oxygen.

What had he done? God help him, what had he done?

Images of his father's smiling face, always smiling, the charismatic bastard that he was, rose up to torment him. *Join me, Lucian, you're blood of my blood. We're the same.*

How many times had he told Lucian that over the centuries, reminding him of his heritage, that he'd been created by a psychopath. Lucian knew, deep within his soul, that of all the brothers he was most like Daniel, created in his image.

Claire, I'm so sorry, but I couldn't help myself.

And there it was, the absolute truth that Lucian hadn't wanted to stop taking from Claire, so he hadn't.

Claire. Please come back.

Claire.

Claire.

Claire.

Claire heard a man's voice, but he sounded so far away. Her mind seemed to be drifting in some kind of fog.

Where was she? Lying down, but too weak to move. She moaned softly and the arms that held her tightened suddenly.

You're alive.

Of course she was alive. Sort of. She felt so strange, as though she could barely make her mind work.

Where am I?

Just lie quietly. My serum will restore you in a few minutes. You'll be weak for a couple more hours, but no longer than that, I promise.

Why was this man promising her anything?

Why did he sound so desperate?

Who was he?

The gray fog started lifting from her mind. Her bare breasts were smashed against the hard planes of a man's chest, of Lucian's chest. She was on top of him.

Why?

Maybe that was the dumbest question she could ask.

The smarter one came to her: Why was she so damn weak?

Oh, that's right. Lucian had been drinking from her.

He'd sexed her up that way, made her feel impossible things.

She opened her eyes, looking at a nightstand and a lamp. She was essentially in bed with a vampire.

She tried to lift up and off Lucian, but she couldn't move. She was too weak.

Oh, my God, he'd drained her.

Lucian, you almost drained me dry.

He didn't answer her, but his arms grew slack. He patted her shoulder. "I was out of control. I'm sorry. It won't happen again."

As the memories came flooding back of what the sex had been like, she moaned softly. He had been amazing. He'd come more than once, and because of it so had she. Sex had never been like this before.

"I'm going to lift you off me now, okay?"

Then she felt him low. They were still connected. "That's fine."

He slid his hands under her arms and lifted her, glid-ing out of her at the same time. He swiveled and laid her on her back next to him. He sat up and released the ankle restraints.

When he was free, he once more stretched out next to her, then turned to caress her face. "I'm so sorry, Claire."

He looked sunk in his guilt, and she didn't want him to feel that way. Her blood-chain vibrated with his shame.

He watched her for a long moment, then finally rolled onto his back as well, pulling the sheet up at the same time.

He stared up at the ceiling, but remained silent.

Then she felt it, a stream of sensation that she'd only sensed in small pieces. For a long moment, as the dark waves rolled over her, she tried to understand exactly what he communicated. Shame and remorse had all but drowned Lucian. He'd fallen deep into the pit of those feelings, one of the reasons the chains barely spoke to her. Old wounds surrounded him, spoke to him, assaulted his mind.

She looked up at the ceiling as well, the beautiful light-blue waves, like the ocean, flowing over the top of the room.

She felt better. The serum in her blood was working quickly, giving her more strength than she would have thought possibly in such a short time.

Lucian had been right: She was recovering at light-speed. Drained to the point of death, yet she lived.

But above all, she needed to remind herself repeatedly of what had just happened, that she'd almost died because Lucian had lost control. She had no intention of dying before she had a chance to rescue Zoey, and then to return to her former life in Santa Fe, to see her parents and brothers again.

She sat up, further indication of her progress, then slid

off the bed, heading into the bathroom. A shower sounded like exactly what she needed.

She felt the warning tug at her neck, letting her know that she'd reached the proximity limits of the blood-chain.

As she stepped into the steaming shower and lathered up, she knew she had to do better with Lucian, to suppress what was proving to be a profound attraction and desire for the man. She washed her hair and applied a crème rinse, all the while searching for some means by which she could resist him. Unfortunately, nothing very specific came to her.

Toweling off, she was almost dry when she turned to find Lucian standing in the doorway, the sheet wrapped around his waist. He leaned an arm against the upper jamb, which revealed the powerful angled line of his chest and waist. Just looking at him, however, caused her resolve to falter.

She felt a flush cover her face and neck that had nothing to do with embarrassment. His navel was exposed along with his well-defined abs. What he could make her feel just by standing in a doorway. She honestly didn't know what she could do to stem this tide.

She cleared her throat. "Everything okay?"

He held her gaze, nodding. "I just wanted to say thank you."

Her brows rose. "For what?"

"For blood. For sex. For giving me what I needed despite your reservations. I know this isn't easy for you. And it's not easy for me, either, knowing that you're having to do things that you otherwise wouldn't."

Her gaze drifted to the tiles of the floor as she thought about what he said. When she looked back at him, she took a deep breath. "I need to keep this simple between us and sex is never simple, at least not for me.

I tend to get attached, and I don't want that. When all this is through, I'll need to go home to New Mexico."

"I know." His frown formed a ridge between his brows. "Then we'll keep it simple."

She breathed a sigh of relief. "You want a shower?"

"That would be great."

Wrapping herself up in her towel, she gathered up her toiletries. But when she tried to move past him, he caught her arm.

"Claire." The resonance of his voice alone forced her to look up and meet his gray eyes. Right now they weren't steely at all, as they could be at times. Instead they were warm and almost questioning—concerned.

Now more than at any other moment, even through the difficulties of altered flight or having Lucian almost drain her dry, Claire wished the whole thing undone. She felt horribly vulnerable, a state she despised. She didn't want to desire a vampire this much.

Finally she eased past him anyway. "Enjoy your shower."

Lucian moved into the bathroom, acutely aware of what Claire was feeling. This was perhaps the hardest part of the chain-bond, that he always knew what was going on with her. He'd felt her distress as she moved by him, and he thought he understood. She feared getting close, getting attached—and maybe for the first time in his life he felt the same way.

He turned the water on and stepped inside the enclosure. The warm water flowing over his short hair and down his shoulders, chest, and back was a soothing balm. Most of the cramping was gone, at least for now, though he knew he'd need Claire's blood again within the next few hours.

He just wished another woman would do for the blood

service part of their arrangement, as well as the sex. But the blood-chains seemed to invoke some kind of instinctive possessive response that he couldn't override.

He didn't want anyone else but Claire.

So what the hell were they supposed to do?

Neither of them wanted this level of connection. She wanted to go back to New Mexico and her family and he needed to be free to continue working on behalf of his society.

He'd always kept his liaisons with women on a strictly superficial level. At the very least, a man ought to know his limitations, especially where women were concerned. He had no interest in hurting Claire or any female, but if he got much closer, yeah, he'd hurt her, emotionally if not physically.

By the time he left the shower, he'd shored up his resolve to do all that he could not to make a mess of things. He wrapped a towel around his waist, feeling more confident. But when he left the bathroom, the mere sight of Claire overturned his resolve. Even with her hair damp, she looked so beautiful that his lungs seized.

She wore snug black jeans and a double set of tank tops, one cut low and hanging off her left shoulder. She looked damn sexy as she moved in the direction of the dresser. Even in profile she was beautiful. Despite looking away, desire rushed through him so fast that he coughed and sputtered.

"You okay?"

"Sure. Fine."

She settled her brush on the dresser and turned to meet his gaze. "I called Rumy and ordered breakfast for us. I probably should have asked for your preferences."

He waved a dismissive hand. "I'm sure whatever you chose will be fine."

"Good." She smiled. "And as for me, I think I'd eat anything right now. I'm so hungry, probably because I've been feeding you."

He wished she hadn't said that. He looked anywhere but at her because the thought of sinking his fangs in her neck or her wrist, or a dozen other places he could think of, sharpened his needs all over again.

In an effort to distance himself, he searched for his battle leathers and slipped them on. He added a long-sleeved black T-shirt and steel-toed boots. He was now ready for whatever came at them next.

CHAPTER 5

When breakfast arrived, Claire sat opposite a very quiet vampire. She worked her way through a wonderful spinach-and-mushroom omelet while Lucian ate waffles that he speared into bites stacked three high.

And he'd stopped talking to her.

He didn't look at her, either.

Just keeping things simple.

She sipped her coffee and sighed, but the silence didn't seem like a solution. "I like the clothes Rumy provided for me. He really takes care of the details."

"Yes, he does." His gaze shot to the shirt hanging low off her shoulder. He kept chewing, then speared another section of three-high waffles, sliced it off from behind with a knife, and in they went.

Earlier, Lucian had called Rumy and arranged for

them all to meet in Rumy's office to plan their next move. "Did Rumy say anything else when you talked to him? Anything about Daniel's tip line, for instance?"

Lucian shook his head but remained focused on his meal. He looked so damn serious.

He also looked sexy as hell, which she decided was not hard for him at all. She liked his short hair; parts were almost spiked but not quite. His face had a faint stubble, and the dark blue, long-sleeved T-shirt he wore really set off his smoky eyes.

This close, and with him looking away from her, she was free to just take him in. There were permanent tension lines around his eyes. She was pretty sure Lucian held himself together by sheer force of will.

She wondered what would happen if he ever really let loose. What would that even look like? Who would he be?

She blinked and recalled what it had been like riding him. These were errant, dangerous thoughts, of course, because suddenly her mind was full of the sight of him beneath her, before he'd put his fangs on her neck, before he'd almost drained her dry.

You were exquisite.

His gaze flashed to hers. "What?"

Had she spoken? She hadn't meant to, but the word had slipped from her mind, aimed at his. "Nothing."

He scowled. "What's with the rich scent you're throwing at me? I thought you wanted to keep things simple."

She blinked at him, then glanced down at her omelet. Using the side of her fork, she cut off another section. "I want you to know that though parts of what happened over the past twenty-four hours have horrified me, other parts were incredibly beautiful. Sex, for one thing." She chuckled and felt her cheeks grow warm. "I mean before you almost killed me."

Glancing at him, she saw a shard of guilt pierce his eyes and she regretted her words. She shot a hand forward and grabbed his wrist. "I am totally teasing you about that. And you didn't kill me."

"I could've. Hell, I almost did." He looked panicky, and the chain vibrated on her neck heavily. "I was out of control."

She held back a smile. "Well, think of it this way. If you'd succeeded, because of the chains, you would have died as well, so justice would have been served."

At that, his lips quirked. "You have the strangest way of looking at things."

She laughed. "I guess I do. Maybe it's from having taken care of a kid for two years. We played video games a lot, and the movies he thought were the funniest drove me crazy and might have affected my ability to reason. Imagine."

He seemed to relax. He even separated the three-part stack so that he only ate two segments at a time. "I want you to know that I will do everything in my power to make sure you get home. I know we have a mountain to climb between finding the extinction weapon and rescuing Zoey, but we'll get this done."

She nodded. Suddenly tears touched her eyes. "I've missed my family so much, my mom and dad, my brothers, even their horrible teasing." A vivid memory came to her about how she'd go into the bathroom and when she came out, both her brothers would be waiting there as though standing in line. Her mother would just laugh when she complained.

"You were robbed of precious time with them. Unforgivable."

She sipped her coffee, considering him. "So why exactly haven't you become an Ancestral?"

He shrugged, adding more syrup to his waffles. "For

the simple reason that power corrupts, especially vampires. You have to understand, I'm Daniel's son. I'm like him in more respects than Adrien is, and more than Marius ever was. I fear that I'd become like him— that instead of helping my world, I'd become the asset to Daniel he's been hoping for all these years. You don't know how much it plagues my mind."

"Lucian, I don't think you see yourself clearly at all. You could never be that man."

His brows rose and his lips parted. "I'll always be grateful that you've said that to me. But I want to change the subject just a little, something for you to think about. When the day comes that I take you back to Santa Fe, you'll have the option of having your memories stripped. You won't remember a thing. Your human specialists will call it selective amnesia because of what you've been through. I can do that for you, if you want."

Claire sat back in her chair, pondering his offer. Her gaze drifted back to the bed, to being with him. She'd lost the past two years, and yes, she wished her life had unfolded in a different way. But would she truly want to forget that she'd cared for Josh, or that she'd seen Lucian through a terrible bout of blood-madness, or that she'd had the most amazing sex of her life with him?

What was the measure of a life except all the combined memories, good and bad? She was a social worker by profession, which meant she'd seen a lot of bad stuff touch the lives of other people. They often had to keep enduring child or spousal abuse, or the chaos of alcoholic parents, or drug-addicted family members who kept stripping a household to the bones financially.

Not a single human she knew had the power to get rid of their memories forever.

Why should her experience be any different?

"You're thinking about this really hard, aren't you?"

She shifted her gaze back to him. "You felt that from the chains?"

But he nodded in the direction of her lap.

Glancing down, she saw that her legs were crossed and so were her arms. She smiled. Body language really didn't lie. "I was thinking about whether or not it would be truly wise to let all these memories go. I'm not sure I want to go that far."

"It would be a difficult judgment call, that's for sure. But it's available if you want it."

"Thanks." She thought about picking up her fork again, but the remainder of her omelet had grown cold and she was no longer hungry.

He wiped his mouth with his napkin and glanced at her plate. "Are you done? If so, we can head to Rumy's."

"I am. Just give me a sec." She took time to brush her teeth, which prompted him to do the same.

Then, like any old couple, he held the door for her.

But just as she would have crossed the threshold, she looked up at him, grabbed the front of his shirt, and pulled him down to her. Kissing him once on the lips, she said, "You're a good man, Lucian, one of the best I've ever known. Don't you forget that."

She saw the doubt that flickered through his eyes, but rather than let him argue the point, she headed back up the hall in the direction of Rumy's office.

Once there, Rumy seemed oddly nervous, this time grazing the tips of his fangs with his index finger.

"What's going on?" Lucian asked. "You look like a mouse staring down a snake."

Rumy sighed heavily, turned around, then picked something up off his desk. Claire saw that it appeared to be a display board covered in green velvet.

"What is this?" Lucian scowled, but Claire could

feel through their shared chains that his heart rate had jumped a notch. He must already have an idea what they were looking at.

"Gabriel had these delivered about two hours ago. They're for you and Claire—but only if you want them. He said to tell you no pressure."

Claire drew up beside Lucian and watched as Rumy lifted back the velvet cover. Mounted on another piece of velvet were two sets of elegant silver chains, each made up of two rows of interlocking loops.

"Hell the fuck no." Lucian crossed his arms over his chest and glared.

"Are these the double blood-chains?" Claire was so intrigued.

"Yep, and only Ancestrals can wear them—and their partners of course. They also have the ability to jump-start Ancestral power. Gabriel had them made up special for Lucian and for you, if you want them. So what do you say?"

Lucian snorted. "For starters, I'd rather be hung upside down and zapped with Tasers for the next century than put these on."

But Rumy smiled ruefully. "Okay, but tell me how you really feel."

Claire wasn't surprised at Lucian's response, since he'd told her of his reservations so recently. But she'd probably never get a chance to see this kind of blood-chain again, so she drew close. Power vibrated through her, even called to her from the chains. Unfortunately, she made the mistake of reaching out and touching one of the links. The next thing she knew, she was flying backward.

Lucian felt power surge through him from the double-chain the moment Claire made contact. He crossed to her quickly and picked her up in his arms. She was out cold again.

She was breathing steadily, however, so he could at least relax about that. He wouldn't have been surprised if the sudden burst of power had stopped her heart.

Claire?

Nothing returned.

Yep, out cold.

Though he had little enough experience with blood-chains, he still didn't understand why Claire touching them would have resulted in such a swift, unexpected power boost. Even his chain sang with new energy and power flowed through his bones—an addictive, dangerous kind of power, the kind that lived in Daniel. What the hell had Gabriel been thinking to tempt him like this?

Of course, the double-chain meant exactly what Rumy had said: If Lucian put it on, he'd become an Ancestral, something Gabriel had wanted him to do for a long time. Gabriel, an Ancestral in his own right, had been a surrogate father to him and to his brothers when they'd escaped Daniel's house all those centuries ago. Lucian respected him, but he couldn't take this step.

Claire came around slowly, her eyes opening as she turned toward him. "What happened? And why do I feel so good? Like I've been drinking or something." Absently, she plucked at his shirt just above his right pec.

"Do you remember touching the chain Gabriel sent over?"

"Vaguely. Hey, you're holding me in your arms."

"I am." Between the power surge and the fact that she'd recently fed him, his desire for her rose once more.

His gaze fell to her lips and images suddenly filled his mind, of taking her to bed and showing her that he really knew his way around a woman's body, being generous with her the way she'd been giving up her blood for him.

Despite their recent agreement to keep things simple, if they'd been alone, he would have said exactly those words to her.

But they weren't alone and Rumy was grinning at him in that lascivious way of his. Worse, Claire was now rubbing Lucian's pec with a sensual swirl that made him think if she dipped any lower and touched his nipple, he wouldn't be responsible for the consequences.

He knew by the shared chains that she was feeling it, too.

Desire. Pure desire.

And all because she'd touched the double-chain.

How hard are you?

Oh, God, Claire's voice in his head really didn't help, so he responded in kind. *How wet are you?*

Enough to handle what you've got. Her voice sounded loose and needy inside his head.

We're both feeling too much right now. Must be because of the double-chain.

Maybe. Or maybe it's just you, Claire. And how much I want you.

Aloud, he said, "Rumy, would you give us a minute and turn off your damn security cameras."

"You got it, boss."

The moment he left, Lucian lowered Claire to her feet, then turned her in his arms, slanting a kiss over her waiting mouth.

In turn, she grabbed hold of him, her fingers digging into the muscles of his arms, shoulders, back, whatever she could reach and fondle.

His hands went straight to her bottom. He cupped her and pulled her against him, grinding into her. His tongue drove in and out of her mouth, mimicking what he wanted to be doing to her.

When she suckled his tongue, he groaned.

Finally he pulled back, breathing hard. Her lips were swollen, her light-brown eyes dilated. His gaze drifted over her face, memorizing her features that, because of the damn chains, seemed to have gained critical, life-altering importance to him in only a night and a half.

He wasn't sure what to say, but he would never forget this moment, her beauty, her long wavy auburn hair, her creamy skin, the small indentation in her chin, the laughter in her soft, light-brown eyes.

She caressed his face. "You're driving me crazy, you know."

"Same here."

He'd smiled more than usual in the past few hours. He couldn't remember the last time he'd done that. Even with his brothers, smiling was rare. Marius had been able to make him smile, and on the rare occasion to laugh until his sides ached.

His thoughts fell hard to that other reality: Marius. Now dead.

What is it, Lucian?

Just thinking about Marius. My brother is gone. Sometimes it hits me hard. I was thinking of him just now.

She hugged him, and he returned the embrace.

After a minute of just holding her, and once his body had calmed the hell down, he brought Rumy back in.

At the same time, the landline on Rumy's desk rang. He crossed the room to answer it, but after a moment he turned in Lucian's direction, frowning. "What's her name, the one asking about Zoey?"

"Zoey?" Claire's voice sounded small in the room. She glanced at Lucian and instinctively drew closer to him. He took her hand, holding it tight.

Rumy kept nodding. "Repeat that last bit." He paused.

"Okay. And you're sure they're from a club in Santa Fe? What did you call it? The Prickly Pear?"

Lucian heard a sharp intake of breath from beside him. "Oh, God, no," Claire murmured.

Rumy pressed two fingers to his temple, concentrating hard. "Tell me where they're at again?" Another pause, then, "Thanks, Sam. I owe you one."

Lucian leaned close to Claire. "You were abducted from that club, weren't you?"

"Yes. This does not sound good."

Rumy settled the phone on its cradle. "Claire, were you taken from The Prickly Pear?"

"I was."

"Shit. A vampire known to have connections in Daniel's sex-slave operation owns that club. But one of my informants, who works at the Hawaiian cavern system, said a couple of girls arrived recently and they've been asking about Zoey and you. They said they were from Santa Fe. It can't be a coincidence. Anyway, this system is a suspected trafficking center."

Lucian lifted a hand. "But the disguising effects there are some of the most powerful I've ever seen. We could never break through to see what was going on, because an Ancestral created the fields."

"Which means I might be able to help." Claire squeezed Lucian's hand.

Rumy nodded. "That's what I'm hoping. The owners of the pineapple-exporting firm are a couple of major slimeballs. I'm pretty sure they paid the Ancestral a huge fee—and maybe a percentage of their trafficking business—to get that level of protection and secrecy. Anyway, the informant talked to one of the guards about half an hour ago and here we are."

"What are their names? The girls who were taken, I mean." Claire squeezed Lucian's hand.

"Amber and Tracy. Do you know either of them? Apparently Amber has straight black hair almost to her waist, if that's any help."

"Oh, God."

Lucian felt Claire's sudden horror and wasn't surprised, as he glanced down at her, to find that she was trembling.

Who is she? Who's Amber?

Claire turned toward him slightly. "Amber is Zoey's younger sister. Lucian? Is it possible vampires just kidnapped Zoey's sister?"

Lucian frowned. "It's possible, especially if she'd been hunting for information about Zoey."

"Doing her own investigation."

"And asking the wrong people."

"But what are we going to do?"

Claire still held Lucian's hand. She had never felt so solemn in her life. This simple phone call to Rumy, a communication from halfway around the world, had just added a new layer of complexity. Not only was someone she knew in trouble, but the whole situation reminded her yet again of the dark forces she and Lucian fought.

She knew Amber well, because she'd practically lived at Zoey's house for over a decade and had even babysat Amber when she was a kid. Right now, she had to be eighteen, a very tender age for most young women.

And if something wasn't done right now, Amber would disappear into the vampire world's sex-trafficking nightmare, just like Zoey had. Both women could be dead within two weeks. If not, they'd probably perish sometime in the next eighteen months.

She looked into Lucian's steely gray eyes. She felt

his distress, even his anger at the abduction, at more innocent lives taken.

He ground his teeth.

"Lucian?"

His rage made the chain at her neck feel hot, as though his anger burned within the metal and now scorched her skin.

Then she felt it, an answering rage within her own spirit: at having been abducted herself, at losing two years of her life, at Zoey's fate and now Amber's.

Still holding Lucian's hand, she realized they shared the same understanding, as well as the same purposeful reaction.

His gaze left the floor and slid in a long slow trek toward Rumy's desk, landing finally on the green velvet display board.

Claire felt her chain vibrate with another pulse of sudden, quick anger followed as swiftly by Lucian's resolve. On every level, she saw what needed to be done, not just to save Amber from what sounded like an impossible-to-find trafficking center, but for the more inclusive purpose of tracking and locating the extinction weapon. In order to expand their tracking ability as well as to enhance her own ability to detect and create disguises, Lucian would have to rise to Ancestral status.

Without the increased power, they would struggle to accomplish any of their goals, including rescuing Amber and her friend. Flight would remain unbearably painful for Claire, their current tracking ability was weak compared with their pressing need, and even if they somehow found the extinction weapon, Lucian wouldn't have sufficient power to take Daniel on.

But she recalled Lucian's greatest fear: that in

embracing the full potential of his power he would become like his father.

She met his gaze, knowing he had a tough choice to make and that only he could make it.

His lips turned down, and his gray eyes darkened. "I know the Hawaiian system. No one can get in. The disguises are beyond anything I've ever seen, maybe even beyond your current power, Claire. And that system is far away. I couldn't even fly you there without causing you a shitload of agony all over again."

She looked deep into his eyes and saw everything there, the totality of his determination and how much he would sacrifice, just as she would. And here was a trait they shared in common, something that might be even more binding between them than the blood-chains. Each would sacrifice. Each would do what had to be done.

She had to do this.

So did Lucian.

She might not understand all his reasons, but hers were simple: She knew Amber and she knew Amber's mother. She couldn't let this happen to either of those women, not when Zoey had been lost to her family for the past two years, maybe even forever. The household had endured enough suffering with Zoey's kidnapping. But even beyond Amber's abduction, there were thousands of young women in the same kind of jeopardy.

And Daniel Briggs was behind it all. From what Rumy and Lucian had said, Daniel led the way when it came to sex slavery. And all roads seemed to lead back to him.

She began to understand the impact the extinction weapon could have on her world as well. Once Daniel had full control of the vampire world, he could expand his vile sex-slavery operations so that more and more human women, just like Amber and Tracy, would fall victim to him. More than ever before, she saw the absolute necessity of making sure that Daniel's plans failed.

"Lucian, I want you to know that I'll do whatever it takes to help you stop Daniel. He's set the worldwide stage for this level of sex trafficking. He has Zoey in his power and now his organization has abducted Zoey's sister and her friend. I don't think I really connected all the dots before, but none of this will change until he's brought down."

He closed his eyes, a frown never far from his forehead. She felt how upset he was that the very thing he'd promised himself never to do looked like the only way he could save his world from calamity. Saving Amber would be a side trip, though a critical one. But becoming an Ancestral in order to get the job done would accelerate their efforts on all fronts.

Lucian turned and faced her fully. "The only way we make this work is with your disguising power enhanced with an infusion of Ancestral power. I truly doubt we'd even be able to find them otherwise. But once I rise to this level, nothing will stop us from finding the weapon. I'm sure of it. As far as my biggest concern goes, I have no idea which way this will fall."

"You mean whether the new power level will somehow seduce your dark side?"

"Exactly."

"But you're willing to take the risk."

"I am, but are you? This could backfire and you could get hurt."

She took his other hand and held his gaze with all the ferocity she could manage. "With all my heart, I believe you're incapable of resembling anything like Daniel Briggs."

* * *

From the time he could remember, Lucian had fought his basic nature, the one that matched Daniel Briggs point by point: his level of rage, his desire to hurt, his willingness to fight anyone to the death. He was more vampire than Claire would ever understand, and to some degree, when she questioned his civilization, she had it right about his species. What else could account for such a vast network of human trafficking in his world?

His gaze settled on the double-chain. The new set would hit him about three inches below the well of his throat and were just big enough to slide over his head. And Claire would wear the matching one in order to sustain their bond. She would continue to siphon his power, but otherwise the primary changes would occur within him.

He couldn't believe that after four hundred years, he was making the Ancestral leap. But it had to be done. If he had any hope of stopping Daniel from getting the extinction weapon, he needed to be at Ancestral level right now and he needed Claire with him.

He turned toward her, meeting her steady gaze.

He picked up the set meant for him and for the strangest split second wished Claire stood beside him. Then suddenly she was there and touched his shoulder.

"I can feel the difference and you haven't even put them on."

He breathed hard now, because he was feeling it as well, the potential in the double-chain. His life would change from this moment forward. Nothing would ever be the same—and even more troubling, he'd never be able to go back. He would become an Ancestral. Once his power rose, he would be born into that new realm.

He stared into Claire's light-brown eyes, still breathing hard. He'd resisted and feared this moment his entire life: The double-chains would make him Daniel's equal, his competitor, his true enemy.

And once the chain was on, Daniel wouldn't be far behind.

But would the rise to Ancestral status make it impossible for him to battle the constant evil that threatened to take him over? Or would he become a sadistic killer? Would darkness rule his mind and his thoughts the way it did his father's? Or was he truly the man Claire believed him to be?

Claire's beautiful voice eased through his mind. *Are you ready?*

He nodded slowly. *I am.*

Lucian drew the chains close. He could smell the power of them now, what they would bring him. He wanted that power—and here was another of his truths: He'd longed for Ancestral power from the moment he'd first learned of its potential.

He drew in a deep breath, one that went to the base of his lungs, and without any more questioning of motive or purpose he slid the double-chain over his neck.

On instinct, at the same moment, he took the single-chain off and tossed it onto Rumy's desk.

Then he waited.

He met Claire's gaze.

The first thing he felt was the absolute purity of her soul. The second thing he knew was his complete unworthiness of being with a woman like her.

Then the power struck like a blow to his head, and he fell to his knees. He hadn't known what to expect, but the sheer level of the power felt like a tornado in his body. Some deep part of him resisted.

Claire's hand was on his arm once more, and she

squeezed hard as she knelt beside him. *Lucian, listen to me. I can feel that you're holding back, but you have to let go, let the power become part of you.*

I can't. I'll become like Daniel.

Gray spots flew through his vision. He'd lose consciousness soon.

She shifted to get in front of him, then put both her hands on his face. *Look at me, dammit. Lucian, look at me. You can do this! You're not Daniel. You think you are, but you're not, and that's something both Rumy and I agree on. You're worthy of this power and this power will change your world for the better. I know it will.*

Her words started filtering through the spots. Somewhere in the middle of the power crushing him and his fading consciousness, he decided to believe her.

He opened his lungs wide, arched his neck, and let it come.

Ancestral power, what had been his from the beginning, now flooded him in waves, perfect and beautiful, like an old friend returning to have a long brilliant conversation.

Once his resistance left, his spirit soared. He extended his arms up and out as though embracing all that there was in the world, in life.

Lucian, I can feel what you're experiencing and it's magnificent.

He opened his eyes and looked at Claire. He saw her as though surrounded by a halo of light. Even his vision had changed, sharper, clearer.

He rose up, lifting her to her feet at the same time. He turned to face her. He touched her gleaming auburn hair, letting the strands sift through his fingers. The texture was coarse yet somehow silky at the same time.

He leaned in and smelled her hair, then her forehead.

The scent of her blood came to him like a sharp blade of sensation. He'd loved tasting her blood from the first drop in the Dark Cave system. He wanted more, but something stood in the way.

He eased his shoulders back and stood up straighter. He turned in a slow circle, just sensing his surroundings. He felt the club, even the miles of underground dwellings and theaters, even Rumy's villa hidden in the center behind thick disguises, Rumy's safe place.

So this was what it meant to have Ancestral power, to have all of his powers and abilities heightened. He was astonished at how far he could reach out to gather information.

He retrieved the second double-chain and put it over Claire's head, settling it on her neck. As he'd done with his own, he took the single-chain and removed it at the same time.

She gasped then smiled. "It's amazing, like hearing a choir of angels sing."

Lucian felt nothing but gratitude as the bond between them strengthened. He drew her into his arms. For a long time, as his Ancestral power flowed and began to settle into every cell of his body, he held her close.

After a few minutes he drew back and saw that Claire's eyes were full of fire. "What is it?"

"Let's go get the girls."

"Can you feel them? Do you know where they are? Rumy tells me that when Adrien and Lily formed a tracking pair, she could focus on a specific cavern and get a reading."

He watched her turn her thoughts inward, but he could see that she still struggled to get a reading, despite the new level of power they shared.

"I don't think I have Lily's gift—or if I do, it's not

the same. What I sense when I think of Amber involves deep swirling patterns. I think I'm sensing the disguising pattern that keeps her hidden."

"Can you tell if she's in Hawaii?"

At that, she nodded, then smiled. "Yes, absolutely. I can at least tell you that much."

CHAPTER 6

Suddenly a new voice intruded straight into Claire's mind.

Claire?

A young woman's voice. How was that even possible?

She drew back slightly. "Lucian, I think I'm hearing someone calling to me."

He shook his head. "Who?"

"I'm not sure." At first she thought it might be Zoey. But she focused once more on Hawaii and suddenly, Amber's voice pierced her mind. *Claire, is that you? Claire? Am I talking inside your head because I feel you inside mine? Claire?*

Amber? Zoey's sister?

She thought she heard a scream, or a squeal maybe, and she gripped Lucian's arm hard.

"What is it, Claire?"

She shook her head in disbelief. "I'm communicating with Amber telepathically."

He looked stunned. "This is a result of Ancestral power."

Claire nodded.

His lips worked as though he ran through a quick litany of questions. Finally, he asked, "Does she know where she is?"

Claire asked her, but Amber's response was cloaked in sobs. When Claire finally made sense of what Amber was saying, she addressed Lucian. "She doesn't know. She smelled fruit of some kind, and some of it rotten, but that's the most she could tell me."

"We'll figure it out. Tell her we're coming."

Claire nodded, then turned her thoughts toward Amber. *It's okay. We're coming for you, sometime within the next hour. Be ready. We're leaving now.*

Thank God. Just hurry. Some of the women are getting hurt.

She ended the telepathy and yet again drew in a deep breath. "So, do you know where the Hawaiian cavern system is?"

At that, he smiled, a big perfect smile, something he did so rarely. "Hell, yeah."

He turned toward Rumy. "Not sure when we'll be back. Hold the fort and let me know if Daniel makes a move while we're gone."

"Understood."

Before Claire could prepare for what was about to happen, Lucian switched to altered flight. Suddenly she was streaking through solid rock then high into the dark night sky, gliding through space like it was nothing.

Feeling any pain?

She gasped slightly. *Not even a little.*

I'm so glad, Claire. I was worried.

She glanced down. *Wow, look at the Atlantic. So we're heading west this time?*

Yep. Flying into the night.

The flight was so fast—even faster than when he'd flown them both out of the Dark Cave system—that she watched the earth below her in amazement. The Atlantic gave way to the Gulf of Mexico to Mexico proper then the Pacific, all in less than a few beats of her heart.

He began to slow, though she wasn't certain why until she realized how easily he could overshoot the Hawaiian Islands.

He dropped closer to the earth as well.

Okay, Claire, you're up. There are several disguised caverns along this side of the island, so focus on Amber because I'll need you to guide me in.

She settled her thoughts on Amber as Lucian's movements grew slower and slower.

I'm trying, she sent, *but this tracking thing isn't working for me.*

Then try your disguising power. Maybe that's the key.

The moment she shifted her focus toward her ability to create and detect disguises, the direction she needed to guide Lucian suddenly arrived.

Head toward the volcano. The caves nearby have unique, powerful disguises. I haven't seen this kind before.

Once she'd set the end point, Lucian sped up. The next moment he said, *Create a strong disguising shield around us.*

The funny thing was, when her thoughts became fixed on Lucian, what followed was a sudden powerful

need to protect him. Was this the chains talking? Or
something more typical of the vampire culture and
experience?

She was so intent on what she'd created that she
didn't realize he'd come to a stop, that they'd touched
down at what looked like an enormous docking bay
carved out of an equally large cavern.

She glanced around. *Oh, my God. This is a real
business. But where are they shipping all those pineapples to?*

He moved her off his foot but kept a loose arm
around her waist. *We have thousands of legitimate
businesses in our world. These pineapples are shipped
everywhere. But I have to say that this new disguise
you created around us is amazing. There's actually a
color now, sort of violet.*

You're right. But I wonder why that is.

Just probably part of your gift.

Well, I think that's interesting.

What? Why are you frowning at me?

*Because I'm starting to understand you. You're gen-
erous with me, but not with yourself.*

He stared at her for a moment, then shrugged. *Not
sure what that means, but let's see if we can find Amber.*

Good idea.

She turned her focus on Amber and extended her
senses into the Hawaiian cavern system, searching as
best she could for Zoey's younger sister. From what she
knew about all the systems in the vampire world, the
caves could go back into the earth for miles, with layers
of caves one on top of another, at times opening to massive caverns or at others shrinking to tunnels that would
need work before being usable.

But as she focused on Amber and her long, thick
black hair, she found herself moving yet not moving, as

though some internal visionary part of her could see. A second-sight window opened, and she reached for Lucian's hand. He gave her a reassuring squeeze so that while she experienced this strange split viewing, she felt grounded and secure.

What met her was one disguising shield after another, each one with a different texture. Some swirled, some moved in strange waves back and forth, but none of them was in color.

As she witnessed the various disguises, she related them to Lucian, who remained very quiet. She sensed he was letting her explore without commentary or question—maybe to keep her centered, she wasn't sure. She could sense, however, a certain amount of astonishment as he occasionally gave her hand a squeeze.

Keeping Amber at the forefront of her mind, she traveled deeper and deeper into the system, one mile then two, until she knew she'd reached the last disguising layer, though she couldn't say how she knew.

This is it, the last barrier. I can feel it.

Break through, if you can. Let's see what we've got here.

The final disguising layer proved more than Claire could manage, however. She moved up and down searching for a way in, but nothing budged. *I don't know what's going on, but this last shield is stubborn. And I know Amber's there, I can feel her.*

Lucian remained quiet, a sign he was thinking about the situation. *I wonder if you can access more of my power. I'm going to try something.*

Do it.

He let go of her hand. She glanced at him as he stepped behind her, moving in close. He surrounded her with his arms. *Lean back against me and try again. Just think about Amber.*

Easy for you to say; I have a gorgeous vampire with his arms around me.

He chuckled again.

So what's the plan?

I'm going to funnel as much of my power into you as I can, holding you like this. Okay?

Ready when you are.

The power flowed in a strange zing of energy. As she concentrated on the second images in her strange split-vision, the disguise began falling away in bits and pieces.

It's working. Or starting to. I can see the tops of what look like jail cells. The floor is a dark slate and extends at least fifty feet in length. I hear the women now, all the slaves, some talking quietly, others weeping. They seem to be somewhere in the middle of this part of the cave system. The tunnel isn't broad but it's wide enough for a row of cells on each side, with bare lightbulbs overhead, that's it. These women must be scared out of their wits.

No doubt. Do you see any guards?

More of the disguise floated away, disappearing like mist. The lower portion of the west end of the space came into view.

At least one man is standing in front of a desk. I can see the backs of his legs. Two more guards are off to his right and one, to his left. I hear them laughing now. But a woman is screaming. More of the disguise lifted. *Oh, God.* She gripped Lucian's arms. *They're raping one of the girls right there. Right now. On a desk.*

Okay, take it easy. We'll get to her, but I've got to call in reinforcements first.

He released her, slipped his phone from his pant pocket, and the next moment spoke to Gabriel. Within seconds he'd relayed their position, called for a large team including medical personnel, then hung up.

This is it, Claire. We're going in, but don't worry. I've been fighting for centuries and I can handle all five of these bastards. Set us down in the middle like you said, then find your friends. I'll do the rest.

Do it, Lucian.

"Do it, Lucian."

Just like that. No fear.

Lucian was amazed by Claire's courage. He didn't know if she'd always been this way or whether the struggles of her abduction had created her confident spirit.

Of course, once she witnessed the carnage soon to follow she might change her tune, but right now she had a warrior's mentality.

I should warn you, I'm going in to kill, not to save these vampires. They're bad men. Do you understand?

She turned to look at him, her soft brown eyes suddenly hard with an emotion he understood quite well. *The young woman is still screaming, so beat the shit out of each one of them and cut their balls off if you need to. I don't give a damn.*

He nodded and something like respect flowed through his chest. Then he ignited his Ancestral power, used Claire as a beacon, and took her straight to the center of one of the biggest abduction cells he'd ever seen.

That part of him familiar with battling evil in his world came alive, a twisted creature that enjoyed doing what he did best.

Just as he said, he left Claire in the center so she'd be away from the guards and could help the other captives. He then headed toward the desk and the five bastards.

From behind him, he heard Claire calling for Amber and Tracy.

One of the vampires had just finished, and the girl had stopped screaming. She lay with her eyes closed, breathing hard, blood smeared over her face, her neck having been pierced more than once, her features twisted in pain.

Lucian felt his rage overtake him. They got off on it, the way his father had gotten off on hurting his sons, slicing them open with blades, beating them until they were a mass of vivid red, black, and blue.

He shifted to flight mode and went for the first man, now zipping up his pants. His new Ancestral power, combined with his rage, had an unexpected effect. He grabbed the vampire, yes, but his movements as he shifted to altered flight took him through the cave wall and suddenly he was over the Pacific Ocean. He still had a proximity issue, though much longer than previously, because of the double-chains. He felt a profound tug on his neck.

But his instincts kicked in and he snapped the rapist's neck, then dropped him into the water, returning swiftly.

He found that two of the men had remained by the desk but the other two now headed in Claire's direction, looking around as if confused.

He landed in front of Claire. These men didn't deserve to live one second longer for their crimes, so he did what he'd been able to do since he was young: He split into two separate battling entities. His secondary self drew a knife and headed to the top of the room after the remaining two vampires near the desk.

The ones closest to Lucian's primary self started backing up.

"We've got an Ancestral in here," one of them shouted,

reaching back and pulling out a knife. The men were fighters, and even though they were scared, they weren't going to back down.

Lucian laughed and with a wave of his hand beckoned the man forward. He drew a long battle chain from the pocket of his leathers and began to spin it quickly.

The vampire sprang forward with a low growl, slashing at the chain with his blade, hoping to disrupt the spin. But Lucian had worked the long battle chains for centuries now and with the slightest flip of his wrist moved it away from the blade. The vampire rushed in, a big mistake, because another flick of his wrist brought the chain wrapping around the man's throat.

He slashed out with his hands, but Lucian used the chain's strength and flipped the man over, then struck his lower spine hard, breaking it. His body went limp.

He let the battle chain fall to the floor, then stepped over the dying vampire. The dark part of him that loved to make war caught the other vampire's gaze and held on tight.

The man looked scared, just as he should. He had the woman's blood all over him, on his face and down his neck. On his hands as well. Looked like he'd already had his fun.

Rage reached Lucian's fingertips. He drew his second battle chain from his leathers and got it spinning. This time he lunged suddenly, and in a quick, arcing bite, he cut up the vampire's face. He screamed and flew back against one of the cell doors. The young woman within also screamed then dove under her cot.

Lucian let those chains fall as well, then slipped a dagger from the right side of his battle leathers. He could feel his second self punching the remaining two vampires near the desk, taking turns on each with a speed that came directly from his rise to Ancestral status.

His primary self, now bending over the vampire whose hands shook near his cut-up face, thrust the dagger at a low angle through the rapist's chest, reaching upward until the sharp point connected with the tougher flesh of the heart.

He screamed one final time, lost air, and arched. Lucian held the blade steady until the vampire lay still, his hands falling away from this face.

For a long moment, he stared down at the man he'd just killed, breathing hard. But as his adrenaline eased back, his hearing opened and he heard the weeping of the young women in the cells. They'd had to witness these kills.

He stood up, stripped off his shirt, and threw it over the corpse. The captives had had enough trauma for one night.

He turned and saw Claire put her arms through the bars of a cell and embrace a young woman with black hair. He made his way back to his second self, looked into his own eyes, and with a powerful vibration rejoined.

All four vampires were dead, and the woman on the table lay very still. Her clothes hung off her in ragged, torn pieces. She'd lost a lot of blood, but she hadn't died, and for that he was grateful. How many times had he found human women in this state: gang-raped, drained, in terrible pain, traumatized? And how many times had they died because of it?

He didn't dare try to touch her. She wouldn't understand he meant to help. He called for Claire, who took charge of her, lifting her from the desk, putting an arm around her shoulders and speaking in a low voice. "We'll have help here soon to get everyone out, medical assistance as well." She drew the woman to a corner away from the desk as well as the cells and held her as she sobbed.

With the victim taken care of, he turned to getting the dead bodies out of viewing distance. He moved them into an adjoining room, a task that, given his increased physical strength, took less than half a minute to accomplish. He didn't want the women staring at this much carnage.

He withdrew his cell and called Gabriel.

"What's your ETA?"

"We're already here, though we're looking at a bunch of astonished dockworkers."

"I'm sure you are."

"So what have you got?"

"One rape victim who will need medical attention and it looks like at least a hundred recent abductees. The guards are dead. They'll need to be processed, and I'm sorry to say one of them got dropped in the Pacific."

"I'll send someone out to retrieve the body."

They would do everything they could to keep the vampire genome a secret from the human world.

Gabriel continued, "I've got my people with me, but this is some serious disguising power. There's even a trace of something violet. Just a trace."

"Can you follow that trace?"

Gabriel was quiet for a moment. "I sure can. I take it this is Claire's signature."

"It is. Just follow it and you'll find us."

"We're on our way."

A moment later Gabriel arrived along with this team.

Claire turned the rape victim over to the physician in charge, but continued to hold her hand until the woman could let go. A shot of morphine for her pain helped a lot. Claire wasn't surprised that by the time she was strapped to a stretcher, she'd passed out.

Only then was she able to rejoin Lucian, who stood beside a vampire almost as big as he was. Lucian introduced her to the man called Gabriel, the one she knew Lucian thought of as his real father. He had short spiked black hair and gray eyes, similar to Lucian's, but they held more tenderness than she'd seen in any of the vampires she'd met before.

She liked him already, but mostly because from what Lucian had told her, Gabriel had taught three teenage boys to function with a conscience even though they'd each gone through hell at their father's hands.

"You've done a wonderful thing here, Claire." He gestured down the long row of cells.

All the young women were now clustered together in the middle of the room as his team began making its way through their number, tending to each one.

"I was only too glad to help." When she heard Amber call to her, she excused herself and hurried in her direction.

Now that all the cells had been opened, she caught Amber in her arms and held her tight. Amber wept against her shoulder, then gestured for Tracy to join her. Claire had never met Tracy before, but she opened her arm and all three women embraced.

Claire, though having boasted to Lucian that she wasn't a weeper, found tears streaming down her cheeks anyway.

After a moment, Amber drew back, linking arms with Tracy. "What's going to happen to us?"

"You'll be taken home."

"But won't they come for us again? The ones who took us in the first place?"

Claire glanced back at Lucian, who had remained near Gabriel. The men appeared deep in conversation, their expressions serious. "I'll talk with Lucian, the one who battled your captors. I'm sure he'll fix things so that you will never have to worry about being abducted again."

Amber nodded, but she had the skittish look of a woman who'd been taken against her will, her gaze bouncing around from the cells, to the medics, to the other young women.

Claire didn't say anything. She just let Amber find her own pace with the situation.

Finally Amber's gaze settled on Claire. "Do you know where Zoey is? I thought maybe she'd be with you."

Now the next hard part. "No, I'm afraid she's not. It's a long story, but after we were abducted, we were separated. Right now, however, I'm finally able to start looking for her. And I feel very confident that I'll have the means to find her within the next few days."

"But it's been two years? Why are you just looking for her now? I don't understand."

Claire debated just how much to tell her but finally sketched out her own experience, adding that Lucian was now working with her to find Zoey.

Amber kept shaking her head, and more tears streamed from her eyes. Claire hugged her once more, drawing Tracy in as well, then reassured them both that all would be well.

As she held the girls, she glanced once more in Lucian's direction and found that he was still talking quietly to Gabriel.

Later, Lucian met Amber and her friend, but he moved away shortly after. He could tell his sheer size and the fact that he no longer wore a shirt intimidated the young women.

While he waited for Gabriel's medical team to wrap things up, he watched Claire as she continued to comfort Amber and her friend and as she extended herself to many of the other young women around her. The new set of chains gave them both a much greater range of movement, one of the many benefits he was already experiencing.

Other aspects were similar to the single-chain, especially that he remained driven as ever to follow her with his gaze, to desire her, to long for some alone time. His need to feed rose as well, a typical response to having been in a recent battle. Splitting into his dual selves, something he often did while fighting, also tended to use up his reserves. But because of his blood-madness recovery, he already felt twitchy.

Claire caught his gaze and tilted her head, an inquiring expression. He smiled ruefully, knowing he'd been caught essentially lusting after her again.

The new chains grew very warm there for a moment. Where were your thoughts?

In my home in the Ozarks. Did I tell you I have a place there?

No, one more indication how little we know about each other.

I thought maybe you'd like to see it once we take Amber and Tracy home.

Sounds like a plan. But do you know what is amazing?

What's that?

Only that we're standing at least thirty feet away from each other and it's as though you're right next to me.

It's pretty amazing.

Amber said something to Claire so that she turned her attention to the younger woman, once more taking her in her arms. But over Amber's shoulder, Claire's gaze traveled to Lucian. *Do you know if they'll be going home soon?*

I'll check with Gabriel.

When he approached Gabriel, he saw the man smile, after which he tossed him a fresh shirt. "When I saw you in just your battle leathers, I thought we couldn't have you frightening all these women. In case you haven't noticed, you're one big sonofabitch." After Lucian and his brothers had escaped from Daniel, Gabriel had taken them under his powerful wing. He'd trained them as warriors, helping to focus all that they'd endured into a force that could help the world. Lucian thought of Gabriel as his true father.

"Look who's talking. And thanks." Lucian shrugged into the shirt, grateful. "So how is everything shaping up?"

"Really well, I'm glad to say. Most of these women haven't been here longer than a few days, so hopefully we'll be able to get them back to their homes before too long. A few have been hurt, but we'll take good care of them."

"Thanks for coming, Gabriel."

"My pleasure."

In the end the doctors declared most of the women fit to be taken home, including Amber and her friend. Only a handful of the young women would require rehabilitation before they could leave his world. Those who had been brutalized, whether raped or beaten, would remain in Gabriel's charge until each was completely healed.

The whole thing sickened Lucian, this wretched part of his world that trafficked in human flesh. He blamed Daniel, who in the past several decades had built hundreds of clubs across the globe to service a hungry, perverse clientele. Some said his Dark Cavern system, which he personally owned, was dedicated almost exclusively to the trafficking of humans.

The sheer size of Daniel's operation appalled him, one more reason to get rid of him forever.

Once Gabriel's team had processed all the women, Lucian agreed without hesitation to personally see that Amber and her friend got home safely.

Gabriel said good-bye without even asking how Lucian was taking to his new Ancestral status. For that, Lucian gave him credit. Gabriel, of all vampires, knew exactly how Lucian felt about rising to his father's level of power.

Making use of a second and third vampire to carry Tracy and Amber on a slow flight back to New Mexico, Lucian held Claire close. The journey took a very long hour, but because of the less demanding speed, neither Amber nor Tracy complained of headaches or nausea.

Once he had the girls outside Amber's home, he sent the other vampires on their way. Each took off, heading back to continue their service to Gabriel.

Lucian felt the sudden nostalgic shift in Claire as she looked at Amber's low, single-story house made of plaster and built with dark, round beams that jutted out at the roofline. The style was popular in the Desert Southwest.

From inside the house, he heard arguing.

"That's Mom." Amber's voice was hushed, her lips trembling. "She always yells when she's mad or sad." She turned toward Claire and hugged her. "Thank you so much, Claire, for saving us, but please find Zoey."

"I will."

He approached both the young women and after Claire had hugged each of them again, he asked for hugs himself, something he only did when he had a specific job to perform. Claire knew what he needed to do, but neither had felt it wise to tell the girls up front. In this case, they wouldn't remember, not even a little, where they'd really been for the past few days, or that a vampire named Lucian had actually rescued them.

The girls went to him readily, thanking him for getting them home, for saving them.

Just as each would have pulled away, however, he began the process of sweeping her mind clean. What surprised him was how easy it was now that he had new power. What might have been the work of several minutes became a fifteen-second jaunt inside each mind, exchanging traumatic memories for what would no doubt become a case of "selective amnesia." They simply wouldn't remember where they'd been or what had happened to them for the time they were gone.

When he let them go, they turned and walked up the path to Amber's home, not looking back even once. Lucian could feel how hard this was for Claire: They were getting to do what neither she nor Zoey had been able to do. He drew close and slid his arm around her waist.

The screen creaked, a comforting sound all on its own. Amber knocked on the door and a few seconds later, a woman, clearly Amber's mother, shouted then screamed as she embraced first Amber then Tracy. The father came next, doing much the same but without the noise. He then got his cell out and called Tracy's parents.

At that point Lucian's rage surfaced, a blinding heat of anger at what had almost happened to these girls. He promised himself that one day, there would be a reckoning with all traffickers.

What is it? Claire asked, looking up at him. *You're suddenly so angry.*

He wanted to answer her, but for a moment he couldn't even speak.

When the front door closed and both girls were inside, he turned away from the house, glancing down the street. He'd been around. He'd been down a thousand streets like this all over the world. Every culture, in his opinion, was pretty much the same, including his own: Most humans—and vampires, for that matter—worked to take care of their families and their communities. Unfortunately, there were just enough psychopaths around in both species, to destroy hundreds, thousands, and sometimes millions of lives.

We've done some good here, Lucian. You need to know that. I can feel how angry you are.

He met her gaze. *I hate this, you know. All this suffering.*

So do I. And that's what I'd dedicated my life to before I was taken—helping women who'd fallen into prostitution.

He nodded. *I know you did.*

She then smiled, but there was a glint in her eyes. *I've been thinking that there's something I'd like to do right now.*

He glanced at her, frowning. He couldn't quite pinpoint the sensation that the chains gave off, so he wasn't sure what she was thinking. Revenge came to mind, but in what way, he couldn't imagine. *And what's that?*

How about we pay a visit to The Prickly Pear—you know, the club that caused us all so much grief. I understand it's owned by vampires.

At that, Lucian's lips curved. *You have a very wicked mind, and I'm liking it. Let's go.*

He knew the location well and had tried several times to get the club shut down. But the ineffective court system in his world never ruled against Daniel or the other more powerful traffickers, using the "secrecy" directive as an excuse for not taking action.

Tonight, at least for this one club, in this one moment, he and Claire would change things. Dawn was already visible on the distant horizon, so the timing worked well: The club would have been shut down for several hours by now, and wouldn't be open for business for a few hours more. Essentially, there was no one around.

He flew Claire around the back, and after she set up a serious disguise over the whole building, he went inside while she stood guard. He had just started breaking up one of the wooden bar stools when his stomach cramped and a hard tremor went through him again. Fucking blood-madness. He'd hoped that his Ancestral status would have changed that aspect of his current predicament, but no such luck. He really did need a good solid hit of Claire's blood, and the sooner the better.

He took the wood to the greasy kitchen and turned on the gas stove. Once the pieces caught fire, he threw them through the club.

He kept doing this, tearing stool after stool apart, until the building set up a serious blaze and really started to roar. He shifted to altered flight and left through the roof, flying high in the air, admiring the flames as well as Claire's violet disguise that kept the stand-alone facility hidden from human eyes, and therefore the local fire department. As the flames rose higher, he kept rising in the air but stopped when the proximity tug of the new set of chains warned him he'd reached his limit. He went in search of Claire.

He found her at the edge of the parking lot and flew to land beside her. The growing sunlight prickled his skin and the backs of his eyes, clear warnings that he needed to at least switch to altered flight. Once in flight, the damaging rays of the sun couldn't touch him.

He held his arm wide for Claire. She slung an arm around his neck and stepped onto his right foot. The chains vibrated heavily, though, which caused him to focus on her completely because right now a terrible sadness weighed her down.

As the sun crested the horizon and when his eyes burned from too much sunlight, he drew Claire into altered flight.

Sorry, my vampire physiology can't take this much sunlight.

I understand. Can you fly me once around the building before we leave?

Of course.

He took her in a slow pattern around the entire circumference, then high enough so that she could watch the roof collapse and flames shoot high in the sky.

I'm going to remove the disguise from the property now.

Go for it.

He felt her draw her power in, the power she siphoned from him as though it was second nature, and the disguise vanished.

While in the air, he turned in a 360-degree circle, looking at Santa Fe from a bird's-eye view.

She remained silent as she leaned her head against his chest, then addressed his ongoing problem. *You need to feed again, don't you?*

I have some cramping but it's not as bad as before. But yeah, I do.

Then how about we head to the Ozarks? I'd love to see the home you mentioned earlier, and I can take care of you there. How does that sound?

He couldn't tell her what he really thought, but her

suggestion sounded like heaven to him. *And I'm sure you'll be ready to crawl into bed.*

Pretty soon.

As he turned, heading east, she leaned up and nuzzled his neck, then kissed him.

CHAPTER 7

Lucian flew northeast toward the Ozarks and soon passed over the Missouri River. Within a few seconds he hovered over the entrance to his Arkansas home.

It's a very private system, and I keep my home in particular behind about a dozen layers of shielding disguise. And yes, I paid handsomely for it. But my guess is that you can see through them.

I can.

Part of his payment for the disguising shield included a location sensor built just for him. He tuned in and passed through the disguise in a quick blur of sensation that landed him square in a large cavern. Over the decades, he'd spent a lot of time in this dwelling, more than once when wounded to the point of death during a battle.

Lucian released her, watching as she turned in a slow circle looking at the room.

"Wow, this is almost exotic." A waterfall cascaded down one side of the cave and passed through a natural breach to a river below. The entire cavern, about a hundred feet long, was on a thick shelf of stone above an underground river. Teakwood tables as well as low leather couches and chairs furnished the space.

"I can sense that you need to eat. My housekeeper knows to keep my cupboards and refrigerators stocked."

She glanced at him. "You mean, she did this even while you were in prison for a year?"

"It's a rule I have. Don't worry. She makes sure any unused provisions are given to homeless shelters. But the upshot is, I can fix you something to eat."

"Well, I have to admit I'm starving, but are you sure you can wait, I mean, you know, to feed?"

He narrowed his gaze. "It's important to me that you have something to eat when I know you're hungry."

She appeared thoughtful. "Thank you. I appreciate it."

"Will sandwiches do?"

"Of course."

He led her to the kitchen and started pulling bread, deli meat, and condiments from the fridge. She sat quietly at the marble island, but he felt her gaze on him, the chains remaining silent as though she worked to keep her emotions in check.

When he finally placed a ham sandwich in front of her and started in on one of his own, her voice drifted through his mind. *We'll take care of business as soon as we've eaten.* But she didn't look at him. She was being careful, not wanting to set him off, and he appreciated that.

Thank you.

Lucian had never been in this place before, knocked

out of stride by a woman, by the courage she'd shown in doing all that she'd done in the last twenty-four hours, by her commitment to getting Amber and Tracy home safely.

Now she was here, aware of his needs and willing to help, even sensitive to the ongoing trouble he had with recurring bouts of blood-madness.

He ate his sandwich, which didn't exactly help the cramping in his stomach, but regular food was as necessary to a vampire as blood. He needed both to survive.

At least he wasn't experiencing the tremors he had with the last go-round.

He'd already finished his meal when Claire took her last bite, wiping her mouth with the napkin he'd set on the counter.

She turned to him and settled her hand on his knee. "You were wonderful at the Hawaiian cavern. I was too busy with Amber and Tracy and some of the other women to tell you that, but I wanted you to know that I thought you were great."

"Just doing my job."

Claire leaned close and kissed him. "Well, you do your job really, really well."

Lucian thought about what he'd felt earlier, about wanting a chance to prove to Claire that he knew how to please a woman. He searched her gaze and returned her kiss, plucking at her lips with his own, savoring how quickly she responded. He loved the sweet herb smell of her and drifted a line of kisses up her cheek until he teased her ear with his tongue.

She moaned softly.

Claire?

Yes?

Have you ever made love on a marble island before?

She drew back, her eyes widening. She glanced at the smooth surface and patted the beautiful stone. "You mean here?"

"Why not?" He met her gaze, then using his finger traced her cheek, dipping lower to play along the vein at her throat. Her breath caught.

"I'd love to, but you need to be prepared."

She'd surprised him. "For what?"

She slid her hand through his hair. "There's something I want from you, but I'm not sure exactly how to ask for it. From the time I first saw you in the Dark Cave, bound in chains, I've sensed something in you, something dark but exciting. You've even alluded to it a few times and earlier I saw that man while you battled. Right now I want you to show me that side of who you are, nothing held back."

Lucian felt a new kind of tremor pass through his body, tightening his thighs. He shook his head. "You don't know what you're asking or how dangerous this is. Have you forgotten that I almost drained you just a few hours ago?"

"I haven't forgotten, but this is something I need from you."

"Why?"

"Call it an instinct, maybe even something I'm sensing because of the blood-chains, but I think we'd both benefit."

She rose from her stool and slid onto the marble island. "Don't hold back. Let me see all that you are."

In one easy move she took off both tank tops at the same time, then cast them aside. He stared at her full breasts and long line of cleavage, made perfect by her black lace bra. He rose from his own stool and stared into her eyes.

Would she like what she saw or would he frighten her? Did he want to find out?

Show me that part of you, Lucian, that lives in the dark.

Lucian was a vampire, now an Ancestral. He stared into her eyes and felt through the vibration of the two chains at his neck that she was more than serious. He sensed the level of her desire, and he could definitely smell that she wanted this.

He wanted to protest, but the part of him that moved like a caged beast, pacing deep within his soul, longed to get out.

She reached behind her and unhooked her bra, letting it slide away from her body. His gaze fell to her beaded nipples, and his fangs began to descend. His mouth filled with saliva as he stared at her chest, his body heating up as his new Ancestral power whipped through his veins.

He met her gaze. *So you want to see my beast.*

I want to see everything.

Claire had never been so revved up by anything in her life. She didn't even understand what the hell was going on with her, why she was challenging Lucian like this. Except that she wanted him to let loose.

As for herself, she'd never felt so free or so wicked, but something about Lucian, the darkness that resided inside him as well as the toughness with which he battled in his world, had gotten to her.

His vampire nature called to an answering primal response within her body. She wanted him. And by the look of him, by the fangs that slowly emerged, she knew she'd struck the right chord.

She breathed hard as she watched his eyes dilate fully, his lips grow swollen, and his tongue stroke up and down his fangs. Nothing could have been more sensual, more inviting.

She moaned, closed her eyes, and arched her back. She thumbed the tips of her breasts, needing him to understand that she was offering herself up right now and that he could take her any way he wanted.

And that she trusted him.

Claire. Even within her mind his voice had dropped low and sounded hoarse. *This isn't smart. The blood-madness is back.*

You won't hurt me and I'm here to take care of your needs. I trust you.

A heavy vibration hit the space all around her. Then everything happened so fast.

Suddenly a pair of hands drew her arms backward over her head, while a second pair now had hold of her legs and began working the zipper of her pants.

He'd split for her, the way he had when he'd battled earlier.

He was now two men.

Oh, my God. Lucian, there are two of you.

She looked up and a secondary Lucian stared down at her, his expression wild, his fangs heavy on his lips. *I warned you, Claire, now you're going to have to do what we say.*

We.

Two of Lucian, two gorgeous men.

She shifted her gaze to the primary Lucian. His fangs were pressed into his lips, his straight brows low on his forehead.

He pulled off her shoes in quick tugs, then her jeans, her hips more than once rising from the island at his efforts. But the secondary Lucian held her in place, his knees on the island behind her.

She was essentially held captive by two men, two

powerful vampires, and the thought made her clench deep within.

This is Lucian—that's what went through her head. Lucian, all of him, the powerful being that she knew him to be showing the farthest reach of his truest nature. The primary Lucian planted both hands on her, kneading her abdomen, then bending low to lick a long line up her landing strip.

The secondary part of him held her arms taut, keeping her pinned down. And she loved it, she loved letting him have this kind of control over her.

Lucian slid his hands up to hold her waist, then swiped his tongue deep between her legs, moving up and up, flicking his tongue at the top of her clitoris. She groaned long and loud at the pleasure that spun in circles over what he was doing to her.

Encouraged by the sounds she made, he worked her low with his tongue, pushing at her folds, sipping the length of her, dipping inside her at times, then plunging.

Within minutes her breathing was choppy with erratic pants. Claire didn't know how much more she could take.

"Please," she murmured.

Lucian smirked then landed his tongue inside her, shoving hard and fast in quick, long strokes, faster than a human could move.

Pleasure hit Claire like a series of ocean waves that moved through her in heavy pulses, rising to a powerful orgasm. She cried out repeatedly, pulling on the arms that pinned her down.

She felt some kind of communication pass between the split-selves, and the next moment the primary Lucian moved up to her left hip. She felt his blood-needs rise as a tremor passed through him. Feeding would help.

When she understood what he meant to do, what his trembling body demanded, she called out a harsh, "Yes, Lucian. Bite me hard."

He licked along her groin near her thigh, then bit down to her waiting vein. The eroticism of the act sent her to the moon, her body reacting as though he'd just penetrated her with his cock. It all felt so good.

She groaned low in her throat as he continued to drink from her. But it wasn't enough. She needed more.

She tugged on one of the arms that pinned her, but only because she wanted to be free to touch him. The secondary Lucian tightened his grip.

He looked up at her while sucking. *You'll have to wait, Claire. All in good time.*

Her body undulated in anticipation, her hips rising and falling as he kept his lips in place and sucked.

My breasts ache. Lucian, I ache everywhere. I need your touch.

He slid his hand up and rubbed each of her breasts in turn, back and forth. She arched against his hand but began to feel very needy between her legs.

She opened herself up to the shared blood-chains, to his Ancestral power, to his experiences of four hundred years of intense vampire living. He must have felt the shift because he drew back from her vein and rose up over her. He caught her thighs, one in each hand.

Is this what you want? He pushed his hips between her legs but rose up so that his cock, rigid and weeping, rode up her abdomen all the way to her navel. *You want all that I am inside you, Claire, taking possession of you?*

She looked first at his erect cock, then met his gaze. He looked ferocious, his gray eyes glinting, blood on his lips and chin, on his fangs. But he looked beautiful as well, like the warrior she knew him to be. *You're magnificent.*

He flexed his arms, then the thick muscled wall of his chest, which left her weak with desire. So she said the one thing she was sure would keep him in just this state. *Fuck me, Lucian.*

Opening his mouth wide, he roared, a sound no human male could make. He then drew back, placed his cock at her opening, and—because she was so ready for him—drove all the way inside. He held her hips with his hands and pumped, letting her feel the length of him.

She writhed on the marble. Nothing had felt more powerful, more exquisite, more sensual. She angled her head, presenting her throat for him. *Bite me.*

Lucian grunted as he bit down. He struck her vein, then began to suck, the feel of his lips and the sound he made once more causing her to clench. She still couldn't move, her arms held as they were by his second self, but Lucian's hips did the work, driving and plunging.

Ecstasy began to roll toward her all over again. That was the only way she could think of the sensation, as though it existed outside her yet inside at the same time.

The chain at her neck vibrated with his profound arousal, another layer of sensation.

His mouth drank, his hips pistoned, and within her body she pulled on him, her muscles contracting and releasing, working to draw from his cock what he could give her.

She closed her eyes, lost in so many sensations. She cried out repeatedly and as the orgasm struck, she arched her neck and screamed. She felt Lucian's release at the same time that he shouted, his hips in a steady rhythm. Ecstasy gripped her body low and flooded her veins. Waves of pleasure flowed again, crashing through her abdomen and upward to engulf her chest, until she screamed once more.

His shouts reached a pinnacle and after several short thrusts, his hips finally slowed, rolling into her several more times, savoring the last of the orgasm.

She lay panting, and he breathed hard. He released her neck as well and rested his head on her shoulder.

Finally his upper self let go of her arms. She brought them back slowly to surround the primary Lucian who now lay slack on top of her, the weight of him sublime.

She felt his rejoining vibration and afterward how much more solid he seemed as he lay over her chest, still joined to her, his hips keeping her legs spread wide.

She petted the back of his head over and over.

She felt wonderful, extremely well used, but what poured from Lucian distressed her.

I was so into this, but did I hurt you?

Claire chuckled softly.

He leaned back, scowling at her. "Why are you laughing?"

She didn't want to use her voice just yet, but glided her fingers through his hair as she spoke within his mind. *You forget that I siphoned your power. Maybe if I'd been only human just now, but no, Lucian, you didn't hurt me.*

He shook his head. "That doesn't seem possible. I was out of control."

She slipped her finger between the crease of his scowl then rubbed up and down the familiar worried line. She sighed heavily.

She knew he didn't understand himself at all.

"Put me to bed, Lucian. That's all I want now, because I'm exhausted."

Concern swept over his features as he pulled out of her. He reached for a napkin and pressed it between her legs, then he held her close against him and they were flying, a very short flight to a massive, literally cavernous bedroom. He'd left much of the cave in its original shape.

"Shower first," she whispered as he drew close to the bed.

"Right."

"You left a lot of yourself inside me."

She felt his chest swell and sensed a very strong male satisfaction. She chuckled again, but sleep began to work at her consciousness. She made short work of a shower, dried off, then headed straight to bed.

He showered after her and she might have recalled the bed dipping when he climbed in, she wasn't sure, because she fell into a deep and profound sleep.

As Lucian lay beside Claire, he didn't understand what had just happened, but he felt extraordinary. This woman did something for him that he couldn't quite explain, except that he felt more like himself than at any other time in his entire life.

She'd begged to see all that he was, so he'd shown her the part of him that liked control. Yet not once had she seemed afraid of him, or worried that he'd hurt her, not even when he'd split into his two selves. His secondary self had held her in place, and he'd enjoyed her body thoroughly.

He also felt instinctively that she wouldn't have done this with anyone else. At the same time, he couldn't imagine doing this with anyone other than Claire.

He lay awake for a long time, watching her sleep. She had a sprawling style, her arms wide, her lips parted.

He'd never spent this much time with one woman, ever. He knew who he was and he'd avoided close relationships. He'd proven the truth of his nature by splitting and pinning Claire down while he took her, drinking from her. Yet it had all seemed so natural.

What's more, she'd loved it. That's what the chains had said to him, that she'd loved how he'd controlled her and made love to her.

He wanted to do it again.

And again.

He rolled onto his back, sliding his hands beneath his head. He'd left the ceiling of the cavern in a natural state. He liked the jagged edges of the rock, which tended to reflect his state of mind more often than not.

His chain vibrated softly against his upper chest and to the sides of his neck. The sensation eased him, in the same way the recent sex had. For one of the few times in his life, he didn't feel so alone—and damn him for liking the way it felt.

He also realized that the remnant of his blood-madness had disappeared during the experience.

After a while, he fell asleep.

Much later, when he woke up, he sniffed and groaned because he smelled bacon frying. What was it about bacon sizzling in a pan?

Coffee, too.

He threw the covers back and hopped from bed, then paused and looked back at the bottom sheet. He rounded the bed, his heart beating hard in his chest as he pulled back the covers on Claire's side. Even though she'd assured him that he hadn't hurt her, he still worried that somewhere in working her up, he'd gotten too rough.

But when he saw that her portion of the sheet remained unstained, with no sign of blood, he breathed a deep sigh of relief.

You okay? Claire was suddenly in his head.

Fine. At least he was now.

You felt worried there for a moment, through the chains I mean, almost panicky. Any sign of blood-madness?

He actually touched his chest, then his gut. *I'm good, thanks.* And he was. He felt almost normal, or at least as normal as the son of a psychopath could ever really feel.

All right then. Breakfast in ten minutes.

He went into the bathroom and shaved, then showered. He donned jeans and a snug black T-shirt, no shoes. He liked feeling the cool smooth marble of the tiles on his bare feet.

When he walked into the kitchen, Claire had her auburn hair brushed to a shine and drawn away from her face, revealing strong sculpted cheekbones. Her complexion glowed, maybe from the sex or perhaps from the power she siphoned. Either way, seeing her tightened something deep in his chest.

He glanced at the place mats set on the island, right over the area where he'd taken her.

She smiled. "Thinking good thoughts about last night? I am." She chuckled.

Damn, he loved that she wasn't embarrassed. Maybe she'd had a lot of experience, but he didn't like thinking of her with other men. He stopped a growl from forming in his throat.

"Thanks for cooking."

"You're welcome. And you were right, your fridge was well stocked. You have steaks in there, and a nice imported beer."

He smiled. "Yes, I do. Standing orders."

She poured scrambled eggs into a sizzling pan, and toast popped up from the toaster. She buttered the bread, stirred the eggs. "Pour us some coffee. It's a nice, hearty French blend you have there. Love it."

He poured two cups and took them to the place mats on the other side of the island. But his gaze remained fixed to her backside, covered in a fresh pair of jeans, something she must have discovered in one of the guest rooms.

"You went on a hunt, I see."

"I did. I borrowed some clothes and I like these leather flats. Very nice. Do you have women here often then?"

"Nope. They belong to my housekeeper. Apparently, you're about the same size."

"Will she mind?"

"Don't worry. She has a generous spirit and I'll compensate her."

She glanced at him over her shoulder, still stirring the eggs. "She pretty?"

"She's one of the finest people I know, but I'd never use her like that. Besides, she's married to one of our university professors."

He felt her surprise as she gently scooped eggs onto a couple of plates. "I didn't know you had universities."

This time he refused to be offended. "Only three on as many continents. Not everyone is cut out for study."

"Did you attend?"

He snorted. "Gabriel insisted on it, and every fifty years I had to take a new degree. Some of them at human universities, night courses, naturally."

"Naturally."

She put the toast on the plates as well as the bacon, then brought them over to the island and set them on the place mats. He waited for her to sit down and get comfortable before diving in.

"Go ahead." She laughed this time. "I know you're starved. I can feel it through the chains. You can take from my wrist afterward as well, if you want."

He met her gaze and blinked a couple of times. She'd offered him blood, just like that. "You sure seem to have adjusted to things quickly. I can't tell you how many times you've surprised me."

She picked up a strip of bacon and took a bite.

He set his coffee mug down and turned toward her. "Claire, I need you to level with me. Tell me once and for all, did I hurt you last night?"

She chewed her bacon but didn't look at him. A smile curved her lips, and the chains at his neck started to vibrate. He felt something emanating from her, a kind of tenderness he didn't understand.

Finally she turned toward him and met his gaze. "You don't know who you are, Lucian. I wish I could convince you of it, but I know I can't. Did you hurt me last night? No, not even a little. It was wonderful and that's my point. I don't believe you could hurt me even if you tried.

"What I enjoyed so much was feeling your strength, feeling all that you were, that you didn't hold back. That's what I loved. Did you enjoy yourself?"

The question startled him because he realized it had been one of the finest experiences he'd known for exactly the reason she'd stated, that he'd truly been himself with her.

"Now you tell me. What was it like for you, splitting like that and holding me down?"

He couldn't quite pinpoint what he felt as he stared into her light-brown eyes. He laid a hand on her arm. "I'll never forget last night. But I hate just how much I loved having control of you. You weren't afraid, were you?"

She shook her head and took another bite of bacon, then scooped up some eggs. *Not even a little.*

Something inside him gave way, a big piece of fear that he'd hurt her. He hadn't. He ate his breakfast and sipped his coffee.

For the most part, Claire remained quiet as she finished her meal.

Once she'd drained her cup, he rose and started

washing the dishes. She offered to help but he told her he had a rule about the cook getting to sit out during cleanup.

He felt the chains once more, only this time he felt her distress. Scrubbing out the frying pan he turned to look at her. "What gives?"

"Well, Rumy called while you were sleeping. Thought I'd wait to share the news."

"What's that?" He rinsed the pan off and set it in the drainer to dry, then continued loading the dishwasher.

"He said to tell you that Daniel has raised the stakes on his hunt for the extinction weapon. He's now offering three million for *any* information about the remaining weapons, payment made on retrieval of even the smallest part of the weapon, whether design or machinery itself. This is bad, isn't it?"

"I honestly don't know how it could be worse. Just like in your world, there are vampires without a conscience who won't think twice about making a buck any way they can, including selling out the rest of the population."

"So what do you think we should do next? We have to find that weapon."

"I know." He shifted to look at her. "I think we should head back to The Erotic Passage and have a chat with both Eve and Rumy."

"Eve?"

"Oh, that's right. You haven't met her yet. She's as well connected throughout our world as Rumy is, and might have an idea or two about where to look for the weapon. She owns and operates a theater called The Ruby Cave."

"Does she put on plays of some kind?"

Lucian grinned. "Of a sort. She presents sex shows."

"Oh." She sipped her coffee. "And is she a former girlfriend of yours?"

Lucian shuddered. "Hell, no. She's full-on dominance. I'd rather eat glass than take up with someone like her. But other than her sexual proclivities, she's good people and she will probably have an interesting idea or two."

When Claire headed toward the bathroom, he made a quick call to Rumy and set up a meeting with him and Eve. Shortly afterward he flew Claire back to Lake Como and straight into Rumy's office.

CHAPTER 8

Claire sat in one of two oversized leather clubs chairs while the one called Eve, almost equal in height to Lucian, sat in the chair next to her.

Claire tried not to stare, but an absolute vampire beauty met her gaze. The woman had on heavy stage makeup with thick false eyelashes, wide black eyeliner, and varying shades of eye shadow from black to red climbing to her brows. Despite the makeup, Claire saw the exquisite lines of her face, her straight nose and strong cheekbones. She wore her blond hair caught up high on her head and flowing in a long ponytail well past her bottom. She held it wrapped around her forearm, petting it like she would a cat.

But beyond her flamboyant style, Claire couldn't believe what Eve wanted her to do. "An erotica fashion show? You want me to walk down a runway modeling clothing fit for porn stars?"

Eve smiled. "Exactly."

From the vibration at her neck, she knew Lucian had a serious problem with her dressing in a series of fantasy outfits, but he remained stoic. The stakes were incredibly high.

Claire turned to Rumy. "And you're sure these two men, Arsen and Salazar, know where the extinction weapon is?"

He nodded. "My informant tells me that they're trying to get Daniel to cough up about thirty million for the information they have on the weapon."

The figure staggered her mind. "But they don't actually have possession of it?" This just didn't make sense.

"No, but word has it that as soon as Daniel posted his reward, they were on it. Like me, they have a powerful network, though theirs involves every criminal from here to Beijing and they don't mind torturing for information.

"It's my understanding that they've physically hunted for it themselves, but can't quite break through a couple of disguising shields to actually get their hands on it. Still, the fact that the information is hidden behind a powerful layering of disguise is telling in itself. I, for one, believe they've landed on the real deal. Also, they wouldn't be so stupid as to play fast and loose with Daniel by faking it. No, I'm convinced they've got something solid, which is also why they're asking for thirty million."

She considered the amount again, which at first had seemed phenomenal. But given the potential the weapon had, she wondered why they hadn't asked for ten times that amount. "And from what you've told me, a serious trafficker like Daniel would have assets in the billions. He could afford to pay any price."

Lucian crossed his arms over his chest. "I think you're exactly right."

She shook her head. "So the plan would be to lure these two men into coming here—then what?"

Lucian frowned heavily. "We'd basically put them in the same kinds of chains you found me in, then work to get the information out of them."

She looked away from him nodding, thinking things through, then returned to him once more. "Why not go after them?"

Lucian rocked slightly on his heels. "Because they live in a fortress, well stocked with every kind of weapon imaginable. Even if we got in, we wouldn't get out, not without an army. But I'm still not on board, not even a little." He turned to Eve. "You must have a dozen beautiful women you could use, dress up in bits of leather and a few rubber bands—"

Eve glared at Lucian. "Hey, I design these clothes. You're disparaging my creative efforts."

Rumy barked his laughter. "Rubber bands. *Love* it. He got you on that one, Eve."

Claire strove to understand the merits of the plan. "Okay, let's say that it's necessary they come here. Why me? Why would I so tempt these careful, well-armed warrior types that they'd actually agree to come to Eve's theater to watch me parade around in pretty much nothing?"

All three vampires turned to look at her. She glanced at each one in turn. Something was up, something that hadn't been said. Eve turned to Lucian. "You want to tell her, or shall I?"

Lucian's nostrils flared. He appeared disgusted beyond words, but he spoke anyway. "Both these men have a thing for redheads."

She laughed. "What? You're kidding. Why?"

But Eve stepped in. "Just about everyone has a craving for something specific. Some men love feet, can't get enough of them, that's why they're called fetishes. You have red hair, and I'll admit it's a beautiful auburn. You'll have them both panting. We don't have a lot of redheads in our world."

Claire pulled a lock of her hair forward and stared at it, then glanced at Lucian. "Is this really true? I mean, do you believe this?"

"I have some friends who will only date Asian women. Period. Others are drawn to blondes. We're all built differently." A half smile curved his lips. "But in this case I don't see how they could resist."

"So essentially, I'd be the bait."

"You'll be more than that." Lucian drew close, looking down at her. "We'll need your disguising power to surround Rumy's security team. The last thing they'll be expecting is that the object of their lust will be the prime reason they'll get caught in the trap."

Claire took Lucian's hand and lowered her voice. "It will be really hard for me to do something like this. I'm fairly modest by nature. But what about you? I'll be parading around in front of a lot of men, and not just bad guys, but Rumy's security force as well. Are you sure you'll be okay with this?"

He met and held her gaze, but a haunted look entered his gray eyes. "I hate the idea more than I can say, but I keep telling myself that this isn't about me, or what I want, but what needs to be done."

"And there's no other way?"

"Believe me, if I had an army, I'd head to Arsen and Salazar's compound and battle my way in. But I don't. And if what Rumy has said is true, we have an extremely narrow window of time before Daniel accepts their offer and finds his way to wherever it is that their information leads."

He took her arm in his large hand and squeezed gently. "But say the word, and we're done here, no questions asked, no recriminations."

Once more, she took a lock of her hair in hand and stared at it. "I'll never think of the color of my hair in the same way again."

"But you're right. I don't want other men looking at you, and I'm pretty sure I'm going to have a hard time holding my temper."

She slipped into telepathy as she said, *And you're the only one I want looking at me. No one else.*

Memories of the night before came flooding back, of being pinned down on the island. She'd encouraged him to tap into something very primal and so he had. Because of it, she felt even closer to him than ever. Sex had definitely complicated their arrangement. She was a human in a secret vampire world, needing desperately to go home. But every moment she spent with Lucian, getting to know him, to know his fine character yet at the same time his deep sense of unworthiness, the more she felt drawn into something she wondered if she'd ever be able to leave. She'd known the man such a short time, but she already cared about him more than she could say.

She turned to Rumy, then Eve as she said, "Because it's a private show, I'll do it. I know I couldn't walk a runway in front of hundreds of people, but if it would mean getting information like this, about the weapon, I think we have to try." Taking a deep breath, she added, "So, how many changes would I have?"

Eve unwrapped her blond ponytail from around her arm. "I'm thinking three, plus one for the photo shoot.

I'll tell Arsen and Salazar that I'm holding a private auction after the show, that I'll have several clients on the line with photos I've sent to them. I'm sure after the third change, they'll be ready to bid on you anyway."

She glanced at Lucian. "And these vampires are in the sex trade?"

"Two of the most formidable. They process more women in a year than most, though still far below Daniel's average. Which means, if we pull this off, we take them out of the game at the same time. It will make a huge difference on every level. Once we gain control of them, I'll have Gabriel move in and dismantle their organization." His gaze softened. "We'll be saving more lives tonight."

Rumy nodded, suddenly serious. Meeting Lucian's gaze, he said, "All these years, your father has protected both these men, supported them in their slavery efforts. So getting them out of circulation will be a real coup. But this other thing?" He shook his head several times. "Any vampire with even a small piece of sense knows that once Daniel gets his hands on the extinction weapon, he'll hold it to all our heads. He won't stop till he owns everything, which means that he has designs on human-earth as well. Our world is just the beginning for him."

Claire gripped Lucian's hand. He met her gaze and nodded. "All right. Let's do it."

Eve nodded, glancing from Claire to Lucian. "I like your woman, boss, a lot. And if you take my advice, you'll put her on my table. Say the word, and I'll lend you one of my specialty rooms, no charge."

"That's enough, Eve." Lucian spoke the words, but Claire heard the sudden hoarseness in his voice and the chains vibrated heavily against her neck. She felt his desire for her spike sharply, which of course sent hers reeling. The marble island had been one thing, but what would it be like for him to strap her down and have his way with her.

The idea sent desire flowing through her so quickly that she felt dizzy.

Lucian squeezed her hand. *What's going on? What are you thinking?*

Claire looked up at him, but she didn't think it wise to tell him her thoughts, at least not now. She'd come to know him a little, and her instincts told her that he would benefit from exactly the kind of scenario that just ran through her head.

But right now she had a job to do, so she strove to block her desire. *Nothing important.*

It feels important, and remember the chains don't lie.

I know, but this isn't the time so if it's all right with you, I'd like to focus on getting through the next few hours.

He nodded.

Still holding his hand, she turned to Eve. "I think it's time to take a look at your collection." Of course the image of "straps and rubber-bands" made her cringe inwardly once more.

But she drew her shoulders back and when Eve suggested they follow her, that she had the costumes in a special location, Lucian held his arm out for her. She rose to her feet.

Because she'd grown accustomed to flying with him, she stepped up on his foot and slid her arm around his neck. He held her tight against him and with Eve leading the way, Lucian flew her in the sex goddess's wake.

Lucian held Claire close to his side. He trembled, but not from blood-starvation. She kept blindsiding him with things, like how easily she slid her arm around his neck and stepped up on his foot as though she'd been doing it for the last century.

And she felt so right against his body. She fit him, her height, the curve of her hip resting against him, his hand splayed over her flat, tight stomach.

He liked having her there too much.

She'd also proved her worth again, willing to sacrifice her modesty to bring a couple of lowlifes to earth, maybe get information that would help locate the extinction weapon and possibly save the world.

Rumy was right. His world was on the brink of falling under the control of the worst vampire to rise to power in its long history.

And Arsen and Salazar were on the brink of handing over the location of the extinction weapon to a psychopath. They needed to be stopped, and Lucian needed to find that weapon first. He couldn't allow Daniel to get hold of it. If Lucian was clever enough, he'd set the trap for Daniel and get rid of him once and for all. That Daniel held Zoey captive was an issue he had no idea how to resolve, but he couldn't think about that right now. God willing, there'd be enough time down the road to separate her from Daniel before things went south.

Then there was Claire.

Feeling so right in his arms.

Did she realize that with her free hand she was fondling his chest again, rubbing over his pec? God help him if she tweaked his nipple.

He thought he should warn her. *Careful.*

About what? The costumes?

No, what your fingers are doing to me.

She drew them back, clearly startled. *I'm sorry. I was touching you. Again.*

As he flew, he caught her hand and pressed it back to his chest. *I liked it. That was the problem.*

He heard that sound of hers, like *unh,* as she nuzzled beneath his chin. *This is nice, flying with you. I can't believe how quickly I got used to it once you became an Ancestral.*

I admit, it's pretty great.

Yeah, it is. And it's fun taking it slow as well.

The absolute worst thought went through his mind: He could get used to this, used to having Claire next to him, flying with him. He could get used to heading into a dangerous situation with a woman who could handle the pressure.

Which brought him full circle, to that slice of anxiety that lived inside him. He needed to guard himself against Claire because he had no future with her—not with any woman. He couldn't be trusted, not when he'd already proven more than once that he had a monster living inside him, a dark entity that liked dominance and control, that would take and take until he had Claire at his mercy.

He flew through another tunnel and cave, following Eve's glittering ruby-red signature. Eve was taking it slow as well, maybe thinking, planning, strategizing. Eve always had one card up her sleeve, always a new idea, a twist on things.

He wasn't surprised when she doubled back more than once, finally landing them in a really dark cavern suite, without drywall, something that had been carved out of a shelf of black granite with lots of rough edges and a tall, rugged ceiling. There were hooks in the walls and several sets of thick iron chains, similar to the ones he'd been bound with in India.

He stiffened as Claire stepped away from him, her brows high on her head, her eyes wide. He watched her turn in a circle then did the same. Eve had told them to stay put, that she'd be right back with her team to get things started. First up, they'd need to do a quick photo shoot, with Claire in costume. Her picture would be Photoshopped into an invitation and emailed to Arsen and Salazar. Hopefully, the men would take the bait and come to The Ruby Cave for the private show.

He also thought he understood part of what Eve was up to. He was pretty sure she wanted him to have a good look at this room, at the chaining-up potential. Eve had more than once told him that he could benefit from a few dominance sessions, just to clear his head from some really rotten memories. He thought she was out of her mind.

On the other hand, as he glanced at Claire, something inside him warmed to the idea, especially as memories from the night before rolled through his mind.

Claire walked away from him exploring a secondary room through a short, arched hall opposite.

When she returned to him, her eyes glittered and the chains at his neck vibrated in a way he'd never felt before. "What's going on?"

He knew whatever had set her off was in the adjoining room, but she drew close then slapped a palm hard on his chest. "You're not to go in there, not yet. We have work to do, but when the time is right, I want to bring you back here with me. But I have one question."

"What's that?"

"Do you trust me?"

He looked into her light-brown eyes, dilated and heady with a desire for more sex. Did he trust her? Something inside his chest gave way. "Yes, Claire, I do. Even more than most vampires."

"That says a lot." She was tense head-to-foot as she continued, "Do you trust me enough not to go in there right now? To wait until the time is right?"

He moved back in her direction and caught her arms

in his hands, gripping her firmly. "What's in there? Is someone in there?"

She shook her head. The sweet, rich scent of her sex poured off her now. "Just something I want you to do to me, that's all."

Something she wanted him to do to her.

His chest seized.

Maybe it was her aroused state, or that he could smell her desire, or the glitter in her eyes, but another tremor went through him, of hunger and blood-need, that lingering blood-madness that had turned into some kind of crazy Claire-madness.

He drew her into his arms and kissed her. He needed this—being with a woman who desired him as fiercely as he wanted her, who even sought his darkness, encouraging him to let go.

She moaned softly as he deepened the kiss and drove his tongue into her mouth. He shifted his right foot and pressed his hips against hers so that she could feel him.

I love how you feel, your cock so hard, right against me. Lucian, I don't understand this madness between us because all I want you to do is jump me again.

He forced himself to draw back. Eve would return any second and he wasn't in a state that could be easily hidden. He leaned his forehead against hers, then drew her tight against him.

He just held her. She kept things simple as well. She didn't rub up against him, or dip her hips into him, or fondle his arms or back.

He felt her thoughts, her feelings, grow very quiet.

When he'd calmed down, he drew her to the side of the room where a bench sat against the wall. Clearly this was one of Eve's workout suites, where she either brought her private clients or enjoyed her own liaisons.

He supposed in human terms Eve would be considered a high-class escort. But she was so much more than that, a businesswoman in her own right, with a very free lifestyle, who didn't mind accepting large amounts of cash to entertain her special people. But she always stayed in control, preferring to dominate, which was probably smart in her profession.

He sat directly across from the short, arched hallway and wondered if he'd find one of her tables in there. Probably.

He cleared his throat and crossed his arms over his chest. Like hell was he going to start thinking about something like that, or even doing it. Maybe he should set Claire straight. After all, how wise was it to keep tempting the darkness that lived inside him?

He was about to address the subject when Eve returned with an entire crew, including a rack of clothes that had, yeah, straps and a few narrow bands and some feathers attached. A string of curses flipped through his head. He stood up and paced in front of the bench.

Eve, however, was nothing if not professional. She knew what she was doing. Her makeup team took charge of Claire and whisked her away, taking her into an opposite suite of rooms. Staff kept arriving, including a lighting expert.

Eve approached him. "This shouldn't take long, but it has to be right to tempt Arsen and Salazar to leave their fortress." She smiled suddenly, "Your woman's good people, Lucian. You need to think about keeping her."

Before he could start arguing the point, however, she disappeared into the makeup room as well.

Lucian wished he smoked, wished he had something to do to occupy his mind.

It got worse.

Claire emerged, surrounded by at least one cross-dressing vampire and two who swung for the other side, proclaiming how fabulous she looked. And she did, like a dream that would wake him up in the middle of the night.

She wore a deep purple bustier that lifted and pushed her breasts into two beautiful swells of flesh divided by a heavy line of cleavage. A small ruffle of lace lay against her creamy skin. He wanted his tongue beneath that lace.

Must gain control.

She wore sheer black thigh-highs, the tops lined with a narrow purple ribbon. At least she had on some kind of underwear that covered her cleft, but even that was sheer and showed the auburn landing strip he knew so well.

She had on black lace, fingerless gloves, with long purple feathers that reached the length of her forearms. His eye was drawn, however, to the small silver chains that looped from finger to finger, the sight of which, maybe more than anything, got him going all over again.

His heart rate increased so that she came to him first and planted a hand on his face.

It'll be all right. I'm thinking of Zoey and getting that weapon. You need to do that as well.

He nodded, a sort of rapid-fire jerk of his chin. The makeup *artistes* led her in the direction of the photographer, telling Lucian they'd take good care of his woman. But because she walked away from him, he saw that she was bare-assed with the tiniest line of a thong rising to the back of the bustier above. She wore purple stilettos as well, with shiny silver heels.

This was too much, all of it, as though fate had intervened in his life just to tempt the hell out of him. He had to stay focused, had to remember who he was, why he was here, why she was dressed like this. He had a job to do, and once they'd somehow found a way to wrest Zoey from Daniel, Claire could go home for good. He'd be rid of her and he could go back to his life, to battling on behalf of his world.

But right now, he was in pain.

He worked on his breathing, one in, one out. He ordered himself to hold it together.

Eve positioned Claire on the simple stage with a gray background, a dark ladder-back chair, and smoky gray carpet. Eve positioned her with one knee on the chair, encouraging her to lean forward while arching her back.

Lucian experienced a new kind of torture as desire raced through him and new tremors started up.

Suddenly Claire's voice was in his head. *Lucian, how about you turn the volume down a little. I'm starting to ache for you in a way that will soon be obvious to everyone.*

She shifted slightly to catch his eye, but frowned at him.

Lucian had been so lost in his lust that he'd forgotten about the blood-chains and how they communicated everything he was feeling.

Sorry. I'm going to find some cold water.

Good idea.

He turned away from her, grateful that the double-chains gave them a good sixty feet of distance, and headed to the only bathroom in the suite. He took a few more deep breaths, then literally splashed cold water on his face and neck. He was a mess, a hungry, needy mess, and unable to do a damn thing about it.

Did Eve know that she tortured him like this? The woman was devious in unexpected ways. He could easily imagine that she'd suggested this whole operation just to heighten his awareness of Claire. But my God, he was in pain.

He stayed put. He had to, otherwise he'd be punching out part of the cave wall or, worse, hauling Claire away from the photo shoot and taking care of business then and there. He only left the room when someone else needed the facility. But he returned right away each time to splash more water on himself, afterward to sit on the floor, trying like hell to hold it together.

He laughed at himself more than once. He realized he'd never really been in this place before, this connected to a woman, not in all his four centuries. The chains had forced him to it, of course, but now that he was here, being with Claire wasn't anything like he'd expected. On some level, he now knew what he'd been missing.

At last the shoot ended, and when he returned to the main room, he found Claire covered in a white terry robe, thank God. She chatted quietly with Eve, and because Claire seemed so intense and because Eve looked conspiratorial, he didn't extend his hearing. He was afraid he'd hear something that would once more put his groin in agony.

That each, more than once, glanced in the direction of the forbidden room told him Eve was probably explaining a few things to her, like how things worked.

A few minutes later Eve and Claire approached him. Eve had a knowing smirk on her face. "Claire did really well, though I know this must have been so *hard* on you." Of course she emphasized the word *hard*. Of course. She was Eve. "But you can be proud of her. I've already shown her the outfits she'll wear."

"So what happens next?"

"I'm going to keep working with Claire on the runway part of the show, just a few tricks. We've already sent the invitation out." Eve had a great staff. "Now all we can do is wait and hope. I'll give Rumy a call and let him know what's going on." She stepped away, pulling her phone from her snug leather pants.

Claire drew close. "Hey. How are you holding up?"

She swept her hand up and down his arm so that he felt the small chains hooked to her lace gloves. He repressed yet another groan.

The photographer and her crew passed by, so he spoke quietly. "The gloves you're wearing are magical."

She smiled, her light-brown eyes carrying a warm, affectionate light. "You really are in a sad state."

"I am, especially since all I can do right now is imagine what your costume actually looks like beneath all this terry cloth." His gaze drifted down the fabric covering her chest.

Claire looked around. Seeing that everyone had left, she slowly pulled apart the upper lapels of her robe.

He groaned softly, his gaze landing on what had tempted him from the moment she'd first walked into the room. She had a beautiful cleavage. He licked his lips, wanting to be licking her.

I can feel your desire. It's hitting me in waves through the double-chain. I'm not sure anything could be sexier, especially seeing the look on your face right now.

He lifted his gaze back to her lips, then finally her eyes. *This is new for me, desiring a woman like this, repeatedly hungry for you with an intensity I've never experienced before. I think what this really means is that we need to get your double-chain off, the sooner the better.* He needed her to remember just how temporary their relationship was.

She smoothed a finger over his cheek. *Well, we definitely need to get something off.*

His brows rose. Had he heard her right? Then he laughed all over again, which reminded him of the other side of the coin, the other reason he felt in danger around Claire: She made him laugh. Just when he was getting serious, reminding her why they needed to split up, she made him laugh.

He took her hand and she squeezed his fingers. He squeezed back, smiling. *Thank you for everything, Claire, but especially for the way you tend to lighten things up. Thank you.*

I guess that means you owe me.

He met and held her gaze. *Just name it.*

Oh, I will, and soon.

He might have asked her to be more specific, but Eve reentered the room and called out, "Salazar said yes. They'll be here in two hours and they're ready for us at The Ruby Cave."

CHAPTER 9

Claire tucked herself against Lucian, grateful all over again for his sheer size, which comforted her when nothing else could. Maybe it was a false sensation, but his powerful, muscular frame made her feel safe. Right now she was nerved up like crazy.

Salazar had said yes.

The fashion show was moving forward. On some level she'd hoped the whole thing would fall apart—that her auburn hair wouldn't have been enough to tempt the two crime buddies out of their fortified compound. Guess she was wrong. But then again, she no doubt underestimated the typical trafficker's desire for new product.

After the photo shoot, Eve had talked her through the show. Essentially, she'd don three different outfits, saving the worst for last, and she'd walk down about thirty feet of runway to sexy blues music. In between, Rumy's carefully selected wait staff would ply Arsen and Salazar with some of her finest whiskey. Eve was pretty sure they'd have one powerful security contingent with them.

But this wouldn't be her only audience. She'd have to conceal Rumy's entire team behind one of the largest disguises she had yet to create. Would she even be able to pull it off? She honestly didn't know, although siphoning Lucian's Ancestral power helped.

Still, it was her scantily clad body that a whole bunch of vampire-warrior-types would be looking at for three full jaunts down a black tile runway. What flashed through her mind was that her previous wardrobe had been made up of fairly conservative clothes. Her job as a social worker had never required a pair of black lace gloves adorned with feathers and chains.

Or vampires flying her through solid stone walls.

Once at The Ruby Cave, Lucian flew her off to the side of the theater. Lily had expected to see rows of seats; instead there were just a few tables and chairs arranged in clusters here and there. The rest of the angled floor was apparently designed for a standing-only audience. She wondered if this was typical of sex shows, or if it was just Eve's preference.

The ceiling looked like it was made of black onyx, but the walls were the real jewels. Crushed red crystals had been pressed into a resin on both the side and back walls. *Ruby Cave* proved the best description possible for the space.

Eve had already started calling out orders to more of her staff. Used to her commands as well as to obeying, the stagehands drifted into altered flight, flying left to right, up through the rock or down, never once bumping into one another. They hauled set pieces of every size and shape imaginable, letting Eve make a series of judgments about how she wanted the stage set.

The runway emerged with floor-to-ceiling pillars of red and purple crystals and sequined swags in similar colors that draped from one side of the stage to the other.

After a few minutes, Lucian stepped away from her, moved into the theater seating area, and got on his iPhone. The chains vibrated, sending a distinct hard-edged sensation that Claire knew meant he was finalizing his plans with Rumy.

She drew the lapels of the robe closer together, trying hard not to think about what she had on beneath the terry or the performance she would soon give.

An hour or so later, Eve emerged from behind the theater drapes, glanced around the stage, then at Claire. She gave her the thumbs-up.

Claire's heart leapfrogged, which brought Lucian whipping in her direction. He held his phone away from his ear staring at Eve. "And?"

Eve waved her hand in Claire's direction. "Time to start getting ready. They'll be here in half an hour."

Claire's heart sank low in her chest as new anxiety rose. Could she pull this off? She'd be walking in five-inch heels and putting herself on display for men she loathed for their crimes. She climbed the three side stairs feeling like she was heading to her execution.

"Hey," Eve said, taking her hand and squeezing. "You'll do just fine. Remember that they'll be looking at your body, and I'll be on stage as well."

"You will?"

"Yes, in the background, in shiny black leather, so that if anything goes wrong, I'll catch you. Now let's get them, Claire. Let's make them pay."

These were the exact right words because they bolstered Claire's courage and reminded her what was at stake.

And all she had to do was model some sexy clothes.

Lucian's voice pierced her mind. *Rumy's coming with twenty of his best guards. We're going to line them up along the back wall away from the double doors. As soon as you're ready, you can create the disguise.*

Got it.

She held her shoulders back as she followed Eve into the dressing room. Her courage didn't waver until she saw the first outfit she'd be wearing for Arsen and Salazar.

Lucian had called it right: bits of leather and a few rubber bands.

Lucian gritted his teeth. He'd been feeling the chains vibrate every other minute as Claire's anxiety mounted. He knew that she was getting a look at the next three outfits and he could only imagine what Eve had planned for her.

But he tried not to think about that right now.

He released a stream of air, forcing himself to calm down.

The part of him that liked a good fight had already started gearing up, the familiar adrenaline that coated his veins when he faced the enemy.

Arsen and Salazar had a smart organization with some of the toughest vampires around. They rarely visited The Erotic Passage, for the simple reason that they preferred their dark world of pain and slavery, of dominance and death, lots of death. By comparison, The Erotic Passage must have looked like a trip to the mall.

A moment later Rumy called to alert him that Salazar

and Arsen, along with a detail of two dozen of their best, had left the compound and would arrive in the next few minutes.

"Get your men over here."

"They're already on their way."

He let Eve and Claire know the ETA and asked that Claire come to the stage to create her disguise.

When Rumy's team started arriving, he had them line up at the back of the theater to the left of the double doors. Without Claire's disguising ability, the plan wouldn't work, not even a little, since the theater had no place for Rumy's detail to hide.

Rumy chose to stay out of the fray. He wasn't a warrior, and he didn't want to inadvertently alert either Arsen or Salazar that anything else was going on besides a simple fashion show followed by a would-be auction. He'd also provided wait staff to serve drinks, two vampires who also belonged to his security detail, but who were short like him and knew how to carry off a servant's attitude. When the fighting started, these men would join in.

When Claire arrived on stage, she looked ill at ease in the tall stilettos, though he wasn't surprised. He was, however, thankful that she still wore the robe.

Time to set up the disguise.

Okay. Then she smiled. *Let's get this party started.*

He smiled in return, his chest swelling as he watched her straighten her spine. He felt her nerves, which only made him all the more proud of her for doing what he knew to be way outside her comfort zone.

Lucian turned and explained the situation to Rumy's men: From this point forward the security detail was to remain at attention and in place. Only when Lucian gave the signal could the men move. Claire heard his directives at the same time. Though she'd be able to see all of the men, Salazar and Arsen, as well as their guards, would have no idea what awaited them.

Rumy didn't allow guns of any kind in The Erotic Passage, and Salazar's men would have to go through an initial security check. But all that meant was that the weapons of choice would be a variety of switchblades, daggers, and battle chains.

He watched Claire close her eyes. His double-chain sang at his neck, and the next moment a violet wave flowed in his direction. He stood in front of the ranks, at a central point, then glanced left and right, watching as the disguise covered them all. He could see through what looked like a wave of violet streamers. The men glanced at one another, brows raised, then resumed their positions. Rumy had trained them well.

Claire stood behind a screen and peeled herself out of her robe. Her fingers shook. She tried to calm herself down, but it was a struggle. How could she do this?

The music was already blaring and a video set up showed the theater to everyone backstage. She saw the wait staff, just a couple of men in what looked like leather pants, white collars with black bow ties, and bare chests. Chippendales came to mind.

Eve helped a lot, though. She just kept laughing at Claire's nerves and said, "Hey, if you're shaking out there, they'll love it. They like their women scared to death—*death* of course being the goddamn operative word. Bastards."

The first costume was made up of a few straps of sequined hot-pink reinforced spandex that ended up conforming to her body like a glove. Naturally the one-piece had a thong, and a strange one-inch hot-pink ruffle at her waist that just reached to the top of her ass-crack. It covered nothing, but then again, that was the point.

In front, another tiny ruffle ran in a slight curve at her abdomen. At least that part of her was covered, though not by much. The cut was French-high so that the straps ran across her pelvic bones, then split at the waist to rise to a strap across her back in support of a bra-like structure in front.

There wasn't very much fabric in front, just enough to cover her nipples.

When she stepped out from behind the screen, Eve clapped her hands. "Beautiful. I think we're ready. Now just try to relax." She left the room, taking the last of her people with her.

But she couldn't. She shook from head to foot.

Then suddenly Lucian was right there. "I could feel you trembling like a leaf."

Claire had never been so glad to see him. He was exactly what she needed right now. "Look at this." She held out her hands, her fingers shaking.

She gestured down at the costume, but she'd forgotten the other side of the coin—how Lucian would feel seeing her dressed this way.

He seemed to freeze, his gaze taking the same long journey as when he'd first seen her at the photo shoot. He shook his head side-to-side repeatedly. She felt the war within him start: desire, refusal, desire, anger, desire, need-to-punch-something.

She plastered herself against his chest. *I need your courage, Lucian. I'm trying here, but I'm scared to death and what Eve takes for granted, what is so easy for her, is like lava on my skin.*

Slowly, his arms went around her, enfolding her as his desire-rage combo slid away. She felt him shift his focus to her. *I can't imagine how hard this is for you.*

It feels impossible. I'm not quitting. It just feels bigger than me right now.

I know what you mean, but you can do this. His chest rose as he took in a deep breath. *We'll both get through this. When we have those bastards, it will be worth it. You'll see.*

Okay. I'll toughen up here, but thank you for coming to me. I just needed to take a moment.

I know. It's okay.

When she'd recovered, she spoke against his chest. "Listen. I want you to just leave. Don't look at me, okay?"

"Okay, but I have one problem here."

"What's that?"

Lucian frowned slightly. "I won't be able to see the men at the back of the room. Can you guide me back in?"

"I'll do better than that." She walked him out to the stage and rolled back just the central portion of the disguise. He flew quickly. The moment he took his place and nodded to her, she sealed up the disguise.

Eve waved her off stage, a panicky look on her face. "They're coming."

"Oh, God."

Eve led her to the side stage and whispered, "You have great presence, Claire, even if you don't know it. You have a natural confidence that I admire like hell. Focus on that for the next half hour." She slid her hand through a slit in the stage draperies. "Oh, and the boys have arrived. Arsen's wearing a yellow silk suit. He looks like Tweety Bird, you know, from the cartoons?"

Claire smiled. "Well, that helps a lot." When Eve waved her forward, Claire moved closer so that she could see these vile traffickers. Eve was right. Arsen wore yellow head-to-toe. He was also blond, which made his whole ensemble a bit of overkill.

Salazar had thick wavy black hair to his shoulders. He had a menacing look enhanced by the large contingent of oversized, bulked-up vampires that ranged behind the two men in a protective arc.

Once the men were settled, drinks in hand, Eve would lead the way and introduce her, then begin the fashion show by enumerating the lines and unique qualities of each costume.

Claire wondered briefly what supermodels thought about just before they walked down a runway. Probably admonitions not to trip and break an ankle.

"Showtime," Eve whispered.

Lucian, here goes nothing.

You'll be great.

Thanks.

Eve moved onto the stage first, a real Amazon in her own pair of stilettos so that she stood close to seven feet tall. Her stride was about a mile long. And talk about presence.

She stopped center stage, but cracked her whip with tremendous precision, hitting neither the pillars on each side of her nor the sheer swags overhead.

Eve made her introduction, welcoming Claire simply as "the auburn beauty."

Claire took a deep breath and focused on what Eve had said about her natural confidence. Still, she trembled, blinked, and tried to remember exactly how to put one foot in front of the other.

Eve waved her forward, bending her knees and slinking backward, dragging her whip with her.

Then Eve's voice was suddenly in her head. *You're doing fine.*

Talk me through it. Tell me exactly what to do.

Eve told her how many steps to take, when to pivot, where to put her hands, when to dip her knees or slink a little as she moved.

As Claire headed down the runway, she kept following Eve's directions but couldn't bring herself to look Arsen or Salazar in the eye.

When she reached the end of the runway, Eve told her to make a very slow turn to be sure both men got an eyeful.

Claire, you're doing incredibly well and the guards are so focused on you that they won't feel this train when it hits. Head back toward me, not too fast. Time for costume two.

The next outfit, all black and white crystals, with a choke collar and platforms seven inches tall, became a different kind of trauma. But Eve stuck close, using her whip for effect until Claire got to the top of runway once more.

Good news, Claire. The men have each had three drinks and some of their excitement has given way to that glazed look, more lascivious than alert. We're almost there.

Claire took her time, giving the whiskey a chance to do its work.

The last outfit, however, freaked her out all over again. "There's nothing to cover even an inch of my breasts."

"Yeah, I debated about this one, but the side panels will push everything together."

Claire stared at her. "And that makes things better, how?"

Eve shrugged. "Not one of their guards will be looking anywhere but at your assets."

She focused her attention on Lucian. The vampire needed to be warned. *Eve says you're set to attack as soon as I appear on stage in this third costume, is that right?*

Yes. His voice sounded edged-up.

I'm ready but listen, don't look in my direction. Got it?

Why?

Eve saved the worst for last, and by "the worst" I mean there's not much there and what is there is pushing things around. Lucian, just don't look. I'll get off stage as fast as I can. You have to stay focused. How's the disguise holding up?

Like a cloak I've always worn.

Perfect. Now let's get us some bad guys.

The music changed, and Eve beckoned for her.

Claire trembled as much from the fact that she was all but naked as from the knowledge that an attack was about to follow. She focused on the latter, on how important it was to keep the attention of the bad guys focused on her and to sustain the disguise.

Eve's commands flowed once more through her mind. Claire began to move, slinking and turning, knees bent, back arched, down the runway.

She hoped to hell somebody did something soon because she was ready to bolt as Arsen leaned forward in his seat and shouted, "I need some of that and I need it now."

As the two vampires started to levitate from their seats, she met Lucian's gaze. *If you're going to do something, do it now.*

Lucian's rage flowed hot toward Arsen and Salazar as each levitated toward Claire. His blood boiled and a red hue covered his vision.

Drop the disguise, Claire.

The next moment the wavy violet lines disappeared. Rumy's team went straight into action as each man shifted to levitated flight and let out a war cry. The guards turned, startled, and a flash of blades ran up and down the line.

Lucian flew faster than he ever had before, landing in front of Arsen, whom he gripped around the neck, then flung off the stage. From his peripheral vision he watched Claire hurry from the stage, Eve with her.

But Salazar, the bigger of the two, had more fight in him. He lowered his arms and shoulders, bending his knees, a knife in his hands.

Lucian drew his own blade from his battle leathers. He circled, watching Salazar's dark eyes as he turned his blade in his hand. Salazar lunged. Lucian shifted away from the strike, but Salazar's momentum brought him close. Lucian struck down hard on Salazar's arm. He heard the snap of bone. Salazar shouted in pain then began to shift to altered flight.

But Lucian caught him midair, preventing his escape, and with his Ancestral power kicking into high gear he threw Salazar against the red-crystal wall to the right of the stage. Dislodged crystals flew everywhere.

The entire theater was alive with battling vampires, but Lucian needed to make sure that he had control of both men. He glanced to his left and saw that Arsen was out cold; one of Rumy's men stood guard over him, nodding to Lucian.

Turning, Lucian saw that Salazar was rising up quickly. Lucian body-slammed him back into the wall. Salazar's head connected and a cracking sound ensued. He slid the rest of the way to the floor and fell inert.

Lucian reached down and felt for his pulse. Good. The bastard still lived.

At the same moment he sensed an attack coming from behind him. He went with his instinct and dove out of the way, which sent a bodyguard's dagger hard into the stone wall of the cave.

Lucian, on the floor, flung his dagger before the vampire had even turned in his direction. He halted mid-flight, dropping to the tile floor, both hands on the hilt of the blade. Lucian took out his thinnest chain, got behind the man, and decapitated him. Blood spurted everywhere.

Killing like this was damn messy work.

He turned and saw that Rumy's men fought hard. Time to get to work. He whisked one of his long battle chains from his leathers and started the weapon spinning. Using levitated flight, he maneuvered swiftly, up and down then sideways.

One of Salazar's men had just killed one of Rumy's.

Lucian gave the whirring chain a jerk of his arm, a flick of his wrist, and the chain wrapped around the vampire's throat. He tugged swiftly, pulling the man backward. The man struggled trying to get the chain from around his throat.

Lucian drew close and drove his blade deep. He left the chains where they were, felt movement behind him, turned and met a ramped-up vampire. He blocked the arm that held one blade, then blocked a second blade in his opponent's other hand.

Lucian threw himself in a quick slide against the vampire's feet, knocking him off-balance and onto the floor. He slammed an elbow into one arm and grabbed the blade; before the man, could bring his other arm close, Lucian slashed deep across his wrist. The vampire screamed.

Lucian continued on in this way, helping Rumy's men to finally gain control of the remaining security force. Within fifteen minutes, the theater fell silent.

Turning around toward the stage, he saw that Rumy

had brought in a second team and that both Salazar and Arsen were bound in preternaturally charged chains. Those two weren't going anywhere.

Lucian headed toward the dominant Salazar.

Leaning against the red-crystal-encrusted wall, Salazar said, "I'd heard you'd somehow escaped Daniel's grasp. But I never imagined you'd fight so dirty given what a Boy Scout you are."

Lucian sneered. "You don't know me at all, Salazar. I've been after you for years and now I have you. Your business is done."

Salazar frowned and his lips formed a tight line, but he looked away.

Rumy called out orders, and his security team stuck close to both him and the traffickers. Shortly after, a medical team arrived to care for the wounded and the dead, followed by a serious cleanup and repair crew. The theater would be restored completely within the next few hours. Rumy had one hell of an organization. He could run a small country.

Approaching Lucian, he suggested they move their party to his interrogation room.

"Good idea," Lucian replied, but his gaze raked the stage where Claire had given her show and distracted the men enough to put Arsen and Salazar in their current predicament. "But I can't go without Claire."

"That's right. Your proximity issue."

Absently, he touched the chains.

Hey, you there? He sent the words softly, not wanting to scare her. But even as he spoke telepathically, he felt a tremor run through him. Battling did that to a vampire, increased his blood-needs. He even felt the familiar sensation of more blood-madness on the way.

Yes. Is everything okay?

He gave her a quick rundown, adding that Rumy

wanted to take Arsen and Salazar to his interrogation room.

I've got my robe on, but my clothes are back at the photo shoot.

His mind wanted to slide all the way there, but he protected himself and pulled his thoughts back, focusing on what was important right now. Her robe would have to do.

Come to me so that I can fly you with the men.

Okay.

She appeared a few seconds later at the top of the runway. Rumy's team had charge of Salazar and Arsen.

Rumy ordered his men to take their captives to the interrogation room, then took off. As a group, the vampires shifted to altered flight and disappeared.

Lucian flew to Claire, then held out his arm to her. With a deep sigh and her eyes filling with tears, she stepped onto his booted foot. She slid her arm around his neck and buried her face against his throat. *I can't tell you how glad I am that the runway show is over.*

Me, too. Understatement. *But you did really well and your shields held, which gave us the advantage we needed.* He drew in a deep breath. *You ready to find out what these bastards know about the extinction weapon?*

She smiled. *Hell, yeah.*

He chuckled softly, then flew her down and down.

He arrived with her at Rumy's interrogation room, a black granite space large enough to house a couple of tanks. Lucian felt the location, deep in the cavern system, which made sense given the downward trajectory.

Rumy had Arsen and Salazar seated in chairs, each spattered with blood.

He didn't want her here, though, not for this, not with the stubborn expressions on the men's faces. *Listen, they're not going to give up their information eas-*

ily. Maybe you should wait in the adjoining room for a while, just until they're ready to talk.

Claire glanced around. *Maybe I should.*

Lucian took her through a doorway into a smaller office. She sank into one of the chairs, looking relieved.

When he returned, one of Rumy's men drew his fist back to punch Arsen, but Lucian called out, "Please. Allow me."

Part of him wanted to beat both these men to a bloody pulp for all that they had done and what they represented in his world. The vampires now gathered around clearly felt the same way.

But he had something far more important to accomplish, and now that he had Ancestral power his approach was completely different.

"You got a new idea, boss?"

Lucian glanced at Rumy and nodded. He ignored Salazar since the man was the stronger of the two and went straight for Arsen's head. He put his hand over his skull and let the power flow.

Arsen blinked then started to scream.

Lucian sent the words straight into Arsen's mind. *Tell me what I need to know and the pain stops.*

Lucian knew exactly what that pain felt like. Daniel had hurt him in a similar way.

About ten seconds later Arsen cried out, "I'll tell everything." Tears streamed down his cheeks.

Salazar tried to argue with him, but Arsen lifted his bound hands and said, "Just how the hell do you think we'll ever get out of this? We'll be lucky to be alive in the next ten minutes."

Salazar's eyes glazed over and his chin sank. "Tell them. It doesn't matter anymore."

Arsen met Lucian's hard stare. "I suppose you want to know about the extinction weapon."

"First, I want to know one thing. Assuming you have information on where to locate this weapon, why would you turn even one scrap of a clue over to Daniel Briggs?"

"For thirty million."

Lucian shook his head. "You fucking bastard. No, let me rephrase that: You fucking idiot. If Daniel gets hold of that weapon, what do you think will happen to you? Do you think he wouldn't be able to find you, or your clubs, or whatever disguises you can create or buy? Do you not understand that ever since Daniel took over the Council of Ancestrals he's become the most powerful vampire on the planet? So what exactly do you think he intends to do with an extinction weapon?"

Arsen stared up at him for a long moment. Even Salazar murmured, "Shit."

Lucian shook his head. "So you're both telling me that until this moment, it never occurred to you that Daniel might use this weapon against you? You never thought it possible that Daniel would show up at your compound one day, hold the weapon to your head, then politely ask for his money back, oh, and maybe the keys to your organization?"

He tossed up both hands, shaking his head. "How the hell did the pair of you build an empire together? No, don't answer that. Just tell me where the fuck I can find the weapon before I kill you both right now for your sheer stupidity."

Arsen spoke quickly. "We went on the hunt ourselves, tortured any number of our sources, and hit on a promising clue."

"A clue."

"Look, rumors have been around for decades about these weapons. Scientists who developed them worried about their potential. Some of them were hidden or left clues to their locations. We tracked one of these rumors all the way to what turned out to be a layering of disguises neither of us could penetrate. Either the weapon is behind those disguises or there's a clue to its whereabouts."

"And where is this exactly?"

"In Siberia at the River of Lights Resort, on the gondola ride. You have to take the tour, then use altered flight at a certain point. First, though, you have to recognize the disguise or see beyond it or something, and neither of us could. We were just putting out feelers to see if there was an Ancestral around with disguise-penetrating abilities when Eve sent us her invitation."

He then coughed up two specific details: a ninety-degree bend in the underground river, and a pillar of stone shaped like a serpent.

"How did you come by this information?"

Arsen shrugged, then spoke oh-so-casually. "We tortured a bunch of different vampires. Each knew something. And we had it confirmed when we went on that ride."

Lucian glanced at Rumy. "I'll want to get over there, the sooner the better."

"I'll arrange for tickets, boss."

"Aren't they booked months in advance?"

Rumy just lifted a brow and made the call. Two minutes later he said, "Thanks." He ended the call, then tapped his phone again. He told one of his team to look for an email from Siberia. "Okay, good. Just print them out and bring them here. Now." He returned his phone to the pocket of his tailored slacks. "Stay tight. I'll have something for you in a few secs."

He rocked on his heels, his brows pinched, an unusual expression for Rumy.

A moment later one of his security team arrived,

passing straight through the wall, and handed him a sheet of paper.

Rumy offered it to Lucian. "You have two entrance passes for the River of Lights at midnight, and you're welcome."

Lucian stared at the piece of paper. "How the hell did you do this?"

Rumy just smiled. "You still have no idea how well connected I am."

"You mean how much dirt you have on everyone."

"Well, that, too."

Without warning, a tremor hit Lucian hard. This time his stomach cramped. "Shit." He looked around, wishing Claire was close.

You need me?

The chains had done their talking so there was no point pretending. *I do.*

Is it okay to come in there now?

It's fine. We've got what we need and the boys are in good shape.

Claire opened the door. At the sight of her, Lucian's heart warmed up something fierce. How had she become so important to him in such a ridiculously short time?

Salazar whistled softly. "Just look at that red hair."

Lucian glared. Salazar lifted his chain-bound hands. "Sorry. Apologies."

Lucian turned to Rumy. "You'll take it from here?"

"I've got a call in to Gabriel. I've decided to let him handle these two. He'll know what needs to be done."

"I couldn't agree more. I'll be in touch after Siberia."

Rumy nodded.

Lucian crossed the room to Claire, unwilling to let her get too close to the captives.

He immediately drew her into his arms, then held her tight for a long moment. *Thank you for all you did.*

You're welcome. She rubbed his back. *So what happened with Tweety Bird and his companion?*

Lucian relayed what they'd discovered, adding that he now had tickets for the midnight ride.

It all sounds so strange. Your world actually has something called a light show in Siberia?

He stroked her cheek. *Yeah, I've never been there. A little too vanilla for my tastes.*

Sounds like it. But it also sounds like the best lead we've had.

Couldn't agree more. He glanced around. *But it looks like we've got a couple of hours to kill. What would you like to do? Want to head back to the suite?*

I could really use a shower, but I left my clothes at the photo shoot. Okay if we head back there first?

Absolutely.

When he drew back, Lucian held out his arm and Claire stepped up on his foot, holding her robe together with one hand. She wrapped her free arm around his neck. Just as he slid his arm around her waist then slipped into altered flight, she kissed him.

CHAPTER 10

Claire let the kiss linger. She'd been wanting to try this for a long time, to see if it was even possible to kiss Lucian while in the middle of altered flight. Apparently, it was.

Claire, what you can do to me. But I'll have to find someplace to land if you keep this up.

She drew back and smiled, hugging him, thankful that the ordeal was over. She held Lucian tight, feeling ridiculously safe in his arms while they passed through all kinds of solid matter. She marveled that she'd only been engaged in altered flight for a few days, but the movement in front of her eyes had come to look like soft swirling mist, nothing that could hurt her at all.

When he slowed and shifted to fly at a steep upward angle, she knew they were drawing near Eve's specialty room, where the photo shoot had taken place. She recalled the short arched hallway leading to the room she had forbidden Lucian to enter.

The timing seemed perfect.

On an instinctive level, she knew Eve had wanted her to see the separate room. The setup spoke of dominance play, and of Lucian, in a way that Claire understood because of the shared chains.

The darkness she sensed in Lucian had resulted from his childhood torture, from the pain he carried around in him because he'd once been bound in chains. He needed to let go of something deep within, and letting him have control of her might just help. She wasn't even sure she understood why this might be true, but she felt a profound need to allow the experience, as much for herself as for Lucian.

She had always lived a kind of safe life, choosing her path carefully, pursuing a profession that made sense to her in terms of building a stable future for herself. On the other hand, her social life had always been a mystery, since she'd never been satisfied with the men she'd dated. And she'd known a number of good men, with strong careers, determined to get ahead, qualities she valued. Yet she'd never felt completely drawn to them, as though something was missing.

Now she flew with a vampire and felt more like herself than she ever had before. So what did that say about her, about what she needed from a man and from life? Another mystery.

He landed her near the bench he'd sat on earlier, during the photo shoot. The hallway was opposite. "So what's in there you didn't want me to see?"

She could feel he was getting worked up, and not just from his desire for her. His blood-madness moved at the edges of his mind once more.

She stood in front of him and put her hands on his face. "We need to get cleaned up. Lucian, look at me."

He dragged his gaze away from the hall. "What?" He scowled, his temper suddenly short. He drew in a quick breath, flared his nostrils, and squinted.

"You're in pain, aren't you?"

"Yes. A little. What's in the room, Claire?"

She slid her right hand down his arm, all the way to touch his palm. She interlaced her fingers with his, then drew him toward the bathroom. "I want you showered up. How about we do that together?"

His eyes fell to half-mast, and a soft growl formed at the back of his throat. It was something only a vampire could do—that soft growl—and she loved it.

She led him to the shower, which turned out to be a deep open space, big enough for both of them.

But right now she had something else in mind. She turned the water on for him, then gestured for him to precede her.

He never took his eyes off her as he stripped, stepped in, and started lathering. She ignored the blood that washed down the drain. He'd been dirty from battle. He'd needed a good scrubbing. "Are you joining me?"

She shook her head. "I just want to watch." Claire had never been so hungry for a man.

When he soaped himself low so that his fist worked his thickening column up and down, she slowly opened the upper portion of her robe.

His gaze dropped to her cleavage and then to her bare breasts, held upright and pushed together by the costume. Her nipples were now like hard beads.

"Get rid of the robe."

That was what she wanted, right now, right here, with Lucian. She wanted him telling her what to do, commanding her. She dropped the robe.

He rinsed, shut the water off, and ran a towel over his body. Drawing close, he stroked the sides of her bare, supported breasts with his palms, then licked down the deep line of her cleavage, thumbing her nipples.

You don't know how much I wanted do this.

I had an idea.

He sucked on her breasts, hard tugs, nursing her, which caused her more agony. She surrounded his shoulders with her arms and flexed her breasts against his mouth and face. He grabbed her waist with his hands, pulling her close.

"Lucian, I swear I could come like this."

But at that, he rose up and looked down at her, his gray eyes glinting. Something very Ancestral, and very vampire, stared back at her as his gaze bored into hers. *What's in that room, the one you wouldn't let me see?*

You sure you want to know?

You know I do.

Very well. One of Eve's specialty tables.

His gaze narrowed. *And is that what you want?* She felt his desire like a strong sudden wind.

She nodded slowly, but before she could say anything more he shifted into altered flight, throwing her over his shoulder at the same time. A second later she stood in that room, now lit with a dozen fat candles. Eve had been there, knowing what Claire intended and how Lucian would respond.

And Claire loved it, all of it.

The darkness in Lucian came alive at the sight of the narrow platform draped from above with a dozen different kinds of heavy black chains, some of them infused with preternatural power. He could trap Claire here forever, if he wanted. She'd never be able to break out, and no other Ancestral would have the power to release her.

He liked the idea.

His cock grew rigid as he slid her down his body and set her on her feet.

She'd seen this room earlier and planned to bring him here. She wanted to be here.

The bed was narrow, meant only for one, and had movable parts that, being a man he understood extremely well. He could place parts of his body next to her. He could reach other parts of her easily. And she couldn't touch him.

Chains hung from a suspended box. More chains hung from wrought-iron loops cemented into the rock wall at the head of the platform. Over the last year, he'd been suspended on similar loops and beaten until his skin hung in strips and he bled in pools around his feet. He'd almost died twice under the whip of the women who tortured him and his brothers.

Now Marius was dead and he was here with a human female, a woman he intended to use. A woman who wanted to be chained down, wanted to be under his control.

She'd already seen the raw state of his dark soul and she wanted more, so that's exactly what he would give her.

First, however, he needed to get the costume off her. He'd hated that other men had looked at her body, especially the two worthless vampires who traded in human flesh.

He needed her cleansed of at least that.

He caught the straps at her shoulders and slowly drew them down over her arms, away from her breasts, peeling them off her hips. He knelt in front of her, and as he removed the patch covering her narrow auburn landing strip, he leaned in and placed a kiss on her cleft.

Are you ready for this, Claire, ready for me?

Yes, God yes.

He rose up and lifted her quickly in his arms. She gave a cry and he smelled her sex. He turned her in his arms so that he held her parallel to the floor, balancing her.

He leaned over her and nipped at her stomach.

Again she cried out.

He met her gaze. "I'll give you a choice right now, Claire. You can leave this room or you can stay, but if you stay, I will bite you, repeatedly."

The sharp scent of her aroused sex flowed over him so that he had his answer before she spoke the words within his mind. *I'm staying, Lucian. I want this more than I can say.*

He looked into her eyes and saw her desire. She was into this as much as he was.

"Last chance. Leave now or stay and take whatever comes at you."

"I'm staying." The double-chains vibrated with her desire.

He threw his head back and roared, still holding her stretched out, barely balanced on the muscles of his biceps and forearms.

He moved her toward the platform, pushing the central portion in and stretching out a leg on each side. He used manacles and chains from above and locked her ankles within, which spread her for him, providing the view he wanted of her sex, of the place where he intended to work her until she came repeatedly. The arrangement allowed her some mobility, but not a lot.

He rounded the sides of the platform then locked her wrists up in a similar way. Again he left her with a short arc of motion: She could reach for things, but she wouldn't be able to leave the table.

As soon as he had her completely chained, he stepped away from the table. He began to feel a swell of power up through his feet, his legs, hardening his muscles and his cock, tightening his abs, his arms, his neck. Again, he roared.

Her gaze tracked him, her light-brown eyes glinting in the candlelight. She streamed an erotic scent.

But the flood of power in his veins ignited his blood-madness. He needed to feed, and he would take from her repeatedly in dozens of places.

And he would start where she was most vulnerable.

Claire wanted this. The chains and being pinned down spoke to something primal, to dominance, and to belonging. That's what she felt, as though the manacles on her wrists and ankles revealed just how much she'd already given herself to Lucian, how completely she trusted him.

What she loved even more was what this meant to him, something the double-chains communicated to her. It fed the desire that flowed in a heady stream throughout her body.

He breathed hard through his nose as he moved between her legs, the outrageous nature of the platform giving him complete access to her body.

With his gaze fixed between her legs and the chain vibrating heavily at her neck, his fangs emerged.

The quick strike just at the top of her clitoris rose to a sharp crescendo of pleasure. Then he began to suck. She arched as pleasure spiked, groaning heavily into the cavernous space.

After a moment he drew back, his eyes glazed, blood on his lips and chin. He moved down the inside of her

leg and bit her again. It felt so good, especially when he
sucked once more and took her blood in these small
increments.

He switched to her other leg and did the same.

Her hips arched each time he drank from her.

He bit just below each knee, then moved down her
leg and struck a vein on top of her foot. Pleasure streaked
up the insides of her legs, making her hungry for his
touch, his tongue, his cock, him.

He rose, then moved away from the center of her,
shifting to her right side. He held her arm up and licked
the inside of her elbow.

"Unh" came out of her mouth as her vein rose.

He bit, then drank, his gaze fixed on her breasts, on
the way they bobbed up and down because her body
wouldn't remain still. She didn't understand all that she
was experiencing or why this turned her on like it did.

She could just reach her breast, and because she
needed to be touched, she stroked her own nipple.

He left her vein and shoved her hand away. "You
don't do anything unless I tell you. Now what do you
say to me?"

"Yes, master."

He growled his approval, then leaned low and bit her
breast above the nipple, sucking at all the small veins,
drinking more.

She loved what he was doing to her. She loved that
he was lost inside the darkest part of himself, that part
of him he worked so hard for no one to see. But he could
show himself to her. This was what Eve had wanted her
to do, to honor all that Lucian was.

Claire understood that in a very essential way, she
was healing him, something Lucian might never understand.

He shifted to her breast and nursed on her, suckling

for a long time until she moaned heavily, wanting to touch him.

She lifted her hand and ran her palm down the back of his neck.

He came off her hissing. "Don't touch me, Claire. You have no rights here. Do you understand?"

She nodded. No touching, no doing anything, unless he gave permission. Yeah, she loved it.

She rocked her hips once slowly.

His gaze fell to the line of auburn hair between her legs. He returned to position himself between her thighs once more.

Then he levitated.

Claire gasped.

He had so much power.

He levitated over her, stretching out prone and moving just a few inches above her body but between the chains hanging from the box overhead. The chains jangled where he touched them, or when she inadvertently moved them.

She thought he would kiss her or take from her throat. Instead he kept moving, sustaining his position in the air until his hips were near her face.

He took the sides of her head in his hands and moved until his cock was close to her lips.

"Open your mouth, Claire, but don't do anything until I tell you."

She panted as the tip of his cock touched her lips.

"Lick me, Claire."

She took her time and slowly drifted her tongue over the crown of his cock, savoring the ridge, swirling. *Let me suck you.*

Just lick, Claire. No sucking. Not till I tell you.

Her chest rose and fell. Her breathing grew harsh. Her body undulated as he teased her with what she wanted deep in her mouth, pushing in and out, making the promise of the pleasure he could give her between her legs.

Please, Lucian.

Yes, Claire, beg me. That's what I want.

Let me suck you, Lucian. I want your cock deep inside my mouth. I want to taste you. Give me every inch you can.

He groaned heavily. She felt the tremendous energy it took for him to sustain himself in the air, but he also loved the control of it.

She licked him in long, slow swipes. The impulse to suck was profound, but she kept her need at bay.

You can suck now.

She wrapped her lips around him and drew him in deep. He groaned heavily, or maybe she did.

Nothing had felt so good as moving her tongue over him, sucking him.

He stopped suddenly and withdrew from her mouth.

She could tell he'd taken himself to the brink; he could have released into her.

He remained prone, breathing hard, but he didn't touch her.

Eventually he worked backward down her body and occasionally balanced himself with a hand on the platform beside her body, even though there was hardly any room.

When he stood between her legs once more, he knelt and went to work on her, feasting between her thighs.

She groaned and cried out.

He suckled and pulled on her clitoris, dipping his tongue to finally penetrate her hard, plunging his tongue in and out, going faster and faster, harder because he was strong and he was an Ancestral.

The orgasm bore down on her so fast that she pushed

into his face and screamed, her legs flailing, chains jangling. Pleasure flowed, searing her veins, rushing up through her abdomen, her chest, her throat, exploding like a thousand stars within her mind. The chains made a strange cacophony of sound against the harsh cries that kept coming out of her throat.

He only stopped when her legs and body settled down and the chains grew silent. She could hardly move. She marveled at the strength of her orgasm. She thought it couldn't get better. Then it did.

Lucian had never felt more like himself in his entire life. He'd kept this part hidden, the part that enjoyed dominating others, that loved having Claire completely under his control.

He'd bitten Claire and enjoyed every wicked response, equally aware that desire flowed each time he struck, the chains telling him the truth, keeping him going and worked up, knowing she loved what he was doing.

He needed this and he needed to do it to Claire. A female vampire could have fought him off, could have blocked some of his power, but a mere human, despite the fact that she siphoned some of his power, was vulnerable; she knew it, he knew it.

That vulnerability, the ever-present knowledge that he could crush her with his bare hands, or drink her dry, or open several veins in the matter of a few seconds and watch her bleed out on the floor—all of that kept his cock hard as a rock.

She had to do what he said. He was master now, in charge of the outcome, whether pain or pleasure, or even death or life.

Most of all, she trusted him.

And he loved it.

His biceps and pecs flexed in response, feeling the

power he wielded. As he looked down at her sex-drenched face, the lethargy in her well-used body, he roared all over again. Claire was his. She belonged to no one but him and right now he could exert his will and do as he pleased.

I love your fangs. Use them again. Drink from me some more.

No, Claire, you don't seem to want it enough.

She leaned up on her elbows. "Please, Lucian, I'm begging you. I need you to pierce me with your fangs. Please take a vein and bite me." Her voice dropped. "Hard."

He felt her desperation, which matched his own.

The time had come. *I'm going to fuck you while I do it, do you understand?*

She nodded, panting.

He moved in tight to her body, holding his cock and looking down at her sex. He pushed against her opening.

Her back arched and she cried out.

She was wet, streaming for him, so that with another thrust he slid inside and pushed to the hilt. He leaned forward and wrapped each of his arms around the chains that were manacled to her wrists. He pulled the upper half of her body a few inches off the table, rolling his hips and thrusting deep. She held her head up, her lips parted, small gasps escaping her mouth.

But he needed more.

He let go of the chains, and she eased back against the table. He split into two parts, as he'd done earlier, only this time his secondary self levitated to the side of the table and positioned his cock against her lips.

He wanted both sensations and he wanted her filled with him, subjugated in just this way. This was how he wanted to come, how he wanted to bring her again.

Suck me again, Claire. You're going to take this with

your mouth and your pussy at the same time. Now do just as I say.

"Unh." That low sound of hers that expressed her desire, made him rock his primary hips.

His secondary self groaned as he slid his cock deep inside her mouth.

He loved this part of being a powerful vampire, of being able to separate into two selves. But he never thought he'd be doing it with a woman, a human, chained down on a table.

Her body moved beneath his, writhing, her hips slamming back into his. He was so ready, needing to come as he watched his cock go in and out of her mouth. He looked down and watched the same thing low as he thrust inside her. A threesome, with only two of them.

I'm so close, Lucian.

His double-chain vibrated with her excitement.

She moved her hand to the exposed side of her neck. She was just able to maneuver close enough to rub a finger down her throat.

He slapped it out of the way. "Do as I say, Claire."

She eyed him while she sucked his cock. She let her tongue drift over the tip so that his secondary self thrust in hard.

His balls tingled.

Her soft brown eyes dared him.

He smiled and began to thrust into her faster. He shifted to the side of her throat and bit deep then began to take from her.

Claire.

His hips pistoned now, the cock in her mouth moving faster.

He sucked her blood, taking this woman who had dared him to bite her. He drank and fucked, taking her hard.

But he felt her response, potent with desire and passion, ecstasy rising in Claire, hotter and hotter.

He was a hard missile now, in her body and in her mouth.

His balls tightened, sending a thrill up through his groin in anticipation of what he was about to give her, the release he'd experience.

His Ancestral power, so new to him, sent him into overdrive. He pummeled, pushed, and thrust. He sucked down her blood. At the same time, she writhed beneath him, groaning heavily, her mouth still working his cock, all the chains jangling.

Let me wrap my legs around you, please Lucian. Please.

The plaintive, begging sound gave him more pleasure. *You may.*

The chains gave her just enough latitude that her legs wrapped around the tops of his thighs.

Let me touch you with my hands. Please.

You may.

But it wasn't just her hands; she dug her nails into his shoulders. The unexpected sensation brought his release. He let go of her neck and roared. His cock jerked as pleasure shot through him, hitting every goddamn nerve in both his primary and secondary selves. His mind spun and his body shook.

His essence went two places at once, and he watched her swallow what he gave her.

But he wasn't done.

He drew out of her mouth and re-formed, becoming one vampire again, all the while keeping his hips working her in quick, deep thrusts, his hands holding her hips, his cock still firm.

She looked up at him, her eyes dark with passion. He felt how tight she was, how wet. He knew he'd be

able to come again, something he'd only done with
Claire.

Do you want more, Claire.

Yes, God yes. Please, master.

He grew tight once more and the small of his back
tensed. His hips moved like lightning and Claire arched
and screamed, throwing her head back, the chains jangling and hitting his ass.

Watching her orgasm, knowing he'd put her there,
filled him with a profound sense of power.

He roared yet again as he came this time, deep gut-
tural vampire sounds of dominance and control. He fell
on her and bit her again, on the other side of her neck
this time.

Yes, Lucian.

He kept pummeling into her and she kept clawing at
him and crying out. He felt every orgasm he gave her,
repeatedly, one after the other. Sometimes he came with
her, sometimes he just wanted to watch her shout and
cry out.

Only when he felt a familiar human weariness come
over her did he finally slow it down, resting his cock
inside her.

She lay panting, eyes closed, the chains quiet at last.

With his hands resting on the sides of the platform,
he felt satiated in a way he'd never before experienced.
He felt good and whole, especially knowing that he'd
brought Claire so much pleasure.

She opened her eyes to mere slits. He felt her ex-
haustion, which would soon pass, because he also felt
her streaming his vampire power and growing stronger
because of it. Her voice came out hushed. "What's going on in that head of yours?"

He stared down at her, amazed by the connection he

felt to her. "I don't know. You amaze me, Claire. This was astounding."

He didn't want to, but his internal clock knew they needed to get on with things, to clean up then head to Siberia.

But he didn't want to leave the well of her body.

As he stared into her eyes, he felt his chest seize. At first he thought the blood-madness rolled again. But he quickly realized it was something else: One day, probably really soon, he'd have to take this woman to Santa Fe.

She put her index finger between his brows, rubbing at his frown line. "What are we going to do?"

He shook his head. He understood her. They were both trapped by the chains that bound them. "Everything will be all right."

Slowly, he withdrew from her, his chest once more feeling tight. He went about his business methodically, but he didn't meet her gaze again as he unlocked each of the manacles. He then helped her to her feet, but she fell limp against him; if he hadn't caught her she would have dropped to the floor in a heap.

He scowled. "You okay?"

But she looked up at him, laughing. "I'm better than okay. You softened my bones with so much pleasure. I think I might even have passed out once or twice."

He smiled in return and ran his fingers through her beautiful auburn hair. He wanted to say something to her, but words wouldn't come.

She put her hands on his face, as she often did. His body stilled for her, waiting, as he looked into her light-brown eyes.

"I loved every minute of this experience."

He nodded, searching her eyes. "I did, too." He put a hand over his heart. "I feel better than I have in decades.

Hell, maybe even centuries, and I have you to thank for that."

"I feel the same way."

"But you're leaving."

"I am."

He nodded. "How about we gather up our clothes and get back to our suite."

"Sounds like a plan."

Claire sat on the side of the bed, her legs and arms crossed. She'd insisted that Lucian shower first because she'd need more time in the bathroom and she didn't want him waiting around for her, especially if Rumy needed him. Men were quick in the shower, and she wanted to wash her hair and strip off all the makeup.

Her thoughts, however, had stayed fixed in the specialty room. She'd loved every second of the experience, which still stunned her. Where had this penchant come from for dominance and sex combined?

All throughout the lovemaking, she'd been so fully engaged, but now, separated as she was from his body, she felt terribly removed from Lucian. The chain at her neck was perfectly quiet. She could tell that Lucian held his emotions in check, not surprising. He'd said it exactly right: She was leaving.

The memories of what had just happened on the platform began to flow in a sudden stream. She watched them almost as an observer, especially each time she orgasmed and what she'd felt: the pleasure, the desire, and something more, something she had a hard time putting a name to.

Then it came to her: *affection*. She'd felt affection for Lucian the whole time, the burgeoning of something greater than mere like or even respect. Dammit, she'd started to love the vampire, the very thing she'd been avoiding.

She leaned over, planted her elbow on her thigh, and dropped her forehead into her hand. Oh, hell, what was happening to her?

She no longer recognized herself, which was part of the problem. She streamed so much of Lucian's power that she didn't know where he left off and she began. In psychological terms she was growing far too dependent on him, on a vampire with a darkness that lived inside him, one needing to dominate. She'd not only let him, she'd savored the experience.

She might even have treasured it, which made matters worse.

Tears burned her eyes. In the space of just a few days she'd grown fond of Lucian—yes, she loved him, or had the beginnings of love for him—but she couldn't be feeling these things. She had a life to return to, a family, a job she loved, and a mission to continue with her social work.

She deserved a chance to be a wife and a mother, married to a normal human man, arguing with him about finances and how to raise their children, not whether he needed his blood-needs met or wondering if this would be the night Daniel would kill Lucian and she'd never see him again.

If this kept up, if she continued to have sex with Lucian, how the hell would she ever be able to part from him when the time came?

Everything okay?

Lucian's voice drew her out of the sudden pain that had engulfed her chest. She sat up and squared her shoulders.

Everything's fine.

You don't sound all right.

I'm trying to be sensible and it's proving difficult.

The water no longer ran in the shower. She rose to her feet, heading to the open bathroom door—and there he was. He stood with a black terry towel tucked around his waist.

She met his gaze, trying not to feel so much for the man.

He stared back, shaking his head as though he understood. "I don't want you to be unhappy."

His words did her in. Claire gave a small cry and went to him. He engulfed her in his arms, holding her tight.

Claire.

I'm sorry, I'm just feeling way too much right now. I loved what we just did together and I shouldn't. I shouldn't be caring for you as much as I am, but I do. And now we have an extinction weapon to find, my friend to save who-the-hell-knows-how, and some kind of River of Lights ride to take.

For a long time, he rubbed her back, just holding her. He said nothing, but the double-chains vibrated with his concern.

Knowing that she needed to get herself together, that they had critical tasks to accomplish, she pulled out of his arms. *Don't pay any attention to me right now. I'll be okay. And I really do need a shower.*

She threw levers and yelped when cold water hit her then yelped when the water got too hot. But she didn't care. She'd made the mistake of getting involved, of wanting Lucian to see himself the way she saw him. And now she cared about him.

Lucian's voice once more broke through her thoughts. *Rumy's sending over some clothes for the trip to Siberia, something warm so you'll be comfortable.*

She took a deep breath. *Sounds good.*

She spent the next several minutes washing her hair then getting rid of all the makeup, trying to find some balance. But the last thing she'd expected, when Rumy had given her the first blood-chain to wear, was that she'd fall so hard for a vampire.

CHAPTER 11

Lucian thanked Rumy for the clothes. His staff was incredibly efficient, highly motivated to please and to do their best at all times. Eve had sent along an iPhone for Claire to use for the duration, and Rumy had provided a long fur coat for her as well. She might be siphoning his power, but it would be cold on the River of Lights ride for her, human that she was. He wanted her to be comfortable.

Rumy took off, asking Lucian to stay in touch and to come back to The Erotic Passage as often as he needed while he continued his hunt for the extinction weapon. He also said he had a few remote connections to the Dark Cave system, where Zoey probably would have lived for the last two years and where Daniel no doubt had her caged up.

"I think it's sweet. The River of Lights. Just precious." Rumy had smiled, but wisely took off before Lucian could smash his face in.

Some vampire couples went on their honeymoon in Siberia, which made Lucian shudder. Just what he needed, to be with Claire in a romantic setting. He didn't want to think of her like that, in any context, and yet how many times had he made love to her over the past couple of days? It had to be some kind of record for a pair of strangers.

And now she was really distressed.

He slipped on a long-sleeved black tee, fresh battle leathers and accompanying weapons, steel-toed boots. He tapped the chains at his neck. Damn chains. This was the real problem. Maybe they didn't lie, but if Claire hadn't bound him in the first place, he wouldn't be stuck feeling so damn much for her. When she'd come into the bathroom, she'd looked beyond upset, so he'd held her. But the whole time, his chest had started to ache in a way he'd never experienced before, which was the exact moment he realized that the woman meant something to him.

So much for keeping things simple.

A string of curses rolled through his head, one after the other, hot bits of invective that summarized his frustration about their present relationship. He desired Claire, wanted her, hungered for her, and it wasn't because of the chains, it was because of Claire herself . . . and there wasn't a damn thing he could do about that. She'd come to mean something important to him, and he was so screwed.

When Claire emerged from the bathroom, a towel wrapped around her, he gestured to the clothes hanging on the rack then turned around so she could get dressed with some degree of privacy.

"Thanks. This is awkward."

With his back to her, he tried not to think about her being completely naked. "I know."

"Am I supposed to wear this fur?"

"It'll be cold. Don't worry, it's faux."

She fell silent but he heard her movements, sidesteps of her feet as she probably put on the thong that he wanted to look at really bad, but didn't. Next, her jeans, which he knew she preferred and looked hot on her. Claire had a beautiful ass. She'd wear a bra, one of several that Rumy's staff had bought for her and arranged in the top dresser drawer. He knew, because he'd checked them out while she was showering

He heard a faint grunt, then, "This is a bit snug."

The comment made him instinctively turn around to look. There were the shapely mounds of her breasts overflowing a low-cut, lacy black bra. His heart might have simply paused for a few seconds, he wasn't sure. His breathing certainly had.

He frowned then looked away. "You want a different one?" He wanted her to say no.

"No, it's okay. I'll be fine."

He waited. She'd already chosen a purple silk top, so she'd be putting that on.

"It's sure a good thing I'll be wearing fur."

Once more, her comment tugged his gaze in her direction. He held back a moan since her perfect cleavage showed through a long cutout in the blouse.

She rifled through the clothes and found a second pullover to solve the problem. He should have been grateful, but he was just enough of a man to admit he liked looking and Claire had great stuff to look at.

She met his gaze, tugging at the hem of the pullover. "What's with all the sexy vibrations? Didn't you take me enough times back there in the specialty room?"

"No." The word left his mouth before he could stop it. He scrubbed a hand through his hair. "I mean sure, yeah, of course. I mean, hell, whatever."

"You said no. Honestly, Lucian, what is it with you men?" But she smiled, and some of the tension left her.

He shrugged, then he laughed, that thing she could make him do. "We're men. Our dicks dictate most of our decisions. I didn't mean anything by it and I know we both need to move on."

The amused light in her eye dimmed. She sat down to put on a pair of socks and soft brown leather flats. "Yes, we do. I'm trying, Lucian, but all this sex is getting to me and making feel things that I know aren't real, can't be real, and can't last. Know what I mean?"

He leaned his elbow on the upper brace of the steel rack, looking down at her. "Yeah, I do. We'll get through this, Claire, and I'll get you home as soon as we have the extinction weapon in hand and after we rescue your friend."

Claire slid her foot slowly into the second shoe. She stared at the floor and released a deep, almost labored breath. "It's funny to me how what we each wanted to accomplish dovetailed like this—your father having bought Zoey, I mean. Now I have yet another reason to detest Daniel, as if what he had already inflicted on your world and on you and your brothers wasn't bad enough. God, Marius . . ."

She shaded her face with her hand.

He kept forgetting that she'd witnessed his brother's murder. Another shard of pain took a slice off his heart for a brother lost, one he'd loved for four centuries.

But he couldn't dwell on his loss, not yet, maybe not until he had Claire safely home. Right now she had to be the focus, as well as the extinction weapon and Zoey.

"Sorry," Claire murmured. She then rose and jerked the fur from the rack. "So, have you got the tickets?"

He patted the inside pocket of his long leather coat.

She glanced at his chest, then her gaze skimmed him head-to-foot. "This is a different look for you. It's nice. Your other jacket was shorter. I like this long look, kind of Old West."

His lips curved. "Yeah, I'm a real cowboy." For fun, he flashed the tips of his fangs.

She grinned then laughed. "The cowboy vampire. Okay, that just sounds weird."

"Yeah, it does." He reached out and caught her arm through the thick fur. "We good, Claire?"

She put a hand on his face. "We'll always be good, you and me. You're my kind of peeps." She nodded several times then drew back. Pulling on her gloves, she added, "So it's Siberia, then?"

"Yep."

"Ready if you are."

"Your timing is perfect." He held out his right arm, she stepped into him, and as he clamped an arm around her waist, he shifted into altered flight and headed northeast.

The moment Lucian touched down, Claire was more grateful for Rumy's foresight than at any time before. It was cold, way too cold for Claire to be comfortable, but the faux fur, lined with down, kept her from freezing her tush off.

The landing area for the River of Lights show went on for at least an eighth of a mile. Lucian slid his arm around Claire then turned back to look over his shoulder.

She looked up at him. *What is it?*

Jitters. Don't know why.

Do you think we've been followed?

It's possible.

After that, she marveled at the disguise around the entire built-up entrance. "I've never seen so much movement in a shielding disguise before."

Lucian laughed. "Part of it's for show—even vampire children can see through it."

Claire knew that there were children in Lucian's world; vampires were born into the world just like humans. But their long-life genes were balanced out with the difficulty of procreation. Children were a rare occurrence.

Practicing birth control was unheard of. That Daniel had somehow managed to produce several sons from several human women had been deemed a result of his considerable Ancestral powers and nothing less.

Vampire attendants, for what turned out to be a gondola ride experience, directed the arriving guests into four lanes. The guides wore costumes, with tall colorful hats and fur-lined vests.

Soft orchestral music floated across the lanes. Two female vampires levitated, carrying baskets of single red roses to sell to the guests.

Claire frowned, wondering what was going on, then looked around and noted just how many couples there were, some locked in tender embraces.

Hold on. This is a romantic getaway, isn't it? Because I can see a hotel through the disguise on the left.

You can see that?

Sure.

You amaze me, Claire.

I don't think seeing through the disguise is about me; it's about you. Ever since you took on your Ancestral power, my abilities have kicked up a notch.

An attendant approached with a basket slung over her arm. "A rose for your lady?"

Claire met Lucian's questioning brow but shook her head.

Lucian reached into his pocket anyway and withdrew a money clip. He handed the woman twenty euros, but she handed it back and in a quiet voice said, "For you, Lucian, no charge. Keep up the good fight, boss."

He took the flower, and she moved on. He touched the soft petal to his lips then turned to Claire. *The good fight. Is that what I do?*

She slid her arm around his. *Yes, and that defines you exactly, who you really are, boss.*

He frowned slightly, then handed her the rose.

She took it, and just as Lucian had she let the velvety petals glide over her lips, but her thoughts had turned to the mission at hand. *Of all the places to hide a clue to the whereabouts of an extinction weapon, why in a Tunnel of Love gondola ride?*

Lucian smiled. *Last place anyone would look?*

You may be right.

Once inside the initial cavern, couples could purchase a bottle of champagne, served in a silver bucket with two glasses. If done properly, sipping the champagne would last the entire mile-long trip, which apparently required a full hour to complete.

An hour to go a mile.

Every gondola was self-propelled and ran on a track beneath the water, much like rides at a theme park.

The seats were comfortable and semi-reclined, but Claire had reached the limits of her patience. *Lucian, can't you just fly me along the river's course until we find the serpent pillar? I think this is going to drive me crazy. We have a weapon to find, a psychopath to trap, and my friend to save.*

Unfortunately, no. There's no flight allowed. An

electric webbing throughout would cause serious pain to anyone who levitated.

What are we going to do when we reach the pillar?

We'll play it by ear. He glanced at her. *Is this changing your mind?*

Not even a little, but it is making me nervous.

A female voice from a speaker inside the gondola told them to prepare for the magic of the River of Lights, to give themselves fully to the experience, and to be assured that they would have complete privacy the entire trip.

The back of the gondola formed a kind of partition so that they could see nothing behind them. The gondola moved forward and passed through a series of curtains so that when the boat emerged into the first cavern on the river, Claire murmured, "Oh, my God."

"It's beautiful."

"Have you never been here?"

"No."

Unlike the best-known human caves, in which stalagmites and stalactites formed the greater fascination for explorers, the vampire world had an almost opposite sensibility: Caves were meant to be transformed, kept free from damp, with the richest mineral veins polished to a glow. They had teams working on caves constantly to remove all kinds of mineral buildup within their developed cavern systems.

When the walls of a cave were a simple stone, crystals were added, or various exotic granites and marbles. Sculpture had been perfected as a high form of art.

Music played in the background. As the gondola moved slowly around each intricate turn of the river, lights played over more sculptures, intricate stone carvings, and beautiful crystal mosaics.

In the face of the beauty in front of her, Claire forgot her present struggles. She took Lucian's hand, overwhelmed.

Suddenly the hidden world of the vampire looked very different to her, full of beauty and subtlety, romance, and even children and families. She was looking at the opposite side of Lucian's civilization. "I had no idea."

"I guess you haven't seen much beauty in our world over the past few days, have you?"

She shook her head as the gondola left the cavern behind and entered what appeared to be a long, dark tunnel. She heard a soft moan in the distance. *Is that what I think it is?*

These gondolas are meant to be very private.

But this tunnel carries sound.

Lucian chuckled softly. He squeezed her hand. *I wish we were here under very different circumstances.*

I'm trying hard not to think about it.

But the dark tunnel ended, bringing the gondola into an immense new cavern and another display of vampire artistry. Realizing that the ride wouldn't get them to their end point for at least another twenty minutes, and needing to keep from thinking about how she wished Lucian would kiss her, Claire let her mind drift and her eyes take in the sights in front of her.

The entire ride was linked with dark tunnels, which created the ideal preparation for the next extraordinary display.

Just as the fourth cavern opened up, which involved a thematic use of obsidian and white crystals, Lucian nudged her. *Look how the river turns at the exit point.*

She sat up straighter and fixed her gaze at the far end of the cavern. *Yes, it turns almost parallel to the rest of the ride; a ninety-degree turn.*

Exactly. Now all we need to find is the serpent pillar.

Yeah, but have you given any thought to busting through the electrical field? And before you dispute what you'd be up against, remember that I saw what Tasers did to you in Daniel's Dark Cave system. You were incapacitated.

I wasn't an Ancestral then.

But she felt his doubts and maybe his remembered experience, the pain of having had that much electrical current disrupting his vampire circuitry.

She forgot about the black and white crystals, her gaze now fixed across the cavern despite the switch-back path of the gondola or the occasionally extreme height of some of the sculptures.

Setting the rose aside when the gondola made the ninety-degree turn, she held her breath.

There, to the left, it's a disguise, Lucian, can you see it? The most beautiful blue.

I don't see it.

That has to be the hidden cavern.

At the same time, she saw the six-foot stone statue in the shape of serpent.

There's the serpent. Her heart started pounding in her chest. *I see it.*

I'm going to throw us through the field and it's going to hurt. But we don't have to do this, Claire.

Like hell we don't. I'm ready, Lucian. I can take a little pain. Just say the word.

Ten feet remained until they would enter the next tunnel.

Just tell me where the disguise seems thinnest.

Claire's heart thumped in her chest, her gaze rising. *Near the ceiling line, but it's very jagged.*

Give me the distance; it's time to go.

Twenty feet straight up, then over eight feet, no more.

Ready, Claire?

Hell, yeah.

She wasn't exactly prepared for how he simply lifted her up and launched her into the air, holding her only by her arm.

The electrical field burned and jolted her senses. When she landed, she felt like she'd fallen on pillows because her mind was floating, making sense of nothing.

Then she blacked out.

Lucian couldn't move, and the space was very dark. Something sharp pressed into his face, his neck, and other parts of his body. Where the hell was he?

His mind faded in and out, the way his early recovery from blood-madness had felt, when only one thought out of three made any sense at all.

Now he remembered. Shit, that had hurt. Where was Claire?

Claire.

Nothing came back to him.

Claire.

Still nothing. He wished like hell he could see, but he'd been in this situation before, every damn time he'd been Tasered.

Light suddenly flooded the cavern. Oh, now he understood what had happened: He'd short-circuited the light show. Great. They'd probably have security on them soon.

Sure enough, a few seconds later a team of eight tough-looking vampires flew through the cavern, high in the air, searching. The electrical fields weren't functioning yet, either, and the gondolas had stopped moving.

He sat up but as several glanced in his direction, he realized they couldn't see him. He and Claire were behind the disguise.

Hey, you're sitting on my hand.

Claire?

He turned slowly, his mind still like mush, but rose at the same time. She drew her hand back.

"You have a hard ass, you know."

He looked down at her. She had welts across her face, a fine array of electrical burns.

He caught her chin in his hand. "You okay?"

"Do I look okay? Because by the strips of pain in rows over my face, I'd say I got fried."

He peered closely. "You're healing fast, though."

She sat up. "That did not feel good."

"But we made it through."

"I take it if I hadn't been siphoning your power, I'd be toast?"

"Burned to a crisp."

She lifted her right fist. "Go, vampire power."

He chuckled, then laughed. "Claire, you're too much. Does anything ever get you down?"

She rose to her feet, sniffing. "Oh, this is bad. The electricity singed my faux fur and now it stinks."

Still sitting on the ground, he looked up at her, marveling. Nothing about Claire was in the ordinary style. She'd been knocked unconscious and her face was burned, but she acted as though nothing much had just happened. He admired her more than he wanted to admit.

Glancing down at him, she lifted a brow. "Oh, I'm sorry. Do you need me to help your sorry ass up?"

He rose, shaking his head but still chuckling.

Her gaze slid past him. "Those vamps in flight can't see us, can they?"

He turned around, watching them fly over their now empty gondola. "Not even a little. They can't hear us, either."

"Good deal."

He glanced around. "All right, let's get going. Who knows what we're going to find next. Although all I'm seeing is a dead end, a wall of rock all the way to the ceiling." His gaze traveled at least fifty feet to the top of the cavern, then back down. Yet something seemed off. For one thing, he couldn't bring himself to shift into altered flight and pass through it, as though something blocked him.

He started to express this phenomenon to Claire, but she merely smiled, then disappeared right in front of him. Gone.

"Claire, what the fuck?"

She came straight back, grabbed him by the lapels of his leather coat, then pulled him through what turned out to be just another layer of very powerful disguise, one that had confused even his strong, Ancestral mind.

"Impressive," he murmured.

He moved into a small cavern, maybe thirty feet in width and thirty across. The stone floor was very old, ancient in fact, created at least three thousand years ago. This cavern hadn't seen activity in a long time.

He turned in a circle, but even he could see that there was nothing here. "Claire, is this another disguise? Because I'm not getting anything."

She shook her head and the chains told him she was serious as she said, "Not even a whisper of a disguise. This is it. And you're right, there's nothing here. Is it possible Arsen and Salazar were lying?"

Lucian shook his head. "I don't believe they were. They'd done their homework, assembling and cross-checking all the rumors and facts carefully. And they would never have crossed Daniel by lying."

"Do you think someone got the weapon first?"

"I doubt it, only because not even Arsen and Salazar couldn't get past the disguise; no one but you could. And I'm not sure there's another vampire in our world that could do that."

"And why this cavern?"

Lucian shook his head. "Who knows? Maybe the scientists who created these weapons hoped that one day our culture would have evolved enough to have made better use of the basic technology, so they chose remote hiding places like this."

Claire still moved about the space, examining the walls carefully. "What does the weapon do and why were there so many of them?"

"They emit a form of high-pitched sound waves that proved to have the capacity to kill all the vampires in one locale. As for the number of them, my understanding is that in the nineteen fifties there was a kind of secret arms race to develop a weapon that could subjugate large portions of the vampire population all at one time, a kind of riot control. Instead the weapon proved to be a killing machine, damaging the brain through the auditory channels, which as you know are hypersensitive in our kind."

"Like bats."

"Going for the obvious."

"Couldn't help it." She smiled, then, using the iPhone Eve had given her, she started taking a video of the space. She moved slowly around the entire circumference and even covered the floor. "I don't know if the patterns on the stones mean anything, but they aren't anywhere else in your world that I've seen yet."

He remained in the center, staring up at the ceiling, looking for anything out of place, then focused on the walls. Except for the arched opening through which they'd come into the cavern, there were no other entrances or exits.

Claire finished her video and had just put her phone back in the pocket of her jeans when Daniel emerged through the secret entrance to the cavern.

Just like that.

Lucian heard Claire take in a ragged breath as she returned quickly to him, then slipped her hand in his.

Daniel's gaze dropped to their joined hands and he smiled. "How tender. Did you enjoy the tunnel of love, my son? Did you make love to your new woman?"

Lucian met his father's amused, hard gaze. "So you followed us."

"I had my spies watching The Erotic Passage, but I doubled the detail when I learned that Arsen and Salazar had been taken into custody."

He turned toward Claire. "So how are you? Do you miss the boy, Josh? Of course you do. My associate, Mr. Kiernan, chose you over Zoey because you were better educated. But dear Zoey, what a tender spirit, yet a fighting spirit."

"Is she still alive?" Claire gripped Lucian's hand hard, but he could feel her summon her courage, and he loved that about her—the way she faced up to things.

He shook his head and clucked his tongue. "That poor child. She's been deteriorating, you see. She'd stopped eating, not a good thing for a human. And yes, that was several weeks ago, which is why she looked so bad when I let you see her."

Lucian's chains vibrated at his neck. He could feel the impact his father's careless words were having on Claire, tearing her hopes down bit by bit. Daniel would never

just come out and say that Zoey had died; what would be
the fun in that when he could draw it out and let Claire
live it piecemeal, one horrific detail after the next.

Daniel glanced at Lucian. "My son doesn't approve
of my telling you these things. How interesting, Lucian,
that you've taken to a woman, a human like your mother,
very Freudian, though, don't you think? A strong vampire female would suit you much better, give as good as
she got."

But his gaze shifted suddenly back to Claire and he
frowned slightly. "So I take it that you have a special
ability to see through the disguises. Even I barely fi-
nessed the last one, except that I'd watched you pull my
son through a wall of rock. I took it on faith and did the
same. It was rather amazing, going against all the fear
the disguise created in me. I confess, I'm much impressed with you."

But Claire ignored these comments and got back to
the subject that mattered. "Where is Zoey now?"

Daniel turned and walked slowly to his right, just a
few paces. He glanced up at the ceiling, around the
walls, then took in the floor. "Looks like a wild goose
chase, a perfect waste of time, Arsen and Salazar up to
their old tricks."

"Zoey. What happened to Zoey?"

He turned his gaze on her, those light, gold-flecked
eyes of his. "Humans rarely last two years—and do you
know why, Claire? Because they give up. The despair
gets to your people. Even when I told Zoey you'd be
coming for her, that you wanted to take her home, she
just stared at me like she didn't believe a word I said."
He smiled and chuckled softly, bastard that he was.
"Imagine Zoey not believing me. I was rather offended."

Lucian barely registered what he felt as his father
strolled through the cavern, except that the tremors had

started again, the ones that would take him into blood-madness once more. Daniel had been the cause this time, or—more aptly—Lucian's hatred for him.

He tracked his father, mistrusting him for a lot of good reasons.

"Zoey was a good lay, though, I'll give her that. She was built the way I like." He glanced at Claire, then away. "Another reason why you got sent to Florida and I moved her into the Dark Cave system."

Lucian pulled Claire close. He felt her rage building right alongside his own. His instincts told him to get the hell out of there and take Claire to safety, but he remained rooted to the ancient stone floor, his gaze never leaving his father's face.

He'd done that as a small boy, watched Daniel like a hawk, reading all the signs he could to see if he could escape a forthcoming punishment, or take the blame for Marius or Adrien so that he'd go under the whip and not his younger brothers.

A primal, childhood fear moved within him at the sight of the man who had done so much damage, not just to his own body and psyche or even to his brothers, but to his world. Claire was beside him right now because of Daniel, caught in his web as well.

"So, it seems Claire's gift differs from Lily's. Lily had these revisiting visions, you see. But you can see through even the most powerful disguises."

He turned to stare at Claire. "I'm sensing something here, something that I felt when I killed Marius. Now I get it. You were there, weren't you? I couldn't see you and I could barely feel your presence, but I knew something was off. The power you siphon and use from my son has a flavor, something I can taste on my tongue. Yes, you were there. Of course you were, and you got Lucian out. How? Come on, Claire, you can tell me."

Claire's nostrils flared. "The chain-bond did the trick, gave us enough shared power to bust Lucian out of your preternatural charge, you fucking bastard. Now what happened to Zoey? She's dead, isn't she?"

Daniel's eyes took on a familiar darkening glint. Lucian knew from long experience that his father loved a challenge. Claire's spirit appealed to him.

"Your friend Zoey matched you in temper. She was feisty, and those first few days she fought me. Hard." He drew in a deep breath, closed his eyes, clearly remembering and savoring the past.

When he opened his eyes, he bored his gaze into Claire's. "I knew she'd make it and more than anything I looked forward to her six-month death transition. I sold tickets at a hundred thousand euros a pop. She was a perfect performer as well because of course by then she'd fully embraced the lifestyle.

"We were an excellent couple that way; she knew my needs and my preferences and she could take the pain like no other human woman I'd known. But what excited me the most was that she held something back, kept a part of herself alive, something I knew she vowed she'd never let me possess. I tortured her repeatedly, to the shadow edge of death, and it was beautiful to see, to watch, how she never gave in, never said, *Daniel, you can have it all*.

"So you see, you shouldn't pity Zoey; she became my favorite. I even thought about having a child with her, but then one's offspring can be such a disappointment."

Lucian felt Claire go very still beside him. "When did she die?"

Daniel held Claire's gaze in a fierce grip.

"Pity. Just a few hours ago. But then you saw what she looked like, how emaciated she was. And I needed relief. I've been under such tremendous strain since you took Lucian away from me. Zoey died while I was pounding into her."

Lucian knew some part of his father's story was a lie, but which part, he couldn't tell. The tremors moved through him again, heightened perhaps because of the monster he faced.

He would have communicated to Claire that Daniel wasn't telling the truth about Zoey, but she tore out of his arms before he could stop her and launched at Daniel.

She had just enough physical power to knock him back a few feet as she clawed at his face. But he righted himself, then subdued her swiftly, overpowering her to hold her tight in his arms.

Daniel could snap her neck with little more than a thought.

Instead he sniffed her throat. "A fighter like Zoey, and your blood smells like heaven. No wonder Lucian is smitten with you.'"

Claire met Lucian's gaze and held it firmly. She didn't attempt telepathy, maybe suspecting that Daniel could intercept, which was probably a smart move. There was a lot about Daniel that even Lucian didn't know.

She then shifted to meet Daniel's gaze once more. "You know what? You can eat shit and die for all I care."

Daniel grinned. "I want to see you go through your death transition. I want to be the one pumping into you, just like I did Zoey."

Daniel lifted his gaze to Lucian. In that moment Lucian's life flashed before his eyes: his desperate childhood, escaping Daniel's compound, enduring a rigorous retraining process with Gabriel that involved a thousand exercises to purge his rage, then later battling the results of Daniel's criminal influence in his world.

And now Daniel had Claire.

Something greater than rage flew through him, something enhanced with his Ancestral power. In the same split second that he'd watched all the events of his life, Claire fell purposefully limp in Daniel's arm, a signal for Lucian to attack.

He flew at Daniel's head, both hands extended toward his face. The natural protective instinct caused Daniel to loosen his grip on Claire so that she dropped to the floor.

Lucian's momentum carried Daniel across the cavern space and into the far wall with a terrible thud.

The blood-madness tremors took over his body as a rage, built of centuries, poured through his brain and stole his rational mind.

Daniel flung him away, but Lucian roared and launched again. Daniel looked surprised, and maybe a little pleased. He reached a hand toward Lucian and Ancestral power poured from that fist, striking at Lucian hard and breaking his attack so that the blow he struck Daniel slid off his cheek.

He caught Daniel around the neck and dragged him to the ground, but his father flipped Lucian onto his back and pinned him with his millennia-old abilities. He slapped Lucian several times in a row.

Lucian bucked, but filled that movement with his new Ancestral power. Suddenly Daniel flew into the air.

Lucian gained his feet and launched once more, meeting his father mid-flight. He grabbed him and called on his power, pulling it into him as he pinned Daniel's arms to his sides.

You've learned some things, haven't you?

Lucian heard Daniel's voice in his mind, but he operated now on instinct and said nothing in response. He gave himself to the feeling of harnessing what he'd gained by putting on the double-chains.

Daniel drew back and punched him, a hard left to

his nose. The force thrust Lucian into a spin so that he landed hard on his back on the floor.

Lucian! Claire called to him.

He trembled now, but he didn't care. He'd finish this with his father right now. He rose up, slower than before as Daniel drifted down toward him. Daniel's cheek bled, and his left eye was swollen. Lucian had gotten in a couple of good hits.

He intended to get in a few more. Despite the tremors in his hands, he bolted toward his father.

Then he saw something glint.

"Lucian!" Claire shouted. "He has a blade."

He felt the slice deep into his gut. He grunted and gasped for air. He couldn't breathe and now he couldn't see.

Daniel twisted the blade. "I made the mistake of trusting others to kill Adrien and I failed. Now that you've reached Ancestral status, you're a danger to all that I'm building. You need to die, and the great thing is that because you share the blood-chains with Claire, she dies with you."

Daniel pulled the blade out as once more Lucian landed on the floor. He saw Daniel, blade in his fist, smiling at him. He felt his intention: His father would come for him again, probably to sever his head.

The next moment he couldn't see Daniel, but Claire was beside him, her hands on either side of his face.

She forced him to look at her, then sent her words piercing his skull. *Lucian, I've created a disguise, strong enough to hold Daniel off for a few more seconds. Which means you've got to fly us the hell out of this cavern. Straight up will do. Just do it now.*

Tremors racked his body.

Daniel's voice broke through the disguise. "You think you can hide from me, Lucian?"

How many times had he heard that in his childhood?
"Lucian! Now!"

Lucian let Claire's orders reach through to his rational mind. The blood-madness had him trapped again,
but despite the intense pain in his gut, he flew straight
up. He heard Claire cry out in pain at the same time,
though he had no idea why, but he had hold of her and
he kept flying.

He focused as best he could on The Erotic Passage.
He dropped straight into Rumy's office, which set the
alarms shrieking.

He heard Rumy say two things: "Put him in restraints," and "Oh, shit, Claire's been sliced deep."

CHAPTER 12

Claire's back burned.

Lucian.

Where was Lucian?

He had to be nearby and alive, because she wasn't dead.

Something sharp pierced her arm first near her shoulder, a shot of some kind, then another needle into the vein inside her elbow.

Eve's voice. "We've got him, Claire. He just needs some of your blood to get him through again. Focus on healing. Sleep now."

Focus on healing.

Her back hurt and stung and burned.

Her mind grew dull, and she dropped off.

She awoke sometime later and felt a hand caressing her face. "Claire, I'm so sorry."

She turned, but the turning caused a mountain of pain up and down her back. "What happened?"

"Daniel cut you deep but you're healing fine."

"We made it? We're alive?"

"Yes, we're alive. I have to take you to a safe place, though, and it's going to hurt."

She nodded. He gathered her up in his arms. Searing pain sliced through her. She started to cry.

Then she was flying and the pain sharpened so badly that she passed out.

She awoke again on a soft mattress, on her side. She heard sucking noises and felt pulls on her arm. Lucian. She smiled. *You're feeding. Good.*

The madness came back so feeding was necessary, but the serum I'm releasing will rebuild your supply.

I know.

Focus on healing. Try siphoning more of my power straight to your wound.

Okay. She glanced around. *But where are we?*

My home in Uruguay.

She turned her mind toward Lucian's power. With what was left of her pain-and-drug-riddled thought process she funneled Lucian's power. The sensation of a warm wave rolling down her back eased her, and she floated away once more.

When she woke up, she rolled onto her back and stretched. She tensed up, expecting pain to grip her all over again, but nothing happened. Working herself slowly to a sitting position, she reached around as far as she could and she felt as much of her back as she could.

Nothing. No pain. Nothing.

"Lucian?" She glanced around. So this was his South

American home. Opposite the bed was the most beautiful modern mural composed of red, yellow, and blue crystals with splashes of green. She stared at it for a long time, marveling all over again at the world she'd entered.

Lucian appeared in the doorway, sipping a mug of coffee. He leaned against the polished stone wall. "Feeling better?"

"Yeah, and you're not dead. How the hell did that happen? Your father, the sweet man that he is, gutted you."

She glanced at his abdomen. The vampire wore the bottoms only to a pajama set and looked sexy as hell, but there wasn't even a scar on him. "Wow."

"Thank you." His lips curved.

"I meant only that you should have a scar and don't." Her amusement bubbled.

"Ah, I see." He moved into the room, smiling fully now, a nice look for him. "I'm glad you're okay."

She shook her head, arching her back once more, which made her suddenly aware of her bare breasts beneath the sheet so she let go of the provocative position. "I don't hurt at all. I take it Daniel cut me pretty bad."

"He could have killed you but didn't. Instead, he flayed you open, one of his specialties."

Claire had seen the thin scar that ran the entire length of Lucian's spine. Only a repetitive injury in the exact same location could leave a scar on a vampire.

He sat down on the side of the bed. Without asking permission, she took the mug from him and sipped. He smiled again. "You're not afraid of me, are you, not even a little?"

"No, never, Lucian. Not even with my ankles and wrists shackled."

He shifted toward her and met her gaze. His gray eyes

glimmered. He stroked the back of his finger down her arm but didn't say anything. Not that he had to: The chains vibrated, letting her know what he felt.

Desire sparked, but she didn't want to fall down that rabbit hole, not yet. She had some processing to do.

After taking another sip of his coffee, she handed the mug back, but he held up his hand.

"Is it to your taste?"

"Black is perfect."

"I'll get another mug for myself, then. Be right back."

She watched him leave, enjoying the sight of his muscled back and tight butt as he moved. She wondered if she had more chores she could give him that would bring him in and out of the room, just like that, another hundred times or so. Watching could be fun.

She chuckled, but just as swiftly her amusement dimmed. She scooted back up to what turned out to be a leather-upholstered headboard, then bunched her pillows up behind her.

She drew the sheet up and settled in to think about the trip to the River of Lights. She could have started at the end of the trek, but for just a moment she contemplated the beginning and all those extraordinary sculptures, the music, the moving lights.

For some reason, her mind got stuck there and she couldn't let go, but she wasn't sure why.

When Lucian returned, however, her mind connected the dots. It was because of him, because she'd once thought of him only as a vampire and the world he lived in as monstrous. But that ride, including the level of organization, the Tunnel of Love nature of the experience, the absolute beauty, spoke of something she could relate to implicitly as a human.

Which meant that her views had been so wrong about Lucian's world. Initially, because of Daniel, she'd landed in the filth-end of a culture that had the same spectrum as her human world, ranging from scum to saints, and she'd judged his world by her extremely limited experience.

"You look so serious, Claire. What's going on?"

She shook her head and sipped once more. She felt absurdly vulnerable right now and took comfort in hiding behind the small black mug with a four-diamond pattern on the side.

"Just thinking about last night. It was last night, right? Or have I been out longer than that?"

"Just last night."

"And we're both healed."

"Welcome to my world." He fingered the double-chain at his neck.

He sat on his side of the bed this time, angled away from her slightly. She turned in his direction, finally allowing her thoughts to travel farther, to leave the ride itself and move into the separate, hidden cavern, what had happened there, what she'd learned.

"My friend is dead."

He didn't look at her. This time he sipped his coffee. Maybe they both needed to hide a little. So much had happened, so much grief.

Her throat constricted, but she didn't want to cry, not now, not yet.

"I'm sorry about Zoey."

"And I'm sorry about Marius." She drew a deep breath. She'd been grieving Zoey's absence from her life for two years, but her death would change things. The loss of all hope was a terrible thing.

"Hey."

She shifted her gaze to Lucian.

"Would you like to go home now?"

Claire at first didn't understand what he was saying to her. She shook her head. "Sorry?"

He looked away from her and licked his lips. "Your journey is over, isn't it? Daniel finished things with you last night when he told you about your friend. You have closure now."

But even as he spoke these words, Claire sensed a small ripple of his doubt vibrate through the chains. "What is it, Lucian? What are you not saying?"

He shot his gaze back to her. "You could feel that?"

She chuckled and touched the chain at her throat. "Of course. What's going on?"

He looked away again. Glancing upward, his brow creased once more, he said, "I don't know. I guess I'm questioning what Daniel said about Zoey. I don't trust him on any level, especially not to tell you the truth."

"You think she's alive?"

He shrugged and shook his head. "I don't know. Probably not. Forget I said anything. What would Daniel have to gain to tell you that Zoey died? Nothing. Sorry, this is just me never trusting my father. I want you to have closure."

"Closure." The word had no meaning—or maybe it was more apt than she wanted to admit: The door had closed, so it was, therefore, "closure." She wished she could reach for a small piece of hope through Lucian's doubt about his father's statements, but Lucian was right: Daniel would have nothing to gain by killing off her hopes.

No, she needed to face the hard truth that Zoey was dead. "When you're ready, Claire, I'll take you home. Just say the word."

She frowned as she met his gaze. "I won't leave yet, Lucian, not until we've found the weapon."

He seemed genuinely surprised. "No, you only needed to stay long enough to find out what happened to Zoey, and now that you have, you can go home, which is where I know you want to be. I can keep hunting for the weapon, or I can find some other means of trapping Daniel and ending his reign of terror." He rose to his feet, mug in hand. "But you don't need to stay. In fact, I wish you wouldn't. I'm living with enough guilt as it is that you were hurt last night."

Claire leaned back against the pillows once more. Lucian looked worried, and she could feel the level of his distress through the chains. "I survived just fine."

"Yes. You did. But there's no reason why you have to keep being thrown in harm's way. You've helped me so much, but you've done enough. I think we should get your chain off and get you home."

She could feel that he'd made his decision, and the truth was that without Zoey alive, she didn't have a reason to stay. Not a real one. Just a powerful, absurd desire to stick close to a vampire.

She nodded. "You're right. I should be going." But her throat constricted all over again.

She looked anywhere but at Lucian. She didn't want him to know exactly why she was feeling this way.

Her gaze fell on her iPhone. She picked it up. Setting her mug on the end table, she opened up the video from the hidden cavern and let it play.

The distraction helped the tightness in her throat to ease up, then the video caught her attention. "Lucian, look at this pattern on the stone floor in the cavern."

He approached her side of the bed. She handed her phone to him while keeping the sheet pressed against her chest. She wished she at least had a shirt to put on.

As Lucian watched the video, he moved to a nearby chair, turned, and handed her a black T-shirt. One of his. He must have felt her need; the chains were amazing. And Lucian was thoughtful. The man really didn't understand who he was.

She held the shirt in her hands, and since he'd once more turned away from her, maybe to give her a little privacy, she pressed it to her nose. The fabric held his smell, a deep, rich scent that she'd come to associate with him and especially with sex.

Her body trembled head-to-foot with a sudden, overwhelming wash of pure desire.

He whirled toward her and stared at her. "You sure you want to go there?" But he smiled.

She shook her head and held the shirt up. "You have a scent that gets to me every time, and it's in your shirt. But thank you for this."

"Okay, but as you told me during the photo shoot, if you could dial it down a little, it would help."

She remembered. "I will." She unfurled the T-shirt, then slid it over her head, not caring that the sheet dropped to her waist first and she'd therefore just flashed him. The chains at her throat vibrated once more, this time as his desire prickled her skin. But he said nothing as he continued to watch the video.

She swam in the T-shirt, but she loved it. She even thought that if she was very smart, she'd take it home with her to Santa Fe.

Glancing at the iPhone still in his hand, she dipped her chin. "What do you make of that? The pattern on the floor."

He slid his finger over the front of the phone, backing up the video, and played the floor portion once more. "It's a very old pattern."

She glanced at her cup, at the four diamonds. "All except one, which has the same pattern but turned sideways so that it looks like four diamonds, like this." She gestured to the mug on the bedside table, turning it slightly in his direction so he could see the pattern better.

He narrowed his gaze and focused on the video once more. "Well, I'll be damned."

"What is it?" She picked up her cup. "Did this mug come from someplace in particular?"

"A collection of four volcanic islands in the Pacific, owned by a consortium and protected by an intricate Ancestral disguise. On one of the islands is the Four Diamond Casino Resort."

"And you think the weapon is there?"

He ran the video again. "Not at the casino, exactly. I think whoever chose to put the weapon in this location chose extremely well." He brought the phone close. "Do you see how the diamond in the upper-right quadrant is larger?"

"Sure?"

"That's the largest island in the northeast. It has a very active volcano as well as a cavern system that was used at one time as a penal colony for our kind, designed for torture."

"Let me guess. Your father ran it."

Lucian drew in a deep breath. "Worse. My grandfather."

She sank back against the pillows. "Oh, Lucian, no. Please don't tell me there are two of them, father and son."

He shook his head. "No, not anymore. Grandpa suffered a terrible accident at the penal colony, going headfirst into the volcano."

"Let me guess. Your father happened to be visiting."

"Bingo. However, I would have to say on that particular day, my father did a service to our world."

"That would only be true if he'd jumped in after."

Lucian chuckled. "Way too much to have hoped for."

She slid from bed to stand next to him. From her bare feet, he was even taller. She took the phone and looked at the picture of the diamonds again. "Okay, so when do we go?"

"You're not going, remember?"

She put her hands on her hips. "Do you want to get this weapon, or not?"

"I don't understand. What are you saying?"

"I'm saying that if we just figured it out, there's a good chance Daniel will, too, if he hasn't already, and we ought to move fast."

His jaw tightened. "I'm going to take you home first."

"But didn't you just say this whole section of your world exists under a heavy disguise? Then you'll probably need me. Whoever it was that created the layered disguises in the Siberian cavern must have done the same here, at the Four Diamonds system, right?"

Lucian ground his teeth. "Oh, shit, you're probably right."

"Then you'll need me. Besides, together we have a magnified tracking ability. Even if it's not really strong, it might be enough to get a fix on the weapon. I'm sure a facility like this would have been huge in its day."

"It was. I was only there once, but it covered several miles of caverns underground."

She turned into him and grabbed the front of his pajama bottoms, at the waist, and gave a tug. "Then you do need me."

His lips parted as he stared down at her. She felt the chain at her neck vibrate again. Once more, she felt his desire for her, which sharpened her own. Between the T-shirt she wore and his really thin PJ bottoms, too little fabric separated them.

"You should get dressed." His voice was hoarse.

She nodded then sighed. "What I'd really like is a

shower, but my guess is that I don't have anything to wear. My clothes must have been a mess."

"They were, but I had Rumy send over your things from The Erotic Passage. I'll get them." She still hadn't let go of his bottoms, and he hadn't even blinked or moved. "Damn, Claire, I was so worried."

She tossed the phone on the bed, and he caught her up in his arms, kissing her hard, his tongue deep in her mouth.

Lucian.

She kissed him back.

You feel so good in my arms.

Back atcha. She loved telepathy while kissing. But when his hands slid down to cup her bare ass, she drew back and huffed a breath. *Maybe we'd better set this aside for now.*

The left side of his mouth curved, and he looked so adorable. Imagine a monster-of-a-vampire looking adorable? She put a big smacking kiss on his lips.

"I'm getting in the shower now, and you can go find my clothes."

He nodded and left the room.

Within twenty minutes, Claire was dressed, and though her hair was half damp she pronounced herself ready to head to the Four Diamonds.

Lucian held Claire next to him, his arm wrapped tightly around her waist, but not because he needed to anymore. She shared enough power with him right now that linking pinkie fingers would have sufficed. But it felt damn good to hold her close, and the knowledge that his time with her was about up made him take the trip to Four Diamonds slower than maybe he should have.

She didn't seem to mind. She must have been on the

same page, because she nuzzled his throat and sighed heavily about half a dozen times.

Soon enough he arrived at their destination high above the four islands. The smoky disguise came into view so he slowed to a crawl to get a good look. Though he had no problem seeing the disguise, he couldn't see through it. Claire's comment told him all he needed to know about her powers.

The islands are beautiful, and they form what looks like a lake between them.

You can see through the disguise then.

And you can't?

No, but then the consortium that owns the casino designed it this way, to have control over who entered and left their system, timing, everything. But they definitely had Ancestral help to set this up. Anyone arriving to enjoy the casino would have to contact their communication center. Okay, guide us in.

Just stay on this trajectory. You're about a thousand feet out, but the disguise isn't deep—maybe fifty feet, no more.

He trusted her and shot through the gray veil, using regular flight. Two seconds later there they were, all four islands.

The largest island, in the northwest, billowed volcanic smoke. He approached from the south. It was daylight in this part of the world. *We may have to wait, if the weapon is where I think it is.*

What do you mean?

A section of the penal colony that will be a bitch to navigate.

He slowed his flight to approach the large cavern entrance, then dropped them just outside, where the mountainside created a long patch of shade. Even then, the shade helped only a little bit; his skin felt like it was on fire.

"Lucian, doesn't this hurt? The sun's out."

"Like hell, but I didn't want to just fly straight in without checking it out first."

"Good thinking, because who knows what's inside."

"Exactly."

He drew her close. Claire stepped off his foot. He set all his senses on alert to the presence of any other vampires, but nothing came back.

He breathed a sigh of relief. "We're alone."

"Oh, thank God." Claire nodded, but slipped her hand in his. "I'm not liking this place at all given its history." She shuddered. "So which way do we go? Down?"

"My guess is that we'll find the weapon in the worst possible place, but let's give our combined tracking ability a try."

She glanced up at him. "What do I do?"

"Just focus."

"On what in particular?"

He waved an arm to encompass what would be the high, northeastern portion of the island, near the volcano. "There's a series of caves up there, open at dozens of places to the sky above. Those openings were part of the torture process—the prisoners would be exposed to sunlight, pinned there to the point of death. They'd be hauled back to their cells, though often too late to be saved. Think being burned by a welding torch."

Claire shivered. "Got it. You'd have to be a sadist to work here."

"Pretty much. This same stretch, which goes on for half a mile and covers a portion of the base of the volcano, also draws near a lava flow so the heat can become unbearable. And as I recall, electrical grids could be tripped anywhere along the way to give a hefty jolt or two. It was said that as many vampires died by torture as by execution."

"A few days ago, I would have said that made no sense, but then I met Daniel. He strikes me as the kind of man who never really needs a reason to kill. If he has to invent one, his imagination is fertile enough for that."

"You're exactly right." He glanced at her. "Okay, try focusing on the weapon now, and think *northeast.*"

He felt the chains at his neck vibrate softly, the response weak. He supported her as best he could, but nothing much happened. However, Claire stayed with it, which might have just been what defined her best, and after about a minute, her voice moved through his mind. *I'm getting an end point. It's growing stronger. I can see it now. A large metal piece of equipment similar to the one Daniel showed us at The Erotic Passage. Can you picture it?*

Yes. A jolt of adrenaline went through him, firing up the muscles of his thighs and arms, because right now he could see the same image within his own mind.

"We found it, didn't we?"

"Well, *you* found it, but I've just seen a vision of it in my head because of you."

"Seriously?"

He glanced at her, nodding.

"Just to make sure, describe it."

"The same ventilation flaps, same color, but the whole thing has an additional black section on the bottom."

She turned toward him, eyes wide. "That's it. And there's a welded loop on top."

"Probably for hauling by crane."

"That would make sense."

He cupped her face with his hands, then leaned in to kiss her. But that was when a familiar voice called from across the space. "How precious. And look, you both survived. Neat trick with the disguise out in Siberia, Claire, but you won't be lucky twice."

Daniel. Again.

Best to just ignore him.

I agree.

Ready?

She squeezed his arm and he flew her straight through the rock, in a northeasterly direction.

Lucian, I caught a glimpse just before you took us out of there. Your father has brought a whole bunch of men with him, but they don't look right. They look ill, underfed.

Slaves. He's brought slaves, the bastard.

What does he intend to do with them?

You don't want to know.

Fortunately, she didn't ask, but she'd probably soon see for herself.

He brought her to the edge of the torture zone where a low gray metal wall separated what looked like a combined minefield and war zone. There were also several paths they could take, but each of them led beneath the openings through which sunlight streamed.

"Can't you just fly us to the destination?"

"Do you see the webbing that hangs all through the space from the cave ceilings, even the shorter tunnels?"

"Yes."

"Electricity. If I'd flown you in, we could have been zapped and lost consciousness. Part of what's along here are fire pits that lead to lava flow."

"We would've fallen in and been burned up completely unaware."

"Exactly."

"So what do we do?"

"Daniel will be along any second, and it seems to me we've got a race on our hands. We need to start down one of these paths."

"What about the sun?"

He gritted his teeth. "I can take it."

"What if I piggybacked you, created sort of a physical shield, at least as much of you as my body can cover?"

He met her gaze, brows lifted. "That would definitely help."

"You seem surprised."

"I suppose so. I've just never gone on missions with humans before—and definitely not with women. It would never have occurred to me." He shifted his back to her. "Hop on."

She jumped up and he caught her below her buttocks and pulled her up. She wrapped her legs around his waist and slung one arm over his shoulder and chest. The other she balanced on his other shoulder and hung on. "Let's go."

Because he'd seen the end point, his innate sense of direction kicked into high gear. Surveying the pathways, he chose one to the far right. Just as he levitated over the metal barrier, Daniel showed up and took the path all the way to the left.

Daniel sent three of his slaves in front, however, shouting directions. The moment one of them hit an electrical field and fell, Daniel leapfrogged then ordered more of his people forward. He'd brought a hundred, at least, and he'd use all of them if he had to just to keep testing the path in front of him. If they died, Daniel just didn't give rat's ass.

Lucian heard the first scream and set his vision forward. He'd trained for centuries in how to battle with single-minded purpose, and he let all that training serve him now.

Ignore those sounds, Claire. There's nothing either of us can do for those lost souls.

I know. Patch of light coming up. She leaned over him, covering as much of his face as she could, but sunlight streamed, burning through his clothes; he hurt at every point that Claire didn't cover him.

He took deep, heavy breaths as he pushed forward.

Behind him, more screams hit the air as Daniel's slaves formed a shield for him through the distance of several feet of sunlight.

Am I smelling flesh burning?

Yes, you are.

I knew the sunlight-thing was true, but I had no idea. It's bad. We live out our lives at night.

In caves.

Yep.

In extraordinary caves.

It helped to have her in his head, making bland conversation when screams of the innocent filled the air and he had a huge pit to traverse with great care. The heat from the lava flow below would scorch Claire's body, and if he hit the electricity above, they'd both be dead.

He stopped at the edge. *Do you trust me?*

Hell yeah.

Lucian smiled. She did that for him, made his heart light. *Okay, I'm going to levitate like I did while you were on the platform, stretching out prone, remember?*

She purred softly and tweaked his ear. *You gonna take your clothes off? I wouldn't advise it. I can feel the heat from here and I'd hate to think of your cock unable to function even a little.*

You done, Claire? But he smiled a little more despite

the fact that he could see Daniel gaining on him, using up his slaves, plowing through the obstacle course.

Do it.

He stretched out and her body slid out to lie the length of his. Still, he knew parts of her would be burned after this. *Hang on. This will be brutal.*

He felt her take a deep breath then he shot forward.

The heat was furnace hot but he got to the other side.

Claire whimpered. *My arms.*

Damn. I'm sorry.

Just go. I can take the pain.

His heart swelled as he moved forward, levitating past a patch of sunlight. His hands were blistered, probably like hers. He sent as much of his power as he could to her, to heal her. But he was damn proud of her.

Thank you. That's better. She rose up to piggyback him again.

How much farther? Can you feel the distance?

I think it's a quarter mile. Is that what you're getting?

Yes. The word came out with a slight hiss. He ran now, having gained a better feel for the path, and the mind that had set up the horrendous obstacles in the first place.

He got zapped just a little by an electrical field, but it didn't stop him; he'd only caught the edge.

The dirt gave way to sharp rock and he levitated now, summoning his Ancestral power, breathing hard. Claire held on tight, but she'd stopped joking. He knew why. He could feel she was in a mountain of pain, again.

When he reached the next pit of fire, he didn't need to warn her. He could feel she was ready.

Lucian, it's okay. Do it. I'm good. Holding steady.

And she was. God, he was proud of her.

He stretched out and as soon as he felt that she was

balanced he shot forward, faster this time. She didn't cry out or whimper, but her whole body had tensed.

She held him around his chest, with the pressure of her wrists. He didn't want to look at her hands.

He moved faster now, especially since he could see Daniel and a handful of slaves racing along the far-left track. He carried ten of them with him over the pits, but lost at least two each time he had to pass beneath sunlight.

He kept pace with his father through the next eighth of a mile. He kept his head down and ignored the severe blisters on his hands and the deep burns through the parts of the clothing that Claire's body couldn't block.

She shivered now. Burns would do that, send a body into shock. He wanted to offer her more power, but he needed to beat Daniel to the weapon.

We're close, Lucian, closer than I thought. There's a disguise around the weapon that has altered the sense of direction and location. We're close. You need to pull up.

If I stop, Daniel will know something's going on. He'll shift course.

Keep going, but I'm going to start fake-screaming, which will give you a reason to start slowing down, like you're worried about me.

Got it.

Claire let out a scream and held up her hands, which were bloody now. Lucian shifted his gaze toward Daniel as he called out, "Claire. My God, Claire." All a fake, of course. The pain was real, but the ruse worked; Daniel took the bait and raced forward.

Where's the weapon?

Claire slid off him and continued to scream, then let her screams fall to outright sobs. *Off to your right. I'm going to give you directions, but I'm staying put. I'm in a lot of pain.*

Got it.

All you need to do is take ten steps straight ahead.

There's a rock wall in front of me.

No, there's not. Just do it.

Lucian felt like something of a fool. He was sure he was going to slam into the wall and end up with a bloody nose, but the disguises he'd seen today were way beyond anything he'd seen before, except in Siberia.

He walked straight ahead. The next moment he passed through the fog and there it was. Now to do the transport and do it quick. Daniel would figure this out and he would be pissed as hell.

Get over here, Claire. We need to leave. Now. I can haul this with one hand if you can hop on my back again.

She was already with him and jumped up, surrounding his neck with her arms and his waist with her legs.

Hold on tight.

I am and I'm ready.

He took hold of the iron loop on top with both hands, felt the weight, then hefted it into the air. The weapon was four feet tall and three feet wide. He levitated and once he knew that Claire was stuck to him like glue and that he could manage the weight of the machine, he used his goddamn righteous Ancestral speed and took the weapon and Claire straight out the side of the mountain.

And nothing followed him.

Daniel had fallen for the trick.

Lucian sped west, past two continents then through the Middle East, heading to the northern regions of Egypt.

The Pharaoh Cavern system wasn't far, but it was one of the most heavily fortified in his entire world: Gabriel's lair.

He shot a telepathic message to the owner and a

second later landed in the middle of Gabriel's outer entrance cavern, with a dozen automatic weapons leveled at him.

Gabriel, wearing a long, Arabian robe, moved into the space, his hands spread wide, letting his men know everything was okay.

"Lucian, where the hell have you been?"

"Four Diamonds."

Gabriel whistled. "And you found one of the weapons. Is this the one Arsen and Salazar were trying to sell to Daniel?"

He nodded. Gabriel started to ask another question and Lucian really did want to answer, but Claire was shaking now. He pulled her off his back and into his arms. Her hands were bleeding, as was her face. Her hair was singed badly, her beautiful auburn hair. "We need help here. Claire got me through the obstacle course, but at a price."

His own pain, he ignored.

Gabriel shouted a dozen orders, which sent his security team to the edges of the space and closer to the entrance in a protective array.

Gabriel's household staff began arriving on a run, and because Lucian was burned as well Gabriel asked permission to take Claire from him.

Lucian looked down at her. His ridiculous protective instincts didn't want to let her go, but he was in bad shape as well.

Lucian took a deep breath. "Please, take her. You're the only one I would trust with Claire right now."

Gabriel hefted her easily, but kept her head near Lucian so that he could see her. Gabriel then shifted to altered flight. Lucian sped next to him.

A special healing bath had been prepared for Claire, something his kind had designed for burn victims, which had always had a beneficial effect on humans as well. She couldn't speak.

Claire?

I hurt.

We're going to take care of you.

At the same time, Lucian sent his power to her, ignoring the pain of his own burns as he sent his vampire healing in her direction.

Once in the bathing area, Gabriel handed her back to Lucian. The female servants cut her clothes off while he held her, then he saw the level of her wounds and cringed. She had third-degree burns on her feet and portions of her legs, her face, her arms, and especially her hands.

One of the women gave her something to drink, and because the drink contained an opiate he knew she'd be out of pain soon. He settled her into the bath. She whimpered and shook, but the water eased her, and after a few seconds he watched her entire body relax.

He kept sending her his healing power so that with her face covered in ointment and most of her body submerged, she finally spoke to him. *Better. Much better.*

You'll heal fast now. You'll see. And you can sleep if you want to, which might be best.

Sounds like a plan.

Knowing that Gabriel's staff would take extremely good care of her and that few other places on earth were as well guarded as the Pharaoh system, not even Rumy's, Lucian finally left the healing room.

He found Gabriel waiting for him along with more staff to tend his burns. There were women present, but he turned slightly in what would be Claire's direction. Out of respect for her, he asked for them to leave, to send back only male vampires to do the rest.

Gabriel stared at him, his usually straight brows raised. "This is new."

"Tacit understanding until Claire leaves. We've both been having major possessive issues because of the chains."

"And will she be leaving?"

"Of course. She'll rest and recover then I'll take her home tomorrow night."

Gabriel said nothing. He didn't even appear to have an opinion on the subject, and maybe as a long-lived vampire he knew his opinions would have had little effect anyway. No matter the reason, Lucian was grateful he kept his trap shut.

Staff brought in two leather chairs so that he could sit with his surrogate father outside the healing room. Gabriel gave him a questioning look, but Lucian didn't have the energy to explain that he couldn't have left Claire for anything in the world right now. Though the double-chains would have let him move sixty feet in any direction, the truth was he needed to stick close.

Claire had, once again, saved him from a tremendous amount of pain and suffering and had almost single-handedly found the extinction weapon. He shared all of it with Gabriel, including Daniel's fatal use of his slaves—he'd probably killed off four dozen or so trying to get to the prize first.

"But it was Claire's unusual ability to detect and to see through the disguises that gave us the advantage. Even Daniel didn't realize what had happened." He told Gabriel about the ruse, the solid wall that Claire could see through but Daniel couldn't.

"That machine is heavy, Lucian. I went back and checked it out. How the hell did you carry it here?"

He shook his head. "I don't know. Ancestral power, I guess. I just couldn't let Daniel get it. But what do you intend to do with it?"

"Anything relating to the extinction weapon that we

receive here gets destroyed. I personally see to that. We're also offering counterbids against Daniel for any information that pans out. We're determined to put an end to this once and for all but this, what you and Claire have accomplished, is a huge victory."

Lucian nodded but he felt the frown on his face, the pull of his familiar scowl, the one Claire had teased him about.

"What is it, son?"

"I want to use the weapon as a trap. I want to bring Daniel to earth once and for all."

"You want to destroy him."

"I do." Lucian compressed his lips. "It needs to be finished. He killed Marius in front of me while he had me trapped in the Dark Cave system."

Gabriel looked as though Lucian had just punched him in the stomach then landed a heavy blow to his jaw. "Oh, God, not Marius."

Grief boiled in the air between Lucian and Gabriel. His heart ached; his chest felt like it was caving in on him and would never be normal again.

Gabriel took deep shuddering breaths and kept his eyes closed. Lucian sat in the hallway outside the healing room, in the brown leather chair, beside the man who had trained him out of his rage and into his fighting leathers. He suffered the loss of the youngest brother, the one who, like Claire, had always known how to joke and smile.

After an hour, one of the wait staff brought honey-sage mojitos. Lucian thought it an odd drink—he would have preferred whiskey—but right now he would take anything.

The cool light flavor, however, had a softening effect. "Marius would have loved this."

Gabriel started to laugh. "Mojitos. Yes, he would have

laughed, and we would have laughed with him." He met Lucian's gaze. "I will celebrate his life as long as I have years."

Lucian nodded. Gabriel had said the exact right thing.

Lucian refused to fall into his grief, not when he was still worried about Claire, not when he had one final mission to execute. There would be time later when he could make the proper observances and mourn in a way that would be fitting for the loss of his brother, but not yet.

CHAPTER 13

Claire floated, in her mind and in her body. She wasn't real. She was a wispy cloud moving slowly through life, passing through solid objects, unable to be hurt, and hurting nothing.

She liked being a cloud. She wanted to stay in this state forever.

She felt wonderful. No, she felt better than *wonderful*. She felt superb and delicious. She was hungry, though, starved for food and thirsty beyond words. But there was something else she wanted; a man. And not just any man, but a vampire who had carried her on his back, then brought her safely to Egypt, like a parable of old.

Her mind seemed to drift in and out of rational thoughts, but what else would a cloud do?

She had a memory of pain across her back and another kind of pain over the surface of parts of her body: her hands, her arms, even her feet.

All that pain was gone. She floated.

She felt something else as well, a steady pulsing of power that tasted like the vampire she wanted, weighted maleness, dragged down by serious responsibility and guilt and rage. All that weightiness often turned inward into a kind of self-loathing that the vampire could only release while he had her on a platform forcing her legs apart.

She liked being there and she liked being there *for him*.

She wanted the vampire.

She woke up in a bath, only a single candle burning somewhere behind her.

Her vision was dull, not a bad thing. Her head hurt. "I need water?" Her words came out croaked.

A female vampire in a long muslin gown, braids pinned in a circle to the back of her head, turned in her direction. "Feel better?"

Claire glanced at her hands, then opened her eyes wide. "The burns are gone."

"Yes. We understand master Lucian sent his power through your bonding chains. You wouldn't have recovered nearly so fast otherwise."

Damn thoughtful vampire.

She nodded. The servant brought a glass of water over, and Claire sipped from a straw, drinking most of it.

She sat up and stretched, the milky water sloshing around her in what turned out to be a large copper tub. "Thank you." She met the woman's gaze. "Please tell everyone who helped me thank you for what all of you did. I thought I'd be in pain for weeks."

The woman nodded. "I will, and we also want to

thank you for what you did for master Lucian. He seems changed somehow, in a good way, since you've been with him."

Claire didn't want to think too hard right now about anything. And certain very specific thoughts, like returning to Santa Fe, she held as far away as she could.

"I'd like to get dressed. Any chance I have clothes here?"

The woman smiled. "Rumy was here. He brought all that you'll need." Rumy, always thinking of the details.

Claire stood up, feeling a little dizzy. She grabbed the edge of the tub and steadied herself then climbed out, one of her less elegant maneuvers.

The woman held a large purple terry towel wide, nothing but concern in her expression. Claire stepped into it and wrapped up. She gave her head a shake and grabbed for hair that no longer existed, at least not the full length.

She reached up. "What happened?" But then she remembered.

"We had to trim it off. I'm so sorry. Most of it was singed and smelled really bad."

"Right. Of course." But it felt so weird not to have her long hair. She gave her head a shake. "I don't suppose you have a mirror."

"Come into the other room. You can get ready in there. There's a full bathroom with a shower if you want to rinse off. Eve sent some makeup along as well."

Claire felt grateful beyond words. There was something so comforting about having familiar clothes at hand and the ability to put on some mascara and lip gloss. Although under the circumstances, the last thing she really should care about was her appearance, she still wanted Lucian to see her at her best.

She'd be leaving soon.

And now her hair was gone.

The maid left her at the door and said that Lucian was just outside when she was ready. He said to tell her that he'd had a meal and a few drinks, even a mojito, though the woman had said he'd smiled when he'd said that part.

She smiled now as well.

Once the door closed, Claire went into the bathroom and looked herself over first. Whoever had cut her hair while she'd been recovering had done a decent job, but it was short, most of it no longer than two inches. Her hair had always had some wave, and when she saw the mousse and a brush on the counter she burst into tears. She wanted things back the way they were.

After a few moments, she pulled herself together and got the water running. As she stepped under the spray, she thought of only one thing: that she'd be going home soon and didn't want to, which was absurd.

In the end, as she dressed her hair with mousse, giving it a little fluff, as she put on some mascara and lip gloss, she couldn't get rid of the sadness she felt. This was what she'd wanted all this time, to go back to Santa Fe, to resume her life, and now she felt as though she'd been given a prison sentence.

And then there was Zoey, lost to her now forever.

Claire, are you all right?

Lucian's voice within her mind brought the same feelings forward, and tears once more welled. And she'd bragged about not being a weeper. Famous last words.

She dabbed beneath her eyes, catching what she could, with the sides of her fingers. *I'll be fine. I'm fine. I'm all healed up. I'll be out in a minute.*

Only then, as she drew her feelings in, did she begin to take in Lucian's current state, as the chain vibrated against her neck. He was worried about her, probably because the last time he'd seen her she'd been blistered, bleeding, her hair burned.

She dressed in jeans and—damn that Rumy—a pair of flashy black stilettos, the only shoes he'd provided. She could just see him smile, thinking how funny this would be for her. The bra wasn't much better, since it pushed her up and out. The blouse, a soft light-green T-shirt fabric, had a low scoop neck and showed off what she knew Lucian loved.

As she took in her reflection in the long mirror on the back of the door, her hair still freaked her out. But overall, most warm-blooded males would like what they saw, even warm-blooded vampires. Of course the irony wasn't lost to her, yet another indication that she'd come to see Lucian's world in a different light.

Still, she needed and wanted to go home.

Lucian, I'm coming out now, but I think I should warn you, my hair's all cropped off. I'll probably look a little strange.

I don't give a damn about your hair. I just want to look at you, to know that you're okay.

I'm fine. Her heart, on the other hand, told a completely different story.

Taking a deep breath, she pulled the door open.

She was grateful for two things: First, that Lucian was alone, and second, that his eyes lit up when he saw her, but quickly fell to half-mast as his gaze drifted slowly down her body then back up.

Oh, shit, she was going to miss the vampire bad.

Lucian did not recognize the feelings that poured through him in wave after wave as Claire moved in his direction. Yes, her hair was short, but that wasn't what he reacted to. He saw only the woman who had piggybacked him safely over a path that probably would have killed him otherwise. He saw the woman who had thrown a disguise in Siberia, getting herself cut up in the process, but allowing him to get them both back safely to The Erotic Passage. He saw the woman who had rescued him from the Dark Cave system by taking on a proximity-enforcing blood-chain.

She'd thrown herself in the path of danger repeatedly on his behalf and he didn't deserve it, not even a little bit.

Oh, Lucian, you're such a fool.

She ran to him, and he caught her up in his arms and held her against his chest. His throat felt tight, an utter betrayal of every intention of holding it together so that he could let her go. She needed to get back to her life, her real life, not this nightmare world of his that had cost her so much.

Claire.

He felt her tug her hand free and knew she wiped her cheeks. How the hell was he supposed to get through this? In the span of three nights he'd come to feel as though he'd lived a century with her. *Damn blood-chains.*

I know. Damn chains.

She hugged him in response, occasionally swiping at her cheeks. *So how stupid does my hair look?*

He finally released her, but he couldn't see her hair. All he saw was *Claire,* the woman who had come to mean more to him than he'd ever thought possible, though he had no way of explaining that to her.

But she truly looked worried. Women worried about stuff, a lot more than men did.

He lifted his hand and slid his fingers through her short hair. "You look beautiful, and I truly could not give a fuck what length your hair is. It got burned off saving my ass. I'll treasure what I see right now for as long as I live."

"That's a long time, vampire."

He nodded slowly. A long time to live without this human.

He swallowed hard. He needed to feed. Warning tremors had been sitting offshore ready to blow in and swamp him hard for the past couple of hours. But he was sick of feeling this awful need, remnants of the blood-madness that each battle situation kept igniting.

"You need my vein, don't you?"

He nodded. "I can feed elsewhere, Claire. You don't need to keep donating."

"The hell you're going to use some other woman, so long as I'm around."

Her eyes crinkled with amusement but he couldn't respond in kind because all he could see was SANTA FE blinking like a shoddy hotel sign, over and over in his mind. Right now he hated the city and never wanted to see it again, or think about it, or picture Claire living there without him.

She stepped back just a little, but took his hands in hers. "We have to say good-bye, don't we?"

He nodded. "We both know it's for the best."

Her gaze shunted away. "And nothing material has changed except that we both have what we want, what we needed from each other: You have the weapon, and I know now that my friend is dead."

"I can take you straight home from here, if that's what you want."

She gave a small cry and landed on his chest again, throwing her arms around his waist. *I don't want that, not yet. Not yet.*

He petted her head and dammit if he didn't have tears in his eyes as well. He felt like he was losing his best friend and his lover in exactly the same moment. *You can stay as long as you want.*

She held on to him and he felt his T-shirt grow damp. She stayed squeezing him hard for a long time, maybe until her arms started aching. "Claire, I'll do whatever you want. Anything, just name it."

She finally drew in a deep breath and relaxed her grip. But without letting him go, she looked up at him. "I'll tell you exactly what I want. I want you to take me back to Uruguay, where we'll both be safe. I want to have a couple of steaks, maybe a salad, definitely a bottle of beer each, something dark, rich, imported."

He nodded. "I can do that."

"I'm not done."

The smallest smile tugged at the corner of his lips. "I hoped like hell you weren't."

"I want to feed you one last time, then I want you to make love to me, really make love to me, because this is going to have to last the rest of my life, got it?"

He wanted to say something profound, even to beg her to stay with him forever, but all he could do was nod.

"Was there anything else you needed to do here? Talk to Gabriel?"

He shook his head. "Everything's settled. He's holding the weapon for me until I can get the trap laid for Daniel."

"Is his Ancestral crew going to help?"

Lucian shook his head. "No, and I didn't want him to. This is between me and my father."

"I guess we can go, then. I've said my thanks to Gabriel's staff."

Lucian nodded. "Ready to fly?"

She responded with a dip of her chin.

Knowing it was possible Daniel would have Gabriel's Pharaoh system watched, he took off south, shooting high into the air then heading west to South America.

Within the space of four powerful seconds, he brought Claire into his living room, a simple place with a wood table and chairs, a bright, multicolored table runner, and tall solid wood chairs.

He didn't say anything else to her, but he set about pulling steaks from the fridge and the makings for a simple salad. To his surprise, yet not, Claire joined him and silently washed and tore apart lettuce, chopped tomatoes and cucumbers, and put the salad together.

He fired up the grill on a vampire-esque outdoor space, a section of the cave off the dining area that had a stone shelf overhang open to the air. A breeze from within the cave kept the smoke out.

His heart beat heavily in his chest, but he wasn't sure if it was his blood-needs, or his desire for Claire, or the fine smell of grilled meat, or a kind of grief he could hardly bear.

Whatever it was, when Claire moved to stand beside him, he slid his arm around her waist and pulled her close. She sipped her beer and sighed, doing both over and over.

The meal he ate with her was a quiet thing. Every once in a while he'd look at her and she'd look back, her light-brown eyes speaking of her affection for him and how much she'd miss him. He returned the favor, but he couldn't speak. What was the point? The blood-chains told the whole story anyway: He'd miss her like hell, and she felt the same way.

She didn't eat much; he was slightly more successful. Eventually, he rose from the table, carrying the plates into the kitchen. He could have cleaned up, but his tremors told him he needed to get on with things.

Claire had just pushed her chair in when he caught her up in his arms and carried her into the bedroom, the place where she'd healed from the cut on her back.

The room was pristine, the bed made with fresh linens and Claire's earlier torn-up, bloody clothing removed. He needed to give his housekeeper a goddamn raise.

Claire had never been so in sync with Lucian as she was in this moment. She felt his pain at the upcoming separation and knew it matched hers like a reflection in a mirror.

When he set her on her feet, she held his face in her hands and just looked at him, memorizing the cool gray of his eyes, the permanent scowl on his forehead that took his thick brows low, the way his nostrils flared because she knew he smelled her blood, and maybe her sex, and that he wanted her.

The chains didn't need to tell her that, though hers sang against her throat, reminding her of how everything had started. Now she was here, staring into the eyes of a vampire she'd grown to love over three short nights. She wouldn't deny it anymore. She loved Lucian, everything about him, including his scowl, the heaviness of his spirit because of all that he carried around with him, his concern for his world, but mostly his belief that he'd lost his soul a long time ago because he was Daniel's son.

This part of his life she would never fully understand, in the way she couldn't truly comprehend what Zoey had endured, or what it had taken for her to live as long as she had, with tremendous strength of spirit.

But the journey ended here, tonight, with Lucian. Soon he'd take her back to Santa Fe.

She released a deep sigh and leaned up to kiss him, just feeling his lips with hers, memorizing them, knowing this would be the last time. She'd already decided to keep her memories and not have them erased. How wise that would be, she wasn't sure, but she never wanted to forget Lucian. Never.

His arms slid around her, very gently, as he drew her close. She hooked an arm around his neck, fondling the coarse hair at the nape.

She pulled back. "Will you let me have my way right now?"

He didn't smile. He just nodded. He must have understood.

"Let's get our clothes off."

There was no hurrying the process, just a steady removal of shoes and shirts, pants and underwear. He was in that half-aroused state that she found extremely attractive: the cock swollen but not yet upright, getting ready.

Lucian had a beautiful cock. She sat on the side of the bed, spread her legs, and gestured for him to come close.

She explored him, touching, looking, feeling the silkiness and the hardness, the magic of what would fit inside her and pleasure her, what he would release that should make babies, but for vampires rarely did.

His abs flexed as his chest rose and fell in long deep breaths. With one hand around his stalk, she ran her other hand over his stomach. "Flex for me."

He tightened his stomach so that her fingers moved up and down the waves of him. She leaned close and took his crown in her mouth. He shuddered, his muscular thighs quivering.

She focused on the feel of him in her mouth, the ridge over which she moved her lips, and heard him groan, her tongue dipping into the tip then swirling over the rounded head. She sucked him slowly, moving down then back up, over and over, her hands sliding around to grip his firm buttocks.

Lucian.

His hands stroked her short hair, her face, her neck, and lingered on her shoulders. His hips flexed, pushing into her.

She heard his breathing catch, so she pulled back then drew him onto the bed. She had him lie facedown and for the next half hour, she moved her hands and her lips over every inch of his body, sucking different parts, tasting, biting.

Claire. Claire.

His voice through her mind was one thing she'd really miss, the deep resonance that filled her thoughts from side to side and made her feel full. And that was how he made her feel: full.

How was she supposed to return to regular old earth, and human men with bouncing, nervous knees as they looked her over, then boasted about accomplishments she would never again care about?

She tugged on his arm and turned him over. She felt another familiar tremor run through him. He'd had several during the time she'd been touching him. He needed to feed and after tonight other women, probably vampires, would take care of him, ease the remnants of the blood-madness he'd endured, slake his thirst.

She hated all those women. She wanted to be *the one,* the only one, the forever one to feed him, all impossible, of course. So she hated them.

But right now she could feed Lucian.

"Take my blood, vampire, in whatever way you want to do it."

Lucian's mouth watered. Claire straddled him now, and his gaze fell to her throat. Over the past three nights, he'd taken blood from different parts of her body, even through a syringe when he was out of control. She'd given it up for him repeatedly, out of necessity at times and out of desire at others.

He felt so much coming from her, vibrating through the chains and through her touch, a kind of energy he'd never felt from her before. Yet he felt the same way: That this was good-bye. That she was touching him so thoroughly, sucking him so thoroughly as a way to memorize his shape and feel.

He wanted something similar, but in this case he'd be doing things she'd never be able to do with a human.

His fangs descended as he got ready to pierce a vein.

"I need you to stand up." He gestured to the side of the bed.

She slid over the side, gained her feet, then waited for him. He stood in front of her first drifting his gaze over her breasts. He fondled each of them, exploring her as she'd explored him, making his hands do the memorizing. Her nipples puckered and her breathing became a light pant. Her hands floated over his forearms, then up his biceps, over his shoulders.

He moved around to position himself behind her. For what he wanted to do, her short hair helped. He nuzzled her throat, kissing her neck, licking the vein.

She tilted her head in response. "Yes."

He drifted one hand low, catching her between her legs. He kneaded her gently, which by the undulation of her hips he could tell pleased her.

With his other hand, he covered both breasts easily at the same time, teasing the nipples into a firm state.

His cock was hard. He pressed it against her cheeks, rubbing up her ass-crack. She pushed back against him as he licked her throat just above the vein. Her blood, as always, smelled so sweet.

Lucian, do it. Oh, my God, do it. I need you to take from me.

Her voice inside his head almost made him come. He'd loved hearing her from the first moment telepathy had arrived for them. His fangs emerged fully and with the practice of centuries he struck. Her warm blood flooded his mouth.

He created a seal over the wound and began to suck, his hips pushing his cock against her ass, his hands working her breasts and the soft wetness between her legs.

He needed more. *Spread your legs, Claire. Let me give you release like this. I want to feel you come on my fingers.*

She made that *unh* sound of hers as she parted her legs. He slid two fingers inside and started to pump, teasing the place on the upper inside of her well, the place where pleasure sparked for a female.

Lucian. So much pleasure.

Her breathing grew ragged, so he drove his fingers harder. He pinned his arm over her breasts to sustain the hold on her throat because she writhed as she came, crying out repeatedly, deep cries as ecstasy took hold of her body and pleasure flowed.

When her body settled down, he relaxed his grip on her then released her neck. He watched the holes shrink quickly to nothing the moment he let go.

He wrapped his arms around her and held her. She covered his arms with her hands and rubbed back and forth. He'd never had this, not in his long life, the feel of a woman in his arms, someone he'd had more than once, whom he'd fed from this many times in a row.

His throat grew tight.

He didn't want this to end and that was a first. He'd never been so tempted as he was now, but Claire needed to go home, wanted it desperately. And she deserved to be back with her family and to pick up her life.

Making this about her helped, because he didn't want to think about the other truth: that he could never ask her to stay, that the darkness in him would live there forever because of Daniel, that he couldn't really be trusted, that one day the darkness would escape and he'd never be able to bring it back.

He picked her up and laid her out on the bed. Still standing, he leaned close. "What do you want, Claire? I'll do anything you ask."

Tears brimmed in her eyes. She touched her hand to his face, something she did often. She leaned up and kissed him, then thumbed his lips. "Just make love to me like I'm your woman, like we're two regular people who've been together for a while, and just want to make love."

He nodded, despite the fact that he'd never had that kind of relationship. But something about Claire seemed so easy to him, as though he couldn't make a mistake with her, even if he tried.

He climbed on the bed and forced her knees apart. She smiled and took a deep breath, her arms wrapping around his shoulders as he stretched out on top of her.

He kissed her, all the while wishing for what he couldn't have.

She responded, her fingers digging into the muscles of his shoulders, his arms, his back. She suckled his tongue, biting his lips gently, kissing down his throat.

At last he held his cock to her opening, then glided into all her wetness, watching her mouth open wide and a heavy moan leave her throat.

He stayed in just that position above her so he could watch her as he flexed his hips and thrust, driving in and out, fast then slow, then fast again.

He liked working her body and watching her pleasure float across her face: the lift of a brow, a wince that looked like pain but was just the opposite, then another moan.

He lowered himself, forearms to either side. He could still watch her but his body had become demanding. He could have split into two parts, he could have bitten her again, he could have moved at lightning speed, but right now he wanted to give her what she'd asked for, to make love to her just like she'd asked, like they were a couple and had been together a long time.

She was breathing hard and staring into his eyes. He was feeling so much, and the chains vibrated heavily so he knew she was just as caught up as he was.

Claire.

Tears fill her eyes. *I know. Just fuck me, Lucian. Let me feel you come. I want to watch you come. Keep looking at me.*

He pushed deeper, strong heavy pushes, his body ready. He thumbed her cheek.

He was so hard.

He felt her tighten down low and gasp. She gripped his arms, holding his gaze.

I'm ready.

He moved faster, then with a few pumps more he started to release, the pleasure gripping and streaking as his cock jerked.

She cried out, but stayed with him. "I'm coming." Her voice was hoarse, and tears tracked down her face. "Lucian. Lucian." More tears. "God this feels good, so good."

His hips began to slow and her hands moved to his neck then his face. She still looked at him, though tears flowed. "That was perfect. Exactly what I wanted."

"You're perfect." The words left his mouth before he could stop them. But he'd spoken the truth.

Her brows lifted in surprise. She wiped her face. "Thank you for saying that. Oh, God, Lucian, I'll treasure this night forever."

The ache in his chest hadn't eased up, so he took a deep breath and pulled out of her. "I'll get you something."

"Lucian?"

Sitting on the side of the bed, he looked back at her.

She dipped her chin. "It'll be okay. We'll both be okay."

Like hell, but he nodded anyway, trying not to think too much, feel too much.

He left the bed and returned with a washcloth, then without saying anything else he got in the shower. He breathed hard while he soaped up and was grateful for the running water because he'd turned into a weeper. He didn't want her to see him this way. He scrubbed his face and was actually grateful when the soap stung his eyes. He could blame the soap.

He chuckled softly then slammed his fist against the tile.

To Claire's credit and maybe because the chains told the tale anyway, she said nothing in response. In every way possible, she'd grown very quiet.

After a few minutes he set his sights on the trap he meant to lay for Daniel. Time to finish off dear old Dad once and for all.

First, of course, Santa Fe.

Claire showered and dressed like she was in a fog. The chains already told her that Lucian had shut down and shifted focus.

It was time, long past time, to return to her life, to the human world.

Lucian told her that Rumy had already arranged to set her up in a hotel in Santa Fe so that she'd have a place to live until she was ready to contact her family, something Lucian had asked him to do. He'd transitioned a lot of humans back to their world; a separate residence sometimes helped, especially if the captive had been gone a long time, like Claire.

She nodded her appreciation, but her hearing had sort of shut down. When she asked about his plans with the extinction weapon, he brushed her off. She didn't need to worry about that kind of thing anymore.

He was right. She needed to let go of him and of his concerns. She needed to turn her face to the future.

But the fog remained, even as he flew her back to The Erotic Passage and Rumy's office.

Once there, Claire recognized the chain-removal expert and something inside her spasmed, a twist of pain that stunned her.

She didn't want the chains off. They'd become part of her. They connected her to Lucian, and she didn't want to let go.

But she had to.

She closed her eyes and ignored how she felt. She focused instead on the complete blankness that Lucian had become, a wall of closed-off vampire. That was what she needed to do as well, to shut down once and for all.

Removing the chain turned out to be a simple process. The expert slid a thick leather band beneath the chain all the way around, then one by one made a hairline cut through the side of each link, small enough that the chain still held together. With each snip, Claire felt some of her connection to Lucian fade, one by one, link by link.

"I'll be doing the last one now. You might experience a sudden dart of sensation, a little bit like electricity, but nothing more. You ready?"

"Yes. Go ahead."

He made the final snip, cutting through the larger link at the nape of her neck, which broke the chain. A jolt passed through her that arched her neck and made her gasp, but she couldn't describe it as pain exactly.

"You okay?" Lucian asked. He reached a hand toward her, then let it fall away.

She touched her neck as the specialist pulled the leather away, still holding the chains in his hand. Claire took them from him and glanced at Lucian. "I'd like to keep this, if it's all right with you?"

He swallowed hard as his gaze fell to the limp collection of severed loops. He nodded several times in a row. "Of course."

It felt so strange not to have the connection to him anymore. And yet she still felt connected. In fact, she could have sworn she still sensed what he was feeling, but maybe that was an afterglow effect of having been chain-bound for the past several days.

"You really gonna leave us, Claire?"

She turned to Rumy. "I have to go home, to see my family. I have a different life to live." But the words tightened her throat all over again.

He smiled, the tips of his fangs as absurd as ever on his callused lips. "Well, you can always come visit." He handed her his card, which had his phone number on it. She took it and tucked it away in the pocket of her jeans, but she doubted she'd ever see him again.

He snapped his fingers. "Wait, I have something for you, a little going-away present. It's not much, something smallish from one of my shops." He reached into the drawer at his desk and pulled out a box with a big pink polka-dot bow on top. "Just something to remember us by."

"Rumy, thank you. You didn't have to do this."

"Oh, yes, I did, because I want you to look at this all the time and feel guilty as hell about leaving us. No, don't open it here. When you get to the hotel will be soon enough."

"Okay." Tears once more bit her eyes. She felt an impulse to hug the vampire, but she knew, chains or no chains, that Lucian wouldn't like it.

Instead she extended her hand. He shook it once firmly, then let go, because Lucian was suddenly next to her, his hand on Rumy's shoulder, pushing the small Italian vampire back a few feet.

Claire glanced at Lucian, surprised. The connection was gone, but he was still behaving as though she belonged to him.

He looked down at her, equally as surprised. "Claire, I'm sorry. Rumy, apologies."

Rumy waved a dismissive hand, but Claire threw herself into Lucian's arms once more. *I'm going to miss you more than words can say.*

He wrapped her up in his arms and hugged her hard. *I feel the same way.*

The next moment, without another word, she was flying to Santa Fe.

CHAPTER 14

Half an hour later, Lucian stood in the middle of Rumy's security briefing room. One of Rumy's team, Alan, explained the explosives setup for the extinction weapon. He'd spent decades studying and making bombs, mostly as a hobby. Both Rumy and Lucian knew him well and trusted him.

Lucian had left Claire in Santa Fe, but apparently his heart had remained behind. He'd never felt worse in his life and he hated not sensing what she felt because of the chains. He'd gotten used to *feeling* her one minute out of two.

At the same time, he was surprised at how much still came through, apparently a sort of leftover effect of having been bound to Claire for the past several days. He could still feel her, if just to a small degree.

"I'll attach the trip wire to the bottom of the weapon." Alan showed him a diagram. "All you have to do is to lift it up by the crane-loop, the way you did at Four Diamonds. And, boom."

Lucian was only half listening, but he needed to pay better attention. He nodded. "Got it."

Alan would help him rig up the extinction weapon to a boat, a twenty-foot vessel that Lucian planned to take to the center of Lake Como, surrounded by a disguise.

Daniel had already agreed to meet with him, to talk things over.

Lucian had suggested the location: a boat out on the lake.

With his arms crossed over his chest, Lucian's biceps flexed. The plan would work as well as anything else—maybe better, because Daniel wouldn't easily be lured to the depths of a cave where all sorts of traps could be set, especially involving electrical fields. But he could easily flee a boat on open water.

Daniel had indeed thought the idea perfection, no confining cave walls to hinder either of them. Maybe he wanted to pick up where they'd left off in Siberia.

Bastard.

He'd called Daniel, just to let him know he had the weapon and that he wanted to talk because certain possibilities had come to mind.

Daniel had grown silent, then finally agreed. "Son, if you're interested in a trade, I know I have something you'd be more than willing to exchange for the weapon."

His first thought was Claire, but Rumy had a security detail on her in Santa Fe and they'd been reporting in every fifteen minutes that all was well.

Knowing, therefore, that Daniel wasn't offering up Claire, he couldn't imagine what could possibly tempt him. He'd already killed Marius and as far as he knew, Adrien was still hidden away in the Amazon cavern system.

After he'd set the time of the meeting with Daniel, he'd called Gabriel to warn him what was going on and to let him know where Claire was. Gabriel said he'd keep his eye on things until Lucian had finished off Daniel once and for all.

With Claire protected, he stayed with the bomb and the extinction weapon. He watched both put aboard the boat, a job performed beneath several layers of disguises, the trip wire attached.

Dawn crept close—it was an hour away, no more, when Lucian finally piloted the small craft out to the center of Lake Como, alone, to face his bastard of a father. Lucian knew that he sat on enough firepower to get blown into a million pieces, but he really didn't care. He might even have to pay that price, but he'd do it, for Marius's memory alone, if it meant ridding his world of Daniel Briggs forever.

Claire held the curtain back in her room and stared down at twelve, *twelve,* vampires in the hotel parking lot. She could see a variety of disguises around a team that looked like a special ops force.

Lucian's concern for her safety had driven a stake through her heart all over again. And now that she'd admitted exactly how much she loved him, tears had been just one of the effects of her exile in Santa Fe. And she wasn't a weeper. She'd only been in the hotel a couple of hours, and it already felt like a decade.

She kept thinking about her family and returning to them after a two-year absence, what that would be like. She tried to imagine picking up the pieces of her life once more, listening to her friends complain about things like bad haircuts, or the hardship of having to choose a new car, or the price of gas.

She stretched out on the bed and kept staring at the ceiling as though the drywall and texture could give her answers to questions she couldn't quite bring herself to frame in actual words. She longed to see a cavern ceiling again, maybe the one with light-blue wavy lines where she'd first taken care of Lucian.

She couldn't even ask her questions, however, because they were ridiculous. Could she make a life with a vampire in a world on the brink of annihilation? Could she live a life that played out only at night? Could she feed a vampire from her vein for years and decades on end? Could she truly leave her family and her life behind?

She'd already made her decision, anyway, so she didn't need to pose the questions at all.

Rolling onto her side, she saw Rumy's present still sitting unopened on the nightstand. Maybe because she was feeling so low, she thought this might be a good time to see the smallish thing he'd given her as a going-away present.

She sat up and drew the gift onto her lap. She pulled the bow apart and lifted the lid.

What stared back at her was a set of double-chains, exactly like the ones she'd had removed, only the links were all intact.

Then she understood. The moment she put her fingertips to the chain, a familiar vibration passed up her arm. She felt all that Lucian was flow through her like a welcome cool breeze on a warm day.

A card lay within.

She opened it and saw that the author wasn't Rumy at all, but Gabriel. "Claire, this is a second blood-chain forged from Lucian's blood. I wanted you to have it, just in case. I know my son; he'll never bind himself to an-

other woman. He won't want to. I have no expectations—
but should you change your mind, and feel the need,
you'll have the chain in hand. He doesn't know I've
done this; he would be furious. But you have a practical
turn and I know you'll do what you need to do. You've
proven yourself a dozen times over the past few nights.
One last bit of information: I've modified this chain, and
distance shouldn't be an issue. Godspeed. Gabriel."

And Claire's heart started to ache all over again.

A new blood-chain.

And Lucian.

All she had to do was put it on.

The call to do just that was more powerful than she
could have imagined.

Lucian sat on the boat waiting for Daniel. He held a beer
in hand, wanting to look casual, though feeling anything but.

Five minutes till game time.

He wore battle leathers stocked with chains and daggers, no jacket, just a formfitting tee, fighting boots.

He didn't know what Daniel expected to happen tonight, but Lucian intended to go to war.

Once again he crossed his arms over his chest, the
bottle of beer dangling from between two fingers. He
wished that Claire was here, that he was still bound to
her, but only for one reason: He missed the hell out of
her. That damn ache in his chest kept expanding.

And there was the hard truth about Claire and what
the blood-chains had really done to him: They'd forced
a love he'd never expected to feel.

He loved Claire.

He knew that now.

He loved her with all his heart.

Since the chain removal, he could no longer blame

the chains for what he felt, for the intensity of his feelings toward her. He'd been told from the beginning that the blood-chains didn't lie, but he'd never quite believed what he'd felt for Claire, not until this moment. With the chains gone, he could no longer deny that, despite who he was, despite that his DNA gave him the soul of a monster, he'd fallen in love with a human and for the first time in his life he could picture a different kind of life.

Claire. *Claire.*

He'd sent the telepathic word shooting into the void before he could stop himself.

But nothing came back.

Claire.

Still sitting on the bed, Claire tensed up, having heard Lucian's voice, as a clear as a bell, dead center in her brain.

Lucian?

Though she responded immediately, she could tell her reach, without the blood-chain, went about as far as the wall in front of her. As an Ancestral, he could reach her—yet he couldn't hear her.

Was he okay?

She rose up from the bed and started to pace. She kept glancing at the chain in the box on the bed. Her heart started to race.

Why had Lucian called out for her? Was he in trouble? Did he need her?

She thought about putting the chain on, but she wouldn't be able to remove it if she did, so she hesitated.

There was something else she could do, however.

She placed a call to Rumy's office. After being handed over twice by his security team, she finally reached him. "Lucian called out to me. What's going on? I'm assuming you're watching."

"I've got my binoculars, and right now he's okay. No Daniel yet, though. He's thrown a heavy disguise out there—nothing I can't see through because let's face it, Lucian doesn't have your ability in that arena and I have my own awesome level of power. But the lake is quiet.

"Sure you don't want to come back? I can have one of my detail bring you over here right now. None of them can fly as fast as an Ancestral, but they're the next best thing and pretty damn fast." Rumy suddenly paused. "Okay, hold on. Daniel-the-asshole just arrived."

Claire pressed a hand hard against her chest. "What's happening? Rumy, talk to me." She should be there.

"Holy shit, Lucian just pulled out his long chain and he's rising into the air."

"He's going to fight Daniel."

"Yes, he is."

"What's Daniel doing?"

"Smiling. What else?"

"He's going to kill him."

"Listen, Claire, I don't mean to put undue pressure on you, but I think you should be here. You've been our boy's backup from the moment I took you to the Dark Cave system. Sure you don't want to come?"

"Just hold on. Let me think." She held the phone away from her, panic gripping her heart like a fist.

She paced fast now. She didn't know what to do.

Dammit.

Lucian rose into the air, his gaze fixed on his father, who smiled.

Whirling his battle chain, Lucian said, "You don't

really think I brought you here to have a father–son, chat, do you?"

Daniel levitated twenty feet away from Lucian. His smile had dimmed a little. His gaze for a brief second fluttered down to the extinction weapon, widened, then returned to Lucian. "You want me to fight you for it?"

"Yes. I do."

He took on his most patronizing air. "You're making a mistake. I have over fifteen hundred years on you. Do you honestly believe, even for a second, that you can take me?"

Lucian had long ago lost any desire to play by the rules when it came to the master rule-breaker himself. Instead of engaging in conversation, he shot forward, chain spinning, and sent the wheel of silver in an arc that would have taken the head off most vampires.

But Daniel was an Ancestral. He shifted to altered flight and reappeared behind Lucian, using a blade to just graze his shoulder as Lucian darted out of the way.

Lucian's blood was up and he had just enough blood-madness going on to give him a spurt of strength. He brought forward his new Ancestral powers, and his vision and reflexes improved.

He drew a dagger at lightning speed and let it fly. How surprised Daniel looked when it caught him in his right forearm. The momentum of the hit sent also sent Daniel spiraling backward as he removed the dagger.

Lucian flew after him, and saw the same dagger in Daniel's hand flying toward him. He shifted his waist, rolled, and two seconds later he heard the small piece of metal buzz past him, then drop into the lake.

By then he had a shorter chain out. He let it fly above Daniel's head, and wrapped quickly.

But Daniel was fast, and instead of trying to relieve the pressure, he flipped his feet up and slammed into

Lucian's stomach. Lucian somersaulted through the air. By the time he righted himself, Daniel had the short chain from around his neck and threw it toward the lake.

He levitated in the air, smirking at Lucian. *Why are you doing this, Lucian? Can't you see I'm toying with you?*

Like hell you are.

Lucian attacked once more, ready to tear his father apart physically. But as he grabbed Daniel's right arm, he felt the slice as Daniel stuck a blade deep across his ribs.

Lucian had battled for centuries, though, and a little blood and pain weren't going to stop him. Daniel, believing he'd made a serious score, remained where he was in a fairly relaxed stance, still smiling. When he figured things out, Lucian was on him and had him in a headlock, spinning him again over the lake, holding him.

If he could just keep holding him like this, Daniel would lose consciousness. Then he'd break his neck.

Claire stared at the phone. She kept hearing Rumy call for her: "Claire. Claire. They're battling midair right now. Claire!"

She set the phone on the bed next to the blood-chain, still uncertain about what course to take.

She stared at the chain.

She'd felt the vibrations when she'd touched it.

Maybe if she just held it, without putting it on, she'd have a sense of what was happening. Maybe then she'd know what to do.

She leaped and grabbed the chain, holding it with both hands, staring at it, willing it to give up the information she needed.

But what came to her had nothing to do with Lucian at all, or Rumy.

Instead, she could hear a new voice in her head, a woman's voice. *Claire. Oh, God, please hear me, Claire. You've got to get over to Lake Como. Daniel has us hidden behind a disguise that Lucian can't see and once he reveals us, Lucian will die. Please, Claire. You've got to come. Please.*

Claire's lips parted. She couldn't breathe.

For a moment she thought she was hearing Eve's voice. But no, she would have known her friend's voice anywhere: Zoey.

She blinked.

Zoey.

She shook her head. Impossible.

Zoey? she called telepathically.

Claire. Oh, thank God you're there. You've got to get over here. Lucian doesn't know what Daniel has planned. He's lied to you both; I'm still alive, so is Marius. Lucian thinks he's winning, but Daniel knows about the explosives in the boat. He'll make Lucian choose and you know what Lucian will do. He'll sacrifice himself thinking he'll be saving us. Claire, you've got to come. If you don't save him, he'll die.

Claire didn't pause for even a second to figure any of this out. She just accepted what Zoey had told her. Every instinct in her body screamed the truth at her: Lucian was in danger, Zoey was alive, and if she didn't help the man she loved, he was going to die.

Claire?

I'm coming.

She shut down the telepathy, then slid the chain over her neck and felt it lock in place. Lucian's power began to flow, even thousands of miles away from him, just like that.

She contacted Rumy and had one of his men come to her. He saw the chains at her neck and said simply, "My orders are to obey your commands."

"Good."

She had him assemble Rumy's security team, the one assigned to her, and the next moment she held on to the lead man. As a unit they shifted into altered flight, heading east.

They moved fast enough that they'd be in Italy in a matter of minutes. Still, she'd flown with Lucian. Never would she have thought altered flight could feel so damn slow.

Lucian had Daniel pinned, one arm behind his back. With his free arm, he surrounded Daniel's neck in a tight grip, his Ancestral power at full bore, and felt him slowly losing consciousness.

Lucian had achieved the impossible. He'd gained control of the psychopath.

That was when he felt his chains begin to vibrate and an awareness of Claire fill his senses. She was in flight, and somehow she was attempting to speak to him telepathically. But how was this possible?

Despite the slight distraction, he kept Daniel pinned. He wouldn't let go of him now, even though he didn't understand how Claire could have made use of the destroyed chain. He'd watched the expert clip every link then break the chain.

But then he remembered Rumy's gift, and he understood. He smiled and felt the strangest sense of relief: For a little while at least, he'd have Claire back with him.

With Daniel under control and now dangling in the air, his weight growing heavier by the second as the life drained out of him, Lucian opened his telepathy. *Claire, is that really you?*

Lucian, listen; Something's wrong. I just heard from Zoey. She's not dead and she's there, somewhere near you. So is Marius. They must be hidden behind a disguise you can't see. She said Daniel knows about the boat and the explosives and he's going to use Zoey and Marius to guilt you into giving up the weapon. You've got to get out of there.

Just as he returned his complete attention to Daniel, who truly felt close to death, Daniel suddenly shifted, broke out of Lucian's grasp, then whipped into the air. He floated nearby and waved a hand in a wide sweep.

Lucian turned to face him, levitating with arms wide to balance himself, and there they were.

Daniel's other sons, Quill and Lev, the ones loyal to their father, each held a chained-up prisoner. One was an emaciated woman, and the other . . .

Lucian's mind stalled out. He shook his head. Claire had already told him the truth, and now his eyes confirmed it, but he still couldn't believe that Marius was alive.

Lucian. I'm thirty seconds out.

Claire again.

You were right, both Zoey and Marius are here.

Hold on. I can help.

Daniel moved to float in front of him, just a few feet away, barely out of physical reach. "I was sure you didn't bring me here to catch up. So I'm going to make this simple for you. No more games, no more trying to battle me to the death. If you want your brother and this human to live, you'll hand over the weapon now."

Marius called out, "Don't do it, Lucian." Clearly, Daniel had feigned killing Marius while Lucian was caught in blood-madness, but Marius was as dull-eyed as the woman next to him. They'd both be dead soon without help.

I'm almost there.

But if Claire arrived, Daniel would have one more piece of leverage. He couldn't let her get caught.

Claire, stay away. You can't help right now. I've got this.

He met his father's gaze. "Let Marius and Zoey go right now, and I'll give you the weapon."

"You'll have to detach the bomb, or did you think I didn't know about it?"

In that moment, Lucian realized that he'd lost the war. He could accomplish half his goal and save Marius and Zoey, but not his own life. At this point Daniel would never believe that Lucian could choose death over handing him the extinction weapon free and clear.

He slowly levitated away from the boat, pulling his phone from his pant pocket and pretending that it was the detonator. "You have five seconds to choose, Daniel, or I'll blow the weapon up. Let Zoey and Marius go. Now." He started the countdown. "Five, four, three, two . . ."

"Fine." Daniel waved a hand.

Quill dropped Zoey, who started to fall a hundred feet toward the water, her cry more a whimper than anything else. At the exact same moment, Marius fell. But despite his chains, he had enough power to fly after Zoey and scoop her up before she hit the water, then carry her in the direction of The Erotic Passage.

Marius was free, and he'd saved Zoey.

The original plan—to have Daniel take the weapon and blow himself up—had failed. Lucian had only one recourse that made sense to him. He had to destroy the weapon if his world was to survive and right now he intended to do just that.

Lucian dropped into the boat knowing that at least

he'd be keeping the weapon from Daniel's hands. He'd lived four centuries. Long enough, and what better way to go than by protecting his world?

Claire reached the boat at the same moment as Lucian. But she had one advantage her vampire boyfriend didn't. She quickly engulfed him in a disguise that even Daniel couldn't see.

Lucian already had his hand on the heavy iron loop at the top of the weapon, so she said, "Don't do it, gorgeous, or we'll both eat it. Now look up?"

When he glanced up Lucian gave a shout that came straight from his gut. He saw the disguise there, and how furious Daniel was as he flew in quick streaks above them, unable to see the boat.

Daniel roared his fury. His other sons took off in quick bursts of altered flight.

Lucian caught her up in his arms and hugged her. "You came back."

"We can talk later. Let's get rid of this weapon for good."

She felt Lucian's uncertainly through the familiar vibration at her neck. "We can get out of this, Lucian. Trust me. The disguise will hold long enough, even through the blast, for us to get away."

He turned to her, his eyes searching her own.

"Okay, this is how we've gotta do this thing. The second I lift the weapon and trip the wire, I'll shoot straight up. You'll have to hold the disguise tight or Daniel will be after us."

"Got it." Claire smiled then eased into a grin. She shrugged. "Easy-peasy. Ready to go with the disguise when you are." She stepped onto his foot and he slid his arm around her waist, pulling her close. She felt, in this simple way, like she'd come home. All her questions were answered. She knew, in the deepest part of her soul, that this was where she belonged.

Glancing past him, she saw that Daniel seemed intent on their location. "Your father might have figured something out."

"Then we'd better go. Hold on."

"Do it."

Lucian smiled. Claire had said that to him a lot over the past three nights: *Do it.*

He pulled a battle chain from his leathers and with a quick jerk of his wrist caught the upper loop with the chain. He'd need that extra distance to keep from having his feet or legs blown apart. He gave a tug to make sure the chain held and sent a shot of pure power down his arm to secure the hold.

"Ready?"

With her arm snug around his neck, she whispered, "Ready."

Then he headed straight into the stratosphere, shooting skyward with Claire's dense disguise surrounding them. He pulled the weapon up off the boat to trip the wire then, in that same split second, let the weapon fall back to the deck.

By then he was two thousand feet in the air and moving fast.

He heard the explosion then a moment later felt the power of the blast beneath him, but dimming by the split second until Claire's voice reached him. *Hey, vampire, it's cold up here and now I can't breathe.*

Lucian had gone far enough and fell away, heading south and west, in a trajectory toward Uruguay and his secure cavern.

As soon as he had Claire safe in his home, in the living room, he checked her for injuries but found none.

"You are fast," she said.

"Thank God you're okay."

"Yeah, yeah. Call Rumy. Let's find out what happened from where he sat."

He held her next to him as he made the call. "Tell me everything." He put the phone on speaker so that Claire could hear as well.

"Gabriel's guard had orders to stay here until the situation resolved, just in case Daniel made a play for my club. But here's how it went from my vantage. Daniel and his boys kept flying over the lake until the explosion. Each was blown back a few hundred yards, but unfortunately each recovered. They didn't turn in my direction but took off, heading east, probably back to Daniel's lair in the Dark Cave system. So they're gone, as are the boat and the weapon. The lake's a mess. I sent a crew out there, under the cover of my own disguise, to get everything cleaned up."

Lucian huffed a sigh. It was too much to hope for that the blast would have killed any of them. "And Marius? Zoey?"

"Marius said to tell you that he's fine, but he's in bad shape, like you were. He's in blood-madness recovery now. Eve has about a dozen of her girls donating. He'll be out of the woods in a couple of days. He said he and Zoey know some stuff about the Dark Cave system and he has a plan that'll probably involve Zoey—but from what he can tell, she's willing to do her part. She said to tell you, Claire, that as soon as she's feeling better, she'll call, and that she never stopped thinking about you. She said you were the reason she'd stayed alive as long as she had. She wanted to find you, if she could, and help you."

Lucian felt his chains vibrate heavily. He turned to look at Claire and saw tears running down her cheeks. He pulled her to sit down on the couch beside him, holding her close.

"Claire?"

"Just give us a minute, Rumy."

"Got it."

Imagine Zoey worried about me, when she was the one who'd been auctioned and used. She covered her face. *By Daniel.*

Claire, she wouldn't have known what happened to you, that you'd been in Florida taking care of Josh. She would have assumed you'd been sold into slavery as well.

I know.

He gave her another minute to regain her composure. She pulled a tissue from the pocket of her jeans, a wad of them, and blew her nose. "Sorry, Rumy, I kinda lost it, but I'm back. So Zoey's fine?"

"Marius had enough strength to get her to the back entrance, but my staff was waiting for them. She's very weak, but we'll take care of her, you know we will. One of our medics has her on a blood transfusion right now and we've got a healer coming in soon. She's eating chicken broth as we speak and talking about needing to get back to the Dark Cave system; she says five human slaves die every day and an equal number are brought in to replace them. She seems determined. I recognized the fire in her eye. Looked like your fire, Claire. Damn, I'm glad you're back. You staying this time?"

Lucian's heart stopped. He couldn't breathe. Her answer had more significance than anything else he remembered from his four centuries of life.

She shifted in his direction and settled a hand on his

face, staring into his eyes. "Rumy, I'm going to say something to Lucian, but you can listen, too, if you want."

Lucian met her gaze, his heart slamming around in his chest. Claire spoke softly. "I was in that hotel room maybe an hour when I knew I couldn't stay in Santa Fe. The moment I saw the chains, the ones Gabriel sent by way of Rumy's gift, I knew I couldn't return to my old life. I don't understand all the forces that brought me here, that landed me in the middle of your life, but if you'll have me, if you want me, I'll stay."

"Do I want you?"

Lucian forgot about the phone and about Rumy. He turned toward Claire and pulled her into his arms. He kissed her hard, driving his tongue deep.

Finally, he pulled back and stared into her eyes. "Do I want you? More than life itself. I never thought to have a woman in my life, *any* woman, vampire or otherwise. But you came, showing up in the Dark Cave system, in that pit, surrounded with a disguise that fooled even Daniel.

"I didn't want to let you go the first time, but I thought you should have a chance at the life you wanted. I wasn't even sure I deserved you."

"Are you sure now?" She petted his cheek and kissed him, then drew back.

His lips curved up, and he leaned his forehead against hers. "I'll always doubt that I deserve anything. That's the truth of what happened to me, the darkness that will always live in me. But I don't care, either. I want you and so long as you want to be here, with me, that's all that matters." He kissed her again.

Rumy chimed in. "Hey, someone bring me some popcorn. This is getting good. I'm hearing slurping noises."

Lucian chuckled as he drew back and Claire grinned.

Lucian returned to the task at hand, angling toward

the phone. "Let Gabriel know that the weapon's been destroyed. I suppose you've already told him about Marius."

"He knows on both counts, and he'll be here in about twenty minutes. He might take Marius back with him, but something tells me he won't be anxious to leave Zoey. I think she might have fed him, as weak as she was. She has recent, unhealed puncture marks in her throat."

"What does that mean?" Claire asked.

"When the holes don't close up, death is near. Don't worry, we got her in time."

He watched her swallow hard and nod several times in a row.

"Oh, and one more thing, Lucian. Gabriel said he thinks you should join Adrien in the Amazon system. Catch your breath and we'll all figure out what to do about Marius and Zoey, okay?"

Lucian met Claire's warm brown eyes once more. *How does that sound? Could you handle going underground for a while? With me?*

I don't want to be anywhere else right now.

This time, before he kissed Claire again, he ended the call then turned his phone off.

"What happened to your hair?" Josh asked the obvious question and it was such a young-boy thing to do that Claire ran to him and picked him up in her arms. Despite how big he was, she swung him in a circle. Siphoning Lucian's power had a lot of advantages.

So much had happened in such a short space of time that it was hard to remember she hadn't been separated from him for very long at all, just a few days.

He'd reached that age, however, and pushed her away, his cheeks reddening. "Stop it, Auntie Claire."

But he grinned, and his eyes shone. "I want you to meet my mom."

Claire turned toward Lily, and a stream of understanding and affection flowed between the women. They were family now, bonded to brothers.

An embrace followed, and Claire's shoulder grew damp really fast. "Thank you for taking care of him," Lily whispered. "Thank you, Claire, from the bottom of my heart. I owe you so much. I can never repay the blessing that you were in Josh's life while we were separated."

Claire drew back, her own emotions threatening to stampede her, but she didn't exactly think it would help Josh if the two women in the room dissolved into tears.

The Amazon cavern system, though deep underground, had the most humidity of any of the caves Claire had been in. But a breeze blew through, so that the large living area, decorated in bright colors like Lucian's Uruguay cave, was very comfortable.

Lucian and Adrien were deep in conversation, each wearing a scowl and standing with his arms crossed over his chest. They would have a lot to discuss, maybe even plans to make where Marius was concerned—or more important Daniel.

Claire kept her attention fixed on Josh and Lily. She wanted to hear their stories, especially what had happened to Josh after she left the Florida compound. Josh related being taken by Daniel and gave a brief description of what had to have been horrifying events at the Pit, that place of execution where Lily and Josh, as well as Adrien, had almost lost their lives.

"You should have seen Adrien." Josh's eyes were wide, his voice hushed. "He looked like something out of a movie."

Lily explained, "He fully embraced his Ancestral

power in that moment and saved both of us because of it." Her large hazel eyes glowed with affection as she slipped her arm around Josh, then glanced at Adrien. Love lived there now, in this newly created family. "I still can't believe it was only a few days ago. I feel like I've lived a lifetime."

Claire understood exactly what Lily meant. "Same here."

"So what happened when you left the compound?" Lily asked.

But Claire glanced at Josh. There was no way she would launch into a description of everything that had happened, not in front of a child and especially not Josh, who had suffered enough.

Lily picked up on the cue and told Josh he could play video games for half an hour, if he wanted to.

Claire had never seen a boy leap so fast off a couch, but he came to a screeching halt at the doorway. "Claire?"

She turned to look at him, her eyes once more wet. "Yes?"

"You'll still be here, right?"

Claire glanced at Lucian then back at Josh. "Absolutely."

"Good. Adrien bought me a new game. You're gonna love it. Wanna play now?"

"Maybe in a little bit."

"Okay." Then he was gone.

Claire met Lily's gaze once more, and as before understanding passed between them. She suspected Lily's journey had been similar to her own, since they'd each bound a powerful vampire to them with blood-chains.

When Lily asked Claire if she'd like to sit down and share a glass of wine, Claire agreed readily. It seemed so normal a thing to accept a glass from Lily—like talking the day's events over with a girlfriend. In this case, however, events had to do with the monster that was Daniel and the hell he'd put all of them through.

Claire outlined all that had happened, and Lily did the same.

When each fell silent, enough of their histories shared for now, Claire turned to Lucian and Adrien. They still stood together, still scowling.

"Lucian does that a lot. The line between the brows, I mean."

"I know exactly what you mean."

"But he laughs more now." Claire smiled, glancing at Lily once more. "I can at least do that for him."

Lily reached over and took hold of her hand, squeezing gently. "I'm glad you made it and I'm so glad you stayed." She spoke quietly. "These men, what they've been through . . ."

"And they're so deserving."

"Yes, they are."

"What's going on?" Lucian called out.

Claire set her wineglass down and rose to her feet. On impulse—maybe because she was so grateful to be here, to be alive, to be with him—she crossed to him and put her arm around his waist. He held her against him, his expression somber.

The chains at her neck vibrated heavily and she felt a tremor pass through him. He still wasn't past his blood-madness, but he was holding steady. "We're just sharing, that's all."

"Oh, that's all." His lips curved a little, then he kissed her forehead.

She glanced at Adrien. "Please tell me you're not laying plans to go after Daniel."

But Lucian's chain vibrated and carried an edge of rage, something Claire also recognized. "Can't be helped," Lucian said. "With Marius free, we have to do something and we know our brother will go after him."

Claire nodded. "Then what can I do?"

Both vampires stared at her. Lucian glanced at Adrien and smiled. "See what I mean?"

But Adrien turned in Lily's direction, his expression soft as he said, "I know exactly what you mean, and I have a feeling that whatever we do, it won't be done alone."

"No," Claire stated, lowering her chin. "It won't."

At that, both men laughed.

She looked up at Lucian. "I know we've agreed to remain here for a while, but I really need to see Zoey, to speak with her just once. Can you arrange that?"

He nodded. "Absolutely."

An hour later, Claire flew with Lucian back to The Erotic Passage, having surrounded them both with a powerful disguise.

Within a handful of minutes, Rumy led her to Zoey's room. Claire worked hard to prepare herself for how thin and weak her friend would be. But when she opened the door, Zoey was actually sitting up in bed, the adjustable mattress angled to support her. She had a computer open on her lap, her gaze fixed on the screen. Despite the fact that it was clear her friend was out of danger, her skin showed the outlines of way too many bones.

"Zoey?" She moved inside with Lucian.

Her friend glanced up and her blue eyes widened. "Oh, my God, it's you." Her black hair was damp and slicked back away from her face.

Tears started to stream down Claire's cheeks, as she hurried to the side of the bed and gathered Zoey up in her arms. Claire felt the bones of her friend's shoulder blades and spine, which brought more tears rolling. She held Zoey for a long time, unwilling to let her go.

Zoey seemed to feel the same way and held on tight as well. "You're here," she whispered against Claire's shoulder.

"I'm here."

Claire only released her after several minutes. She drew back and asked, "Are you okay?"

Zoey held her gaze. "I don't know yet. I was so sure I was going to die, but now I'm sitting here looking at you. I still can't believe I survived." A haunted look crept into her eyes. "What happened to you, Claire? Where did you go? I mean, Rumy told me you were in Florida, taking care of a kid. Is that true?"

Claire nodded, then gave her a brief history of her time with Josh.

Zoey's gaze fell to the bedcovers. "No one hurt you."

Guilt poured over Claire. She'd lived a relatively safe life in Daniel's compound, but Zoey had endured the unimaginable. "No, I was never hurt. Not like you, but I was as much a prisoner. I couldn't leave. Rumy somehow stole inside the compound and got me out, otherwise I'd still be there and who knows what would have happened to me."

More tears fell down Zoey's cheeks. She fingered the light green blanket next to her. "I'm glad. I thought about you all the time and of course I wondered if you were going through what I was. I lived as Daniel's slave, his mistress, his toy, his fucking punching bag. You need to know that. I'm not clean. He called me his favorite, but he hurt me."

Claire took Zoey's hand and pressed it to her cheek. "None of that matters and there will be time to mend what happened."

Zoey lifted her face to Claire, her eyes almost panicky. "Is it even possible?"

Claire held her gaze. "Damn straight it's possible. And we have time, lots of time to make things right again." She petted Zoey's thick black hair. "I take it you've had a healer with you?"

Zoey gasped. "The healer. Oh, my God. I've never felt anything like it." She spread her free hand to the side, waving it back and forth. "I mean look at this. I'm sitting up, I'm on the computer, I'm talking. By the time Rumy brought me to this room I was about two breaths away from six-feet-under."

Claire didn't bother telling Zoey that she'd also experienced the care of a healer or about anything else that she and Lucian had been through. She might have survived a couple of difficult battles over the past few days, but by comparison Zoey had endured two years of a violent war. There would be time enough in the coming weeks and months to explore all that each had endured.

She shared about Amber and Tracy, which of course created a new wave of tears, though this time of gratitude that both young women had been spared Zoey's fate. When the same dark, uneasy light once more entered Zoey's eyes, Claire told her how Lucian had burned the Prickly Pear to the ground.

A smile curved Zoey's lips and for just a moment she looked like the young, carefree woman Claire had grown up with. "I wish I could have seen it. You did the right thing."

"Slavers owned that damn club so I didn't have the smallest twinge of conscience in burning it down."

Zoey shook her head slowly. "Can you believe this world even exists?"

"It's astonishing."

She glanced past Claire. "And you must be Lucian, Marius's brother." Rumy would have filled Zoey in on everything.

Claire made the introductions, bringing Lucian forward and taking his hand.

"It's nice to meet you, Zoey." Lucian's deep voice filled the small room.

For a moment, Zoey's eyes narrowed as she looked up at him. "I know what you went through. Daniel liked to talk about his sons. I'm sorry."

"And I'm sorry as well."

Claire glanced at Lucian. His gaze was centered on Zoey and it seemed to her that an understanding flowed between them, each having experienced the brutality of the same monster. Finally, Lucian said quietly, "We'll get him, Zoey. My brothers and I are set on that."

Zoey drew in a breath that sounded like a hiss. "I didn't know such evil could exist. I really didn't."

For a long moment, Zoey shaded her face with her hand. Claire didn't say anything. Neither did Lucian.

When she'd recovered herself, Zoey met Claire's gaze, then glanced at the double chain she wore. "You're bonded."

Claire looked up and squeezed Lucian's hand. "We are."

Zoey glanced from one to the other. "Is it love?"

"It is." Claire's eyes grew wet again. She'd sworn she wasn't a weeper, but events of the past few days had proved her wrong repeatedly. "I'm staying with Lucian, in his world. I never thought I'd say this, but I belong here."

"You look really happy, Claire."

Her heart full, Claire nodded. "I am."

Zoey leaned back against her pillows and released a

deep sigh. Claire saw her fatigue and rose from the bed. "I don't know when I'll be able to return. Rumy wants us to lay low for a while until all the plans are made for bringing Daniel down."

Zoey squeezed her hand, then released it. "I'm so glad you came. Rumy had already warned me that you'd have to stay hidden, so I wasn't expecting a visit, but I'm so glad I got to see you."

"I'm only a phone call away, and I'll come anytime you need me. Just let Rumy know."

Zoey nodded, but her eyelids had begun to droop. The visit had no doubt worn her out.

She let go of Lucian's hand and would have left. But Zoey looked pained suddenly as she held her arms out to Claire.

Giving a small cry, Claire embraced her one last time. "You're safe now," she whispered against Zoey's ear.

"I'm safe."

At last, Claire drew back and after turning at the doorway to wave, she left her friend. Lucian called Rumy to let them know they were leaving. As before, Claire wrapped them up in an intricate layered disguise and Lucian held her close as he flew her back to their hiding place.

After sleeping beside Claire all day, in a private suite in the Amazon hidden cavern system, Lucian awoke to his woman's sprawled sleeping style, her arm over his face.

He took her hand gently in his and slid it lower, but only far enough to hold it cupped beneath his chin. She shifted slightly, turning on her side to face him, her eyes closed. She sighed softly but didn't wake up.

His chest swelled. He couldn't believe this had happened to him, this miracle in the form of a human female.

Claire.

His Claire.

His woman.

The double-chain at his neck vibrated softly, and it was all he could do to keep from touching her. Love had come to him, crashing through his life in the most incredible way, washing away the darkness of the past four hundred years.

Claire had done this not by offering him a simple path to freedom, but by binding him with chains.

He dipped his chin and kissed her fingers very gently. He didn't want to wake her up. He was content to lie beside her, to let her sprawl, to watch her sleep.

The coming days would be difficult.

Adrien had contacted him just a few minutes earlier, mind-to-mind, letting him know that rumors had shot through the vampire world to the effect that Daniel had located what was now believed to be the last remaining extinction weapon. The Siberian lead wasn't the only one Daniel had been pursuing.

A battle was heating up, maybe a decisive one that could end with Daniel's subjugation of the entire vampire world—or if luck would fall just this once to Adrien, Marius, and himself, with Daniel's destruction.

Claire's eyes opened slowly. "I really liked the first part of whatever it was you were thinking, and yes, I've been awake since you took my hand, but this last part has tensed me up something bad. What's going on?"

Lucian rolled onto his back, still holding her hand, which caused her to slide in his direction and press her naked body up against his, right where he wanted her. "Sorry, sweetheart. I went from savoring your presence in my life to thinking about you-know-who."

"Ugh. Please don't speak his name, at least not be-fore I've had my morning, I mean *evening,* coffee." She hugged him and sighed. "So what gives?"

"Adrien contacted me a little bit ago." He tapped his forehead. "Woke me up, too, which was fine, just a little unsettling." Their shared Ancestral status was allowing them to communicate more easily than ever before.

At that, Claire shifted to lean up on his chest and look him in the eye. "So why are you so distressed?"

"It's just a feeling, Claire, but I think things are go-ing to heat up. I think we're in for it."

"Oh, is that all?" Her brows rose.

He chuckled softly and ran a thumb down her cheek and over her lips. "Thank you for that."

"For what?"

"For what you always do—making me laugh."

She sighed, pushing herself up to reach his lips with hers. She kissed him soundly. "You're welcome."

"I've been thinking that once this business with Dan-iel is settled, you'll want to reconnect with your family."

He felt her sudden alarm through the chains and wasn't surprised when she lifted up a little more and stared at him. "Lucian, I'm not going back. My life is here, with you. I can't believe you would even think . . ."

"Hey, you've misunderstood." He tugged on her to bring her back against his chest once more. "I want to go with you, at night of, course. To meet your family. We'd go together."

"Oh." She frowned. "Oh, I see. It's possible, then? I mean, I thought I had to choose permanently against returning to Santa Fe."

"I won't kid you, it'll be difficult, but we can manage it. If we need to establish a home base in Santa Fe, and live there part-time, we can do that. But there will come a point, especially as it becomes clear that I'm not aging—and you won't either, by the way . . ."

"Yes, I know. I mean, I talked to Lily yesterday. They said that humans bound by blood-chains don't age as fast as ordinary humans. So that will be a big problem."

"Exactly. And so long as the vampire world is kept secret, at some point you will have to separate from your human family."

"Hey, what if we faked annual visits to a plastic surgeon?"

He laughed. "Okay, whatever. We'll figure this out."

"I have no doubt about that, but thank you." He felt a sudden wash of sentiment flow through her. "I just never thought I'd see any of them again."

"You will. I promise you that, with all my heart. We'll make it work."

She kissed him again, lingering this time, and her voice pierced his head. *So is there any reason why we have to get up right away? Does Adrien need you, or Rumy? Or can we stay here for a few minutes, say about twenty, although with your vampire speed it could be much quicker.* She shivered with pleasure.

He drew back, laughing some more and gazing into her soft brown eyes. "I love you so much."

"I love you, too, more than I thought I could ever love anyone."

He shifted her to lie on top of him once more and held her tightly against him. "Gabriel is coming over in a couple of hours, so we're not expected to show our faces until then."

"Oh, that sounds wonderful. We can take our time." She squeezed him as she spoke.

Yes, he'd take his time. He'd work her body backward and forward, letting her know over and over how grateful he was that she'd shown up in his life and changed everything.

In just a few short days, she'd become his light and his hope, having bound him with a set of blood-chains that had replaced the dark chains of his childhood.

He could never repay her for a kindness he doubted she could ever truly comprehend. But by God he'd spend the rest of his days letting her know he loved her.

SAVAGE CHAINS
Surrender to your darkest desires.

Don't miss any of the installments in this sexy serial.

Now available in eBook, and coming soon to print!

Savage Chains #1: Captured

Savage Chains #2: Scarred

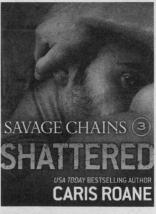
Savage Chains #3: Shattered

Get wrapped up in Caris Roane's
sexy Men in Chains series!

And don't miss a single moment with...

UNCHAINED

(Coming Soon)